ALSO BY SUSANNA KAYSEN

The Camera My Mother Gave Me

Girl, Interrupted

Far Afield

Asa, As I Knew Him

Cambridge

Cambridge

Susanna Kaysen

ALFRED A. KNOPF
New York
2014

THIS IS A BORZOI BOOK
PUBLISHED BY ALFRED A. KNOPF

 Published in the United States by Alfred A. Knopf, a division of Random House LLC, New York, a Penguin Random House Company, and in Canada by Random House of Canada Limited, Toronto.

www.aaknopf.com

Knopf, Borzoi Books, and the colophon are registered trademarks of Random House LLC

Library of Congress Cataloging-in-Publication Data

Kaysen, Susanna, date.

Cambridge : a novel / Susanna Kaysen.—First Edition.

pages cm

ISBN 978-0-385-35025-9 (hardcover : alk. paper)—ISBN 978-0-385-35026-6 (eBook)

1. Young women—Fiction. 2. Intellectual life—Fiction. 3. Art appreciation—Fiction. 4. Cambridge (Mass.)—Social life and customs—20th century—Fiction. 5. Domestic fiction. I. Title.

PS3561.A893C36 2014

813'.54—dc23 2013022216

This is a work of fiction. Names, characters, places, and incidents either are the product of the author's imagination or are used fictitiously. Any resemblance to actual persons, living or dead, events, or locales is entirely coincidental.

Jacket photograph by Della Huff

Jacket design by Gabriele Wilson

Manufactured in the United States of America

FIRST EDITION

For J.D.D.

It was because
probably because

probably because I was often taken away
I was taken away so often
I was so often taken away

I was so often taken away from Cambridge when I was young

that I fell in love with it
loved it

loved it the way that I did
as much as I did

as much as I did.

And it was probably because I needed
wanted

wanted to remember
to construct

to construct a Cambridge from which I could not be taken away,
that would be portable and durable
and that would not change in my absence

Away

It was probably because I was so often taken away from Cambridge when I was young that I loved it as much as I did. I fell in love with the city, the way you fall in love with a person, and suffered during the many separations I endured.

In the summer before our October departure for England, the screen door to the backyard broke and had to be replaced. The new door had a hydraulic canister that hissed when it opened or closed instead of smacking, *thump, thump,* the way the old door had. I didn't like this. Neither did my cat, Pinch. Pinch would use the new door to go out of the house, but she refused to come in through it, and she'd sit by the front door waiting for someone to notice that she'd decided it was time to come home. After three weeks in England, I felt the same way: Okay, let's go home now. It's time to go home. But my parents, looking out their new hydraulic door to England, didn't notice me, and, like Pinch, I had to sit there hoping and hoping.

For my father it was a kind of homecoming. He'd spent the war in London analyzing aerial reconnaissance photographs of German cities to pick targets for the air force. Midnights, he and his comrades stood on the roof of the townhouse where they were billeted and watched the bombs fall, heedless, twenty-three, and abroad for the first time. The damask-and-mahogany hotels, the parks and the Embankment, the Elgin Marbles back from the tunnels of the Tube where they'd been hiding from the Luftwaffe—now he could show all this, his former kingdom, to my mother.

My mother was preoccupied with the oven. She'd been forewarned that there wasn't any heat; nobody had mentioned the oven. The burners worked, but the oven was in a coma. She enshrouded a whole chicken in aluminum foil (alu*mini*um in England) and roasted it over the coals in the living room fireplace in an attempt to make a nice dinner—a nice dinner being something other than a greasy chop or noodles (this was the era before noodles became pasta). It was a failure. It was a poached chicken, pallid, wet, raw in places. The oven, the oven. When was my father going to get somebody to explain or fix the oven?

My father had gone to France for the day to get us a car. It was a tiny English car named a Hillman. How or why it had emigrated to France was unknown. He went with a friend who was a French count, who had found us the car. Why my parents had a friend who was a French count and how they had finagled him into finding them an English car in France were not questions I asked at the age of seven. The car, my father, and the count all appeared at our London doorstep just as my mother was unveiling the disastrous chicken she'd made as a thank-you dinner for the count.

But they were young and full of life and they went out for dinner instead, leaving me with the somber Swedish nanny, who made noodles on the stovetop.

Nanny is a misnomer. Frederika was my mother's aide-de-camp. She came from an aristocratic Swedish family. Her father had dropped the *von* in solidarity with socialist ideals. She had little experience of stovetop noodles, either eating or cooking them. It turned out when she came to live with us in Cambridge that she was a marvelous cook, but she needed six fresh herring or a whole side of salmon or a handful of cardamom and a long twisty ginger root to do her Swedish magic. Though it was ten years after the war, England didn't supply this sort of thing. Noodles and candy, with the occasional tough hunk of mutton, was what was on offer.

She was only eighteen. I thought of her as a grownup, but she was a kid away from home for the first time, just like me. Our family must have been a puzzle to her. Moody. We were all liable to black moods, which we tried to cover up with not much success. My father was best at it because he was always busy. If he wasn't going to France to get hold of a car, he was dashing around London revisiting war glories and teaching at the London School of Economics and on weekends packing my mother into the tiny car to go on expeditions while Frederika and I stayed home with the baby and squabbled about the toilet.

The English toilet was a nightmare. Every day the toilet convinced me—though I needed no more convincing—that we absolutely had to go home.

At home, in Cambridge, we lived in a three-story wooden Victorian house with a square backyard where an old willow hung its whips for me to catch and tear off. The grass grew an inch a day in June, and in January the wind blew around the frames of the double-hung windows with a cheerful rattle. My bathroom had a magnificent claw-foot bathtub fifteen inches longer than I was and my parents' had a blue-tiled shower, and gallons of hot American water gushed out of both of them. We even had a third, extra toilet tucked under the front stairs beside the coat closet, in a tiny room my mother had painted dark red "to emphasize the coziness."

In England we lived in a skinny four-story brick coffin set upright on one short end with a skinny, long, coffin-shaped cobblestoned yard in back that contained some scratchy yews and a million spiders, though once I saw a ball of excitement that might have been a hedgehog. Each floor had two rooms: one that faced the street and one that faced the yard. Some rooms had a fireplace equipped with what looked like the inside of a toaster: the gas fire. The kitchen was in the basement, an arrangement that made no sense unless you had servants. Also in the basement, down a dark hall that felt longer than the house (I knew that was impossible, but still), the sole toilet squatted in porcelain malevolence. Near my parents' bedroom was a tub in what was literally a bathroom, where you couldn't pee, though I'm sure my father used the sink.

The terrible toilet was big and was mounted on a wooden plinth. I could barely get onto it, and once on it, I worried I'd fall into it because the seat was so wide. The room was a nine-foot-high sliver only inches broader than the toilet. Its clammy walls pressed in on anyone who sat there. Up above, mounted like a moon on the ceiling, was the flushing mechanism: a box of water with a chain and pull that wasn't reliable. Sometimes when I pulled it, having made the little hop I needed to reach it, it didn't move. Maybe it was on strike against Americans, like the useless oven. The room smelled of old pee and old plaster and old damp.

Constipation. Psychoanalysis unnecessary.

Frederika got mad at me for using the chamberpot to pee in at night.

"Are you going to clean that?" she asked.

"It's just pee," I said.

"I haff to clean that," she pointed out.

I loved Frederika almost enough to use the terrible toilet.

It was a long trek in the middle of the night, down past my parents' bedroom and the living room to the dank corridor and the prison cell of the toilet room. Some nights I made the whole trip in good faith and then, faced with the plinth and the rank odor, trudged back upstairs to use the pink-flowered chamberpot that lived under my bed. Then Frederika would get mad again. It might take her a couple of days to find it, though.

Then: "I saw vot you did."

"But, Frederika," I was inspired to say once, "why are the chamberpots there if we're not supposed to use them?"

"From olden times," she said. "Now, you must use the toilet."

"Okay," I said. I meant it but I didn't always do it.

· 7 ·

Things improved when I was sent to school.

My parents had found a coeducational day school, wildly progressive for England. By American standards—that is, by my standards—it was out of *Oliver Twist,* a book my father had given me when we arrived in England. It did have pretty good toilets, which halved my visits to the bad toilet at home. The *Oliver Twist* parts were uniforms (pleated plaid skirts for girls, gray flannel shorts for boys, gray flannel jackets for both), lining up for everything (they called this a *crocodile*), including going to the toilet, speaking only when spoken to, and reciting in unison a litany named the "times table."

Every morning the same ritual.

"Two times one is two.

"Two times two is four.

"Two times three is six."

And on up to ten times ten. When twenty-five seven-year-olds chanted this all at once it made no sense. It took me a week to figure out that it was English, I mean, that the words were in the language we shared, or pretended to share, or, in fact, didn't share.

I asked my father what it was all about.

"Daddy," I said, "what does *times* mean?"

"Times?" He looked at me. "Times?"

"They say it. Two times two is six."

"Two times two is four," he said.

"Okay. But what does it mean?"

"It's like addition. You can do that. Two plus two is four, right?"

"I guess." I'd never been very interested in addition.

"It's just another way of saying that. Two *plus* two is the same as two *times* two."

"What does it mean, though?" I asked.

"It means, Take two two times, and you get four."

"So two times three is like two plus three?"

"No," said my father. "It's two and two and two. Two times three. So it's six."

"But when are these times?" I asked.

"Why don't you talk to the teacher," my father said. "Ask her. She will be better at explaining it for you."

"We're not supposed to talk," I said.

"Look, it's just a different way of talking about addition. It's a shortcut."

"You said that. The different way. So why not just do addition?"

"It's quicker," said my father.

"It isn't quicker if I can't do it," I said.

"When you're learning it, it doesn't seem quicker. But once you get the hang of it, multiplication is faster."

"What's multiplication?" I asked.

"Times," my father said. "Times is multiplication." He sighed.

"I'm going to stick with addition," I said.

I decided to stick with addition mostly from petulance. Addition was Cambridge. Times, multiplication, whatever it was, was England, and I knew which side of the Atlantic was mine.

Arithmetic and language affected me in different ways. Arithmetic had a stately, rhythmic progression that I could appreciate. But something about the static truth of numbers hurt my brain. Numbers felt sharp. Words felt elastic and springy. Language had an unpredictable, quicksilver quality, saying one thing but meaning something else, varying from place to place but maintaining (against all evidence) that it was the same language. Thinking about words was ticklish and amusing. It was also easy, as if they fit into slots and patterns prepared for them in my mind. Numbers, on the other hand, bounced right out of my mind. The longer we stayed in England, the more words I accumulated for my internal dictionary of synonyms: *lorry* and *truck; queue* and *line; lavatory* and *toilet*—and the last two even had second synonyms on the English side of the column, *crocodile* and *loo.* A *sweet* was a candy. *Jumper* meant sweater. *Ra-ther* meant Yeah! Within a few months I'd acquired an English accent and vocabulary. I never acquired the multiplication tables. Ten was obvious; I could do that one. And something about five was memorable as well. The rest of it left no trace.

The accent was camouflage. I was shamed into it by Miss Gravel, the second grade teacher.

I was a dunce at calculation, but I was far ahead of the others in reading. Embarrassingly ahead, I guess, if you were Miss Gravel representing the British Empire's side of the Who Can Read Best in Second Grade competition. The class was still at the sounding-out-words stage. Some of them would hesitate and fumble over things as simple as *another* or *because.* I was reading *The Wind in the Willows* and *Oliver Twist* in bed when I should have been asleep.

"Reading aloud," Miss Gravel announced daily.

Eventually, sometime in the second week, she arrived at me for reading aloud.

"Our American friend," she said. Nasty, smirking—even a child could tell.

I read aloud. I read the page she indicated. I read the next page. I was prepared to read until sunset to prove that I knew how.

"That will do," she said, cutting me off.

There was a pause, during which I waited for my praise.

"That, class, is a perfect example"—I held my breath, excited by what was coming—"of how *not* to pronounce your words."

So we were at war.

I won with the method that's proved effective over the course of my life, though it's shut off what are now known as options: I refused to participate.

Each year had a theme. First grade: animals of the British Isles. Second grade: early man. Third grade: Romans. This is a common ploy in schools that pride themselves on being progressive. It doesn't fool the children. They still have to learn how to read and write and to add and subtract (and, someday, to multiply), whether they're adding woolly mammoths or abstractions. We were studying cavemen. We spent hours a day learning about bows, flints, pelts. I couldn't stand it. I had absolutely no interest in cavemen.

Soon after Miss Gravel had disparaged my accent, on a day devoted to how to chip flint to make a spear point, I went up to her desk at the front of the room and announced: "Early man is boring. I am going to read."

She looked at me. I looked back.

"What are you reading?" she asked.

"Puck of Pook's Hill," I answered.

"Very good," she said.

This could mean two things. One was a compliment (I doubted that); the other was the English version of *okay*.

I decided it meant okay.

Miss Gravel and I had arrived at an entente, more or less cordial. I could read instead of listening to flint-talk, I could sit mute during the times table, and in return she would never, ever call on me for anything, especially not for reading aloud. I spent second grade with Kipling and Enid Blyton and Schwab's *Gods and Heroes.* There are worse educations.

First hate, like first love, is unforgettable, and Miss Gravel's disdain still stings. But much of that English year is blurry, stylized into phrases and stories repeated until they have no texture.

It was the coldest winter in decades; the toilet was frightening; my parents were distracted. That was how things were. I couldn't do anything about any of it, not even pay enough attention so that fifty years later I'd be able to remember how it really was.

I was up against the impotence of being a child. Peeing in the chamberpot, dropping out of second grade, refusing to bathe (in this I was being very English, though I didn't know it): My rage at England and being plonked down in it as if I were nothing but a suitcase made no difference to my parents. My plan was to keep doing bad things so they would give up and take me home.

I'd had the same plan about the baby, and it hadn't worked out. Nobody had told me she was coming. Nobody had explained that now my mother would be too busy to bother with me. I hadn't known that the little room next to my parents' bedroom, where I liked to read on the loveseat, was going to be her room and that I couldn't use it anymore.

Several times a week I suggested to my parents that they take her back to wherever they'd gotten her.

"She has very smelly poop," I said.

"Today her poop is green," I told them.

"She makes a lot of noise in the night," I said.

They smiled and chuckled and agreed with me, but they didn't take her back.

Her name was Miranda. In protest, I refused to use it. I referred to her, if I referred to her at all, as "the baby." Oddly (maybe not so odd), she didn't want to use her name either; she didn't like it. The day she turned eighteen she had it legally changed to Jaye. But when we got to England, she was only three months old and couldn't even say Mama, and I was pretending she didn't exist. I became good at that.

All the pretending—that we were going back home, that I was still the center of my parents' attention—made me cranky and difficult. To distract me or to cheer me up or to quiet me down, my father proposed a trip to what he called the "real" Cambridge.

Everybody piled into the tiny Hillman, my parents in front, Frederika with the baby on her lap in the backseat with me. Probably we stopped to eat pickles and Cheddar on a terrace overlooking the smooth, boring English hills. My parents had a knack for finding the perfect lunch spot in any country.

"It's the Cambridge Cambridge is named for," my father said. "This is the first Cambridge. You'll see."

When we got there, it wasn't Cambridge at all.

I burst into tears.

"Look," my father said, "here's the river—not the Charles, it's called the Cam—and here's the university, and here are some towers like the tower at home on Memorial Hall."

None of it was any good.

I gave up. I was a prisoner in England, sentence indeterminate. If I'd known that we were going home the following fall, I might have felt better, but either I didn't know or, more likely, knowing that meant nothing to me. When you're seven, one year is the same as twenty.

We'd taken the *Queen Mary* to England. We hadn't left until the middle of October, which accounted for some of my confusion. For more than a month I'd been walking the two blocks to school every day, then all of a sudden, my mother was putting sheets on the furniture and stuffing clothes into trunks and giving the cat (temporarily, she assured me) to our neighbors the Bigelows, and now, here I was, running up and down the stairs between decks and poking into off-duty ballrooms on a floating vacation that, for all I knew, was never going to end.

October is late for an Atlantic crossing, and we had some bad weather. One night the dinner crew soaked the thick white tablecloths with ice water from the silver pitchers so the plates wouldn't slide around as we bumped through the rough seas. I was delighted by the chilly table and the moist impression left by my glass when I took a drink and the way the waiters topped up the dampness with a little tip of the pitcher as they passed by. I was also pleased to be alone with my father. My mother was feeling seasick and had stayed in the cabin with the baby. I was superior, eating in the half-empty dining room. That didn't last. We were all sick by the next afternoon, stuck in our humid, salty, stinky cabin together.

That night we passed through the storm, and the morning was clear. For the rest of the trip I sat in a deck chair on the sunny side of the boat, looking at the horizon unbroken except by the teak-and-brass railing, listening to the lulling waves. The ship thrummed through the water, moving forward to the future but taking its time getting there. Out in the middle of the ocean there wasn't even a gull, nothing but high, thin clouds drifting behind us, a wake in the sky.

When I read *The Magic Mountain* for the first time a decade later, I recognized the rest cure—in a recliner, swaddled by a blanket on a balcony looking at the Alps—as a variation on the *Queen Mary*'s deck. Alps, Atlantic—not much difference. The point was to be immobilized, by blankets and circumstance, to be cold while being warm (the boat had huge steamer blankets smelling of brine piled beside each stack of chairs), and to have a view so panoramic, so nearly limitless, that it made any idea or worry trivial: tranquilization by landscape or, in this instance, seascape.

But when we got there—and so forth.

In the end (and even at the time it was an embarrassment to me after all the complaining I'd done) I settled into English life. I found a couple of things to like.

The candy was the main thing. It was much sweeter than American candy. Compared to Cadbury's Dairy Milk, a Hershey bar seemed like a sketch of chocolate, a description of a candy bar rather than the thing itself. Dairy Milk was so startlingly sweet that it put me in a swoon, with black dots darting around my eyes and my head spinning in a sugar fog.

The other thing I liked was that one time, for less than three seconds, I managed to fly.

Maybe I was tanked up on chocolate that day. I'd tried flying hundreds of times before, jumping off a rock and willing myself to stay airborne, or running across a lawn as fast as I could, copying the take-off technique of a duck in the water. I could get very close to it but I never got *up*. I was a diligent student, though. Sometimes I'd repeat my effort ten or twenty times in a row. If I just tuck my legs in, if I hold my arms closer to my body, if I jump one inch higher. I was always refining my practice.

It was November. I was sitting on the wall outside the school, apart from the others. I didn't have friends, but I'd been careful not to get enemies either. I stayed in my private reading world and avoided conversation. The wall was about three feet high and, like the toilet, required a hop if I wanted to get onto it. The school was at the top of a hill and the wall got higher as it progressed down the street, so by scooting along the top I could sit farther above the ground than I could hop up to.

We all sat there every day after school waiting for our mothers or nannies or chauffeurs to pick us up. Frederika would come for me, pushing the rattly black pram with the baby, and we'd walk the six blocks back to home.

I'd tried several times to fly off that wall, with my usual result: not flying.

One day, something in the universe bent a little and gave in to me for a few seconds. I jumped off the wall, knowing I'd bang onto the ground but at the same time hoping that maybe today I'd get it right. And there it was, finally, what I'd been after: the sensation of rising. My chest pressed against the English air as if it were water, and I was buoyed up, going forward instead of down. I took a breath and hung by my full lungs for one more second. Then, boom, I was scrambling with both feet on the pavement, winded and thrilled.

I was so excited I had to say something.

"I flew," I said.

My classmates, perched like so many crows (they called them *rooks*), turned to look. Quickly, before the law of gravity could be reinstated, I jumped again.

Is there anything today that I would pursue with such fervor?

When Frederika arrived she was surprised and worried by my knee.

"You hurted your leg badly," she said.

"It's just scraped," I said. But bits of English gravel had got stuck in it, and my knee took a long time to heal.

I'd read Barrie. The idea of Peter Pan—and the fact that the real Kensington Gardens was just across town—had something to do with my determination to fly and with whatever did or didn't happen on the day I did or didn't fly. Giving up flying was therefore freighted with an extra sadness: Now I was a grownup.

It was a nasty winter. Everybody said so. There was no snow, just ice and grimy puddles and a damp that seeped into our coffin-house and made things cold in a way that was much colder than winter at home in Cambridge. Sometimes the only warm place in the house was bed, where I'd curl up under damp blankets and read or sleep. I hid in sleep. Because I slept so much, I was rarely tired at bedtime, and I lay staring through the gloom of the streetlight-twilight of my bedroom at an elaborate plaster knot in the center of the ceiling for what felt like hours, waiting to conk out. Strange things began to happen while I lay there, odd sensations and thoughts. It took a while—several months—for them to gain enough momentum to become Something.

It began with falling. Falling asleep, but slowly, being aware of falling asleep, the stages of it enfolding me, and a sense of dropping into it, as if "it" were a place. I realized I could resist and suspend myself above sleep, or even now and then go into it and rise up out of it again. I experimented with that for a while, dipping into sleep as if it were a body of water and I a giant toe.

One night I felt an amazing thing. I became two creatures, one that was my physical self, sliding into and under the lake of sleep, and another that was also me, but a me without the bother of a body, and that rose out of my chest—as if I'd been cracked open at the breastbone to let myself out—and was free to float around as high up as the body-me was down, in the lake of sleep. They were opposites, they had to move in equal measure from each other, so the further I sank into sleep, the further the other me could go up into the air. What was best about it was the feeling of being peeled apart, a moment as rewarding as the one when a scab finally gives way, when the itch stops and the new, naked skin can breathe.

It was a while before I understood that I didn't have to stay in my bedroom.

First I went up and down the street and looked at the neighbors' houses and the edge of Hampstead Heath. But I didn't really want to see that stuff, which was what I saw all the time, although it was fun to look in people's windows. So I went to Cambridge.

I crossed the Atlantic to Boston Harbor and went upstream along the Charles until I saw the Harvard boathouses. Then I took a right up Massachusetts Avenue, past the flooded frozen Cambridge Common, a temporary skating rink that glistened in the dark. There was my school, my asphalt playground where I'd skinned my knees on American gravel. There was the snow heaped on corners and curbs. There was our house and our backyard willow with its branches short and stiff from winter. Up the hill was the penny candy store—who cared if the chocolate wasn't as sweet? I could move quickly with my hovering and encompass the whole of the known city (known to me, that is) in ten minutes. From the swimming pool by the river at Magazine Street where my mother took me in the dog days to the Star Market on the way to Watertown where she dragged me weekly was at least four miles, but I'd get there in a moment with my floating non-body. I wanted the comfort of seeing the wooden houses and their painted shutters and the spread of deciduous trees (in those days there were still elms in North America), even if they were naked in February. I didn't want brick townhouses, iron railings, yews and cobblestones and equestrian statues.

Every night that I could manage to separate myself, I went home. I called it soul traveling.

It was flying, really.

It was some sort of flying. I hovered above my dream-Cambridge, that was sleeping and frozen below me, and I was happy.

And then, on to Italy.

Everything was new and strange and beautiful. The key to the front door of our villa out on the via Bolognese in the hills above Florence was as big as my arm and looked like a child's drawing of a key, a schematic, enormous proto-key, which nobody ever used but which was handed over to us in a welcoming ceremony by the farmer who lived across the way in a house a third the size of ours and looked after the property in a feudal arrangement with the contessa whose villa it was and who was summering elsewhere. In the tradition of Italian contessas she was broke—she must have been to rent out such a house with such a magnificent view and so well situated that it caught any trace of breeze that managed to blow off the Apennines. Instead of doorknobs there were handles you pushed down to open the doors. The windows divided in the center and opened to the outside instead of going up and down. A shutter hidden in the frame clanked down in metal segments, sort of like an alligator. The farmer showed us how to pull it closed while leaving the windows open, catching the air but foiling the sun. The speckled floors were made of marble chips embedded in cement and polished to a shiny finish. Never a rug to get in the way of my sliding down the hall or round and round the dining room, pushing myself along on the dark, high, dusty gnarled furniture that fortified every inch of the walls. Highboys, lowboys, breakfronts, serving tables, linen chests, armoires, extra chairs (eight in addition to the six at the table): That villa had enough furniture for three villas. All of it was carved from black wood, or wood that time had blackened, and all of it was heavy, thick, oily with the touch of hundreds of hands. Walnut, chestnut, ancient fruit trees—these woods felt and smelled different from what I was used to, Scandinavian birch or teak in Cambridge and the cracking oak veneer and dried-out mahogany of the bad, war-torn furniture in the London house.

Once again I had to hop—up into bed. I liked this hop, which landed me in my more-than-double four-poster with curly columns terminating in pinecones that might have been acorns or perhaps the fleurs-de-lis that decorated every aspect of Florentine life from the red leather wallets that smelled of fish (something in the tanning process?) to the waxy, translucent paper bag in which the farmer's wife delivered our groceries twice a week.

The bathrooms were the best of all.

"The Romans invented plumbing," said my father, "and it shows."

The bathrooms were as big as the bedrooms and there were lots of them. They had large windows and spacious bathtubs and skittery white marble floors veined with green streaks in my parents' bathroom and rosy streaks in mine and blue-gray streaks in the one at Frederika's end of the hall. The only disturbing thing about them—and it was puzzling more than bothersome—was that the fixtures were oddly placed. A sink popped up at a peculiar angle, off-center between two windows, and a toilet was too far into the middle of the room, acting as if it were an armchair. Probably the bathrooms had been bedrooms once, before the plumbing was put in at the turn of the century, and before bathroom layouts had been routinized.

In England time had been thick and impenetrable. It might as well have been plaster. It was immovable, obdurate, and sheer. It was also repetitive. Every day was as bad or bad in the same way as the previous day. Going to school was like putting an iron block on my head and balancing it for six hours. When I got home in the brief gloomy afternoon, I didn't know what to do other than flop onto my bed and disappear into a book. Real bedtime was a relief. I could just lie there and hope to take one of my flying trips—except for the toilet worries that constituted a small but unceasing pressure, as if I wore a too-tight collar at night.

In Italy time had an utterly different shape and feel. A day was a long, coherent totality, shining and hot, all of one piece, though the piece was variegated and speckled like the floor.

In part I was transformed by love, because in Italy I fell in love again, this time with a single entity rather than with a city, which, no matter how much I loved it, could never return my affection. I didn't do much better the second time. I fell in love with a statue.

He stood in his niche on the wall of Orsanmichele, the old grain market in the center of Florence. Lots of other saints and heroes stood nearby, but he was striking for his straight, upright beauty: Saint George, the patron of England, emblazoned on flags and walls and letterheads there, but never looking like this.

For one thing, no dragon. The dragon was understood. This was a post-slaying portrait. He was holding his triangular shield between his feet, resting a hand across the top, looking out at the passersby with a faraway, tired expression. Because he was an Italian saint, he was wearing a sort of toga and cloak getup rather than the chain mail he wore in England.

His face was dreamy, not only his expression but his features. It was slightly rounded, with a small, delicate chin and little ears tucked in close. A northern Italian face. I could see the fair skin and light eyes even in the stained, pockmarked bronze.

It happened because the statues were placed around the first story of the building instead of up along the roofline as usual. If they'd been up where they were supposed to be, I wouldn't have gotten a good look at them. These statues were so close they could have been people on the street who'd hopped up to stand on the ledge of rusticated granite that ran in courses along each floor.

I looked up and our eyes met. I blushed. I had to look down at the cobbles right away. Then I looked up and stared. I wanted to drink him. I wanted to breathe his quiet, steady being and smell his smooth, warm metal mouth and cheeks.

An attractive statue, and I was attracted. But there had to be something else—that's the way love is. Something special, something that made me know.

Later that week we were in the Bargello Museum. We were always in a museum in Italy. And standing on a plinth, no niche, there he was again. This time he was made of marble.

He's following me! He loves me too! That's what I thought.

I stood looking at him.

"It's Saint George," my mother said. "You know him from England."

"Uh-huh," I said. I couldn't talk. Also, I didn't like her saying his name, though at the same time I was thrilled to hear it spoken. Saint George, Saint George, I said silently over and over. I couldn't bring myself to say it out loud.

"Donatello," my father said.

"Donatello what?" I asked.

"Donatello made it," he said.

I didn't like this idea.

"This room is full of him. Here's another good one," my father said, moving off to the left.

It was nice. It was a young bronze man with a wonderful little hat, naked except for this crazy, jaunty hat, smiling, and with long curly hair.

"That's David," my father said. "David and Goliath, remember?"

I remembered.

"Like the huge *David* in the piazza where the best gelato is," my mother said. "By Michelangelo."

I was getting a good art education in Italy. I didn't know that, of course.

We'd left the Bargello and were having gelato in another place, not quite as good as the one near the big *David,* before I dared to ask: "Isn't Saint George on the outside of a building too?"

"I'm sure," said my mother.

"Oh." My father started rummaging through the guidebook. "You're right. That one is a copy. They moved the original into the Bargello."

"*David* is a copy too," my mother observed, wiping chocolate off the baby's chin.

"Is that fair?" I asked. "Is it fair to have copies? Are copies okay?"

"You mean the Michelangelo," my father said to my mother. "The bronze *David* in the Bargello, the Donatello—"

"Yes," my mother said. "What do you mean by *fair*?" she asked me.

"If it's bronze," my father said, "you can make another cast and it isn't a copy, exactly. It's considered an original. But you can't do that with marble."

"He comes both ways," I said. I couldn't bring myself to say *it* or to say his name again.

Back to the guidebook. " 'The Saint George in the niche of Orsanmichele is a copy made when the statues were moved into the National Museum—' "

"There's another one?" I was astonished. Maybe he was everywhere, in every museum and on every building in Florence.

"The National Museum *is* the Bargello," said my father.

"Are you sure?" asked my mother.

"There are too many names," I said. "Is it called Orsanmichele or the grain market? Is it the Bargello or the National Museum?" Even though I'd been wondering about this point, I didn't really give a hoot about the answer. The question was a way of diverting attention from my interest in Saint George.

"Everything here is so old it's been different things in different centuries," my mother said. "The Bargello used to be a kind of city hall, now it's a museum. You see?"

"It used to be police headquarters," my father said.

"Probably for the Fascists," my mother said.

I suppose we made an appealing group, dark-haired and dark-eyed, my mother elegant in brown linen, the baby still feathered in soft curls, my father with his penetrating, often terrifying gaze, all bent over our bowls of pastel gelato, trying to eat it before it regressed to cream and eggs and fruit in the heat of noon. Daily my father intoned, "'Only mad dogs and Englishmen go out in the noonday sun,'" because daily we were out there too, doing our rounds in the museums and piazzas and palaces. We were clearly tourists; only foreigners were so silly as to not go home for a decent *pranzo* and a nap. But we were not obviously American ones. French, a diplomat? Maybe a Greek businessman and family. But surely not Philadelphia Jews, scholarship kids (my mother beat out my father to win the citywide competition for full tuition at Penn), with the kind of luck that comes to high intelligence, the mentors who make sure you get to where you should have been all along: on the Harvard faculty, at the lunch table in the Society of Fellows (aping Oxford and the real, fake Cambridge), or under the red-and-white awning of a *gelateria* in Florence on a Guggenheim and a Fulbright too, in the prime of life, in the middle of the century, in full sun.

But in fact my mother's canny disguises hadn't fooled the cannier Italians, alert for centuries to poseurs, interlopers, forgers, spies, *stranieri*. So what if she'd forked over plenty of American dollars for her caramel suede Ferragamos and convinced my father to trade his chunky Brooks Brothers tie-ups for some sleek black slip-ons? She'd replaced my beloved red Keds with rubber-soled, ankle-strapped gladiatorial leather sandals from the open-air market near Santa Maria Novella. Shoes tell all, was her belief, and she wasn't wrong. Leather- and fashion-conscious Florentines looked first at the feet, then at the face. And though there was a momentary confusion, requiring a second look at the whole ensemble, no waiter ever failed to address us in English. The people who couldn't figure out that we were Americans were the other American tourists.

Frederika (not with us on this day) was a complicating factor in identifying us. She certainly wasn't Italian: too tall, too beige, with her hair in a bun and her thick-framed glasses and her homemade, batik-print clothing and ergonomic shoes. A Swedish hippie is what she was, before there were any hippies. After I fell in love with Saint George, I became aware of the clichés of romance, and wondered if Frederika were to undo her bun, chuck her glasses, and put on a low-cut dress, she would turn into Sophia Loren. When she came to live with us in Cambridge, she did many of those things, but she turned into a tall, brown-haired, nearsighted Swedish girl, which wasn't much of a transformation.

That day of my second encounter with Saint George, Frederika was off with her Italian boyfriend, Fulvio. Despite the glasses and the lumpy footwear, she'd proved exotic enough to appeal to the neighboring villa's eldest son, who was studying or doing an imitation of studying architecture at the University of Florence. Fulvio was in his early twenties, spoke rather good English with a German accent (Austrian mother), and had a green Vespa on which he abducted Frederika on Thursday and Sunday afternoons.

My mother did not approve. She had better things in mind for Frederika.

"It's all right for a fling," she said. "But you don't love him."

Frederika had to admit that she did not.

"Thank god," my mother said. "Be careful."

In Italy in 1956 they must have had to resort to the oldest form of contraception. I imagine the cedar-studded, bee-humming acreage that stretched out behind the house fertilized by Fulvio on those evenings he turned up after dinner (which were all evenings except Thursday and Sunday), his Vespa whining with anticipation as he blasted through the massive iron gate that hadn't been open or closed (it was stuck in a halfway position) since the nineteenth century, judging by the extent of the vines that grew all over it.

I could see them from my window, strolling down the path to the jungle, hand in hand, like Hansel and Gretel. This comparison comes to mind because later, in Cambridge, Frederika made a gingerbread house for my mother's birthday, cutting the windows and doors out of the dough before cooking it, plastering the walls together with caramelized sugar, painting tiles on the roof with red-tinted icing. It was a representation of our villa in Florence, an out-of-season, Swedish-Italian hybrid marvel. "We make them for Christmas," she said, "but I thought it would be nice in springtime too."

By then Frederika was in love for real. This time my mother approved, because she'd set up the match. My mother had more fun with Frederika the substitute daughter than she ever had with me or my sister. Behavior that we called "meddling" or "interfering" seemed to Frederika a passionate engagement with her happiness—which it was, in all its instances.

The thing looked unlikely from the outset: a short, bug-eyed Indian conductor just hatched from the Paris Conservatory, name of Vishwa Dal. My mother was right, though. She often was right, which added to the irritation of her meddling. Vishwa and Frederika were a perfect pair. Their love story unfolded and then folded up again in Cambridge, as I watched and took mental notes and learned nothing, naturally, because the heart is unteachable.

While Fulvio and Frederika thrashed around in the undergrowth, I lay in my four-poster bed and thought about Saint

George. My notion of sexual intercourse was a gymnastic exercise in reproduction, not something you'd dream of and yearn for. So when I thought about Saint George, I thought about hugging him. First standing in front of him, looking at him and wanting to hug him, then hugging him, then his hugging me back. I could and did think of these three tableaux over and over: standing and wanting to hug; hugging; being hugged. I varied it by imagining it first with Saint George in his niche on the wall of Orsanmichele, then with Saint George on his plinth in the Bargello. Once I'd fallen in love with Saint George, I stopped making my nighttime flights to Cambridge. In fact, adulterous, I didn't want to go back to Cambridge because I didn't want to leave my beloved.

There were other things I didn't want to leave. I'd become entranced with the piebald, harlequin Duomo, which we could see from our terrace above town. The crazy-colored marble blocks made it look like a vertical chessboard for a game played on black, pink, and white squares by Italian giants. Nearly every morning I sat on our hot flagstones with my box of Crayons brought from home, now missing some critical colors like red and sky blue, and drew a picture of Brunelleschi's dome. I produced dozens of these drawings. My mother thought they were wonderful and kept them all. For years she had one taped to the refrigerator door in Cambridge. When one faded or got mayonnaise on it, she'd replace it with a new one from her store.

I loved the Duomo because it looked as if the Florentines had had fun building it. When we went to Siena, the whole city looked that way—the sloped, scalloped piazza like a tipped-up pizza shell, the black-and-white prison-striped columns in the churches. I thought Italy's elaborate architectural eruptions had been created to amuse and astonish children, and me in particular. But I was wrong about that, like millions before and after me. Italy didn't love me back any more than Cambridge or a statue of Saint George did.

Though she disapproved of Fulvio, my mother had become friends with his mother, Annemarie. Annemarie also disapproved of Fulvio. "He wastes his life," she said in her growly, smoky voice. Annemarie and my mother spent many afternoons under a parasol on our terrace smoking together. "No talent," she would continue. "No talent at all, at all. It is a rebellion."

"Against?" my mother prompted.

"The Businessman."

The Businessman was what Annemarie called her husband, Alessandro. Whatever business he was in, he made a lot of money at it. Their villa had new plumbing, new marble, a sleek, visionary, stainless-steel kitchen, exposed timbers in the ceilings of the large rooms empty except for groupings of antique armchairs reupholstered in Florentine flame-stitch silk (my mother told me it was called a Bargello pattern) commissioned by Annemarie at the old fabricator in town that still produced cloth in the Renaissance manner on ancient looms. Twenty or thirty years later, this was how houses looked in fancy architectural magazines. In the mid-fifties, it was home decor from Mars. The design talent in that family belonged to Annemarie.

My mother also had a good eye. One of her and Annemarie's favorite pastimes was to stroll together through our dark, overstuffed villa pretending they had all the Businessman's money available to fix it up.

Standing in the dining room, Annemarie waved her hand.

"Out! Out!" she said, banishing the extra chairs and china cabinets and hat racks and footstools that had invited themselves for breakfast, lunch, and dinner. "Nothing," she decreed, nudging with her bare foot a yellow-and-blue Majolica umbrella receptacle big enough to hold a dead dog.

"Nothing would be kind of difficult," my mother said. "Not even a table?"

"A daybed," said Annemarie. "A daybed and an *armadio*—that long, low one in the Child's room." She always called me the Child.

"And where do we eat?" asked my mother.

"Buffet-style," said Annemarie.

"Standing up? Come on, Annemarie. That's cocktail-style. There's got to be a dining room."

"Eat in the kitchen. Eat on the terrace."

Because Annemarie was not Italian, she wasn't very interested in food.

"This room would be perfect for napping," she continued. "It's cool and those long windows. Very nice, opening out to the terrace. Lovely. Painted red. Dark red—everything!"

"Like a bordello," said my mother.

"Exactly!" said Annemarie.

They both burst out laughing.

Annemarie fascinated me. I didn't know that she was an example of a type, not all that rare. She seemed as unprecedented and marvelous as if she'd stepped out of a painting. Not *La Primavera,* certainly; she wasn't a beauty. Something later, blowsier, a Caravaggio or a Titian. She was perfectly turned out for every occasion, even the mundane occasion of smoking on the terrace with my mother. One day: black Capri pants, sleeveless white cotton shirt with mother-of-pearl buttons; flat sandals kicked off under the chair (Annemarie liked to be barefoot); auburn hair swept up in a mishmash that teetered between knot and ponytail, impaled with a tortoiseshell skewer; a diamond ring, a ruby ring, a bloodstone signet ring, three gold bangles, and an English Oval smoldering in her left hand. Next day: magenta linen sheath dress, kneelength; hair au naturel (this meant all over the place, tumbling, wavy); aforementioned rings plus amber necklace; and black high heels in which it was impossible to walk the quarter-mile dirt road between her villa and ours. And yet, she did. She was the sort of woman who could walk three miles in high heels.

She was depilated and waxed and creamed and buffed to a glistening smooth finish like our terrazzo floor after the farmer's wife had scrubbed it with vinegar and water and then skated it dry with lamb's-wool slippers.

My mother was more beautiful, but her arsenal of presentation was limited, first by money, second by inclination. She wasn't willing to spend time on what Annemarie called "the constant vigilance." My mother was younger by about five years—crucial years in a woman's life, the ones that separate the thirties from the forties. And unlike Annemarie, who tended toward plumpness, my mother was a skinny person. That summer in Italy, these factors were in her favor. The differences, though, showed up several decades later when I saw Annemarie again. My mother had aged and Annemarie had stayed quite the same, preserved—nearly pickled—by European beauty secrets. Who knows what they were? Bee-pollen injections, high-colonic mineral-water irrigations, once-a-week fasts (she was doing that when we met her). Possibly she bathed in milk and drank crushed pearls like Cleopatra.

My mother thought Fulvio wasn't good enough for Frederika; Annemarie thought the opposite. She knew her son was a bit of a wastrel, but she didn't understand Frederika's "qualities," as my mother referred to them. I was the Child; Frederika was the Girl. As in, "The Girl isn't very good at keeping the baby quiet, is she?"

"Babies cry," my mother said. "She's had a fever."

"You must have the doctor," said Annemarie.

"It's nothing," said my mother.

"It could be malaria," said Annemarie, a robust hypochondriac. She sent the doctor over the next day.

His first question: "Does she coo?"

This flummoxed my mother. "You mean, is she happy?"

"Coo, coo." He demonstrated, coughing a little *rat-tat-tat* a baby might make. Phonetic English.

"Ah," said my mother. "No, no. Just a runny nose and a little fever."

"And what do you feed her?"

"Pureed carrots, things like that."

The doctor threw up his hands. "No pasta? Of course she is sick. She must eat pasta."

"She's not even a year old," my mother protested.

"In soup," he explained.

"That's damned unlikely," my mother said to herself as he drove off in his ramshackle Fiat. "Am I supposed to masticate the pasta like a bird mother?"

"What does *masticate* mean?" I asked.

"Chew," my mother told me. "Bird mothers chew things and then spit them into the baby's mouth."

"Ugh," I said.

"Don't worry—I'm not going to."

"Icky," I said. I couldn't get over how disgusting that was.

Even though it was disgusting, I suppose because it was disgusting, I didn't stop thinking about it until the inevitable happened, which was imagining myself chewing something, chocolate gelato maybe, and then spitting it into Saint George's mouth. Gelato wasn't a good choice, since it didn't really need chewing and would dribble out. So then I had to think about it all over again from the beginning, chewing something that needed chewing, salami and bread, say, and spitting—*poof,*

poof—and by doing this, waking my love from his stone or bronze trance. Soon it was a second chapter in my pattern of Saint George thoughts. First wanting to hug, hugging, and being hugged back; then, while in an embrace, chewing, spitting, and waking him.

I had no idea what I would do with him were he to awaken, and in my stylized round of thought, everything stopped at the moment he opened his eyes, enlivened by chewed salami.

The evenings a-chatter with katydids and locusts as we ate on the terrace while the abrupt sunset blacked out the already-shadowy garden; the lovely arc of the day, bisected by the nap we'd finally learned to take after lunch so as to attack art and architecture with renewed zest in the afternoon, when the museum guards slumped in postprandial torpor on their tiny folding canvas stools; "our" vegetable stand, "our" *gelateria,* "our" *ristorante* on the Lungarno for a festive Saturday night out: We had Italy in the palm of our hand. We were practically Italian!

Many, many years later, the last year of the century, I spent a winter with Annemarie and the Businessman, who was no sort of businessman at all, rather, a cultured, tailored professor of philosophy from a wealthy family in Trieste. Some friends of theirs invited us to a New Year's Eve house party in Siena in their deconsecrated monastery-chapel, transformed into a villa with no heat. The Businessman and I got up early on New Year's Day and, half frozen, decided to walk around town in order to get the circulation going.

It was quiet and chilly. The tippy narrow streets were empty and dark, because northern Italy, in an awkward time zone, is artificially dark in winter. When we reached the piazza, old men in long blue cashmere coats were watching their grandchildren play ball on the half-shell. Streams of people were coming out from church while the bell rang and rang and rang.

"It looks as if it were five hundred years ago," I said.

"It does look the same," said Alessandro.

"Do you think you can know how it felt to live here in 1499? Because you're Italian, I mean," I asked him. "I know that I can't know," I said. "I just pretend I know."

Alessandro looked around and shrugged. "It's not possible," he said.

"Why?"

"It's just not possible. We're not the same as they were."

I looked at the gray tilted stones and the houses leaning in toward the center like an audience waiting for a climax. "Then all this is as mysterious to you as it is to me?" I asked him.

"I'm afraid so," he said.

It was time to go home. Frederika would join us later. She had to return, first, to her family in Sweden.

Annemarie gave us presents. For my mother, a cake plate from Ginori shaped like a tray and made of heavy, creamy porcelain painted with fabulous—as in nonexistent—birds and insects. For my father, a silver-and-boar-tusk shoehorn as long as his forearm. For me, a tiny blue enameled box in the potbellied form of a pirate's chest, "for your treasures, Child," she said.

"Come back, come back," said the farmer and his wife and Annemarie and Alessandro and Fulvio, all standing by the gate waving the Italian good-bye that beckons toward you instead of pushing you away. "Come back, come back."

We never did.

Returned

Back in Cambridge with an English accent and still wearing my leather-tied Italian sandals, I was an exotic third grader for a warm week in September until I was displaced by a late arrival, a girl just home from India, where her father had been years in the diplomatic corps. She wore silver ankle bracelets that jingled when she walked. The teacher asked her to bring Indian things—saris and brass pots and incense sticks—to class and tell us all about her faraway knowledge. I was irritated at first; I too had faraway knowledge, like how to kiss statues and redecorate crumbling villas and use a chamberpot. But I didn't want to share my secrets, so I was happy enough to keep a low profile.

I was no longer going to the public school across the street with its cold brick halls and the asphalt playground I'd flown over from England to visit at night. My parents had put me into the most progressive of the progressive schools in town, on a hill beyond the big intersection on the way to Watertown. One-story gray bungalows, tidy lawns and little winding paths, low-growing threadleaf maples and ornamental plum trees were supposed to make it child-size and comforting. But I could see right away that it was bogus. Woodworking and bookbinding and maypole dances concealed, not very well, the usual Cambridge atmosphere of competition and compulsive ranking of everything and everyone. In England the pressure had been to conform. Here the pressure was to excel.

I missed my old brick school, where, with no effort, I'd been at the top of the class. But that was over. My long, agonizing apprenticeship in failure had begun.

Either my failures in England didn't count or I'd been then (only a year before) innocent enough to feel that my failures were successes, proofs of being special. Now there was no way around it. I wasn't special, I was just lame and slow, unable to get into the spirit, unwilling to apply myself to whatever it was. Unable as well to stick up for myself, the way I'd done in England when I'd told Miss Gravel that cavemen were boring and I was going to read instead.

I hid out in my surroundings, which didn't have any expectations or demands of me. In winter I watched the constellations creaking around in the cold Cambridge sky. In spring I made grass villages in the backyard for the ants to crawl through and poked at beetles with sticks. At school I sat on the banks of the pond and hoped for frogs. There were still enough fireflies back then to catch a bottle full on a summer night. Mostly, though, I rode my bike.

On my bike I perfected my love for Cambridge. This house here with a hydrangea vine clambering all over the front porch, and that one next to it where the stone wall had fragmented from years of freeze-and-thaw, and the little red one with the back garden, and that one I couldn't really see because of the high privet in front. And the street that made me cry: Gray Gardens East. Gray Gardens West, on the opposite side of Garden Street, didn't have the same effect. East was quiet, motionless, as if it were a photograph and not reality; West had bustle. I saved my ride down Gray Gardens East for the end of my circuit, so I could anticipate the overflow of feeling it was going to provoke and thereby intensify it.

I'd turn on to Gray Gardens East and my throat would thicken. The stillness, the dry leaves rattling in an otherwise-undetectable breeze, the small, shuttered houses quietly waiting for nightfall and their owners' return, the yellow lights and muffled voices that, on those brave autumn evenings when I dared to ride at early dark, I could see and hear faintly through curtains and walls—from all this I constructed a monument to an imagined, safe little life I'd never had and was never going to have. I'd stand there straddling my bike and mourning the loss of a completely invented past.

Part of what was sweet about the experience I concocted on Gray Gardens East was the feeling of being left out. It satisfied me to feel alien and neglected, and to play those feelings against a backdrop of charming little houses with combed, tended gardens. Not-having was a more powerful emotion than wanting or having. I didn't want to live in any of those houses. They were all made of brick instead of being proper wooden New England houses. They were small and they were too close together, and their tidy gardens were too pinched for willow trees and grass tracts for ant villages. They had mean, mingy windows with fake leading and they had fake hobnailed doors. They were pretending to be English houses.

And I was pretending to be an orphan looking wistfully in at a coziness I couldn't be part of. The fakery of Gray Gardens East encouraged me in my self-deception.

My bike was a black English three-speed, a Raleigh. It had a curved wicker basket set between the handlebars and a clasp like a huge paper clip over the back wheel, into whose maw I could jam something unbreakable, a jacket or a book. The gears made a lovely soft click when I shifted them, as I had to do to get up the hill between our house and the Bigelows'.

Roger Bigelow was the only familiar item at school and probably the reason my parents had decided to send me there. He was short, wiry, pale-eyed, and pale-haired, and he smelled of the glue for model airplanes, in which he was saturated from his hours bent over kits in the basement. We were exact contemporaries—our birthdays were a week apart—and I couldn't remember back to a time when I didn't know him. He was a kind of brother, who lived up the hill. He had always been there, bullying me into model-airplane afternoons that made me stiff with boredom and letting me bully him into trying out one of my many inventions (like walking around in galoshes filled with cold water, a cumbersome but effective midsummer air-conditioning technique) or playing my favorite game, detective.

The Bigelows' house was jammed with furniture, which was in turn covered with rugs and blankets and piles of all sorts of things: books, mostly, but also half-finished crossword puzzles and Monopoly pieces and Ping-Pong balls and parts of model airplanes. The mantelpiece was crowded with statuettes and whorly shells and fragments of rusted ironwork. Stacks of magazines camped out along the staircase. A large fringed Oriental carpet draped over the piano made an under-the-piano world where two children could easily fit even though they had to share it with a slide projector, ten boxes of slides, several other Oriental carpets rolled up, and a few folded folding chairs. That house was the perfect place to look for something.

The flaw with the detective game was that I didn't always know what we were looking for. Roger objected to this.

"How can we *play* it?" he'd say.

"That's part of it," I'd tell him. "We'll know it when we find it."

It was an excuse for rummaging through the treasure heap of the Bigelows' life and stuff. Roger wasn't interested, because for him these things were just the substance of the everyday, but it was the opposite of what I was used to and therefore enchanting.

Our house was spare and bright and tidy. Piles were forbidden. My father hated what he termed "mess" (which included any evidence that two kids lived there), and my mother, who was an indifferent housekeeper, a literal sweeper-under-the-rug, didn't want her modern aesthetic cluttered with just the sorts of things that occupied every flat surface in the Bigelows' house.

Murano glass ashtrays, for instance. In the living room alone there were at least six of them. A couple of dark-blue ones, one big and one very small, not even large enough for two cigarettes, and a red one of the sort that looked like sliced-open melons or lemons, thick outer skins that revealed an entirely different inner texture and color. Then one I particularly loved, whose inside was orange and whose outside was green and where the two colors met there were gold-green nipples (it was hard to think of anything else they were like) popping out all around. It looked like a starfish. I wanted to smoke so as to be able to use it.

It wasn't only the objects, though they were fascinating; it was the idea of the mess, the confusion, the makings of a personality being on display that thrilled me. It was not okay for me to leave my schoolbooks on the kitchen table, but it was fine for Roger to leave the instructions for his new chemistry set on the black leather ottoman in front of his father's favorite chair. I wanted to understand why this was so. I was looking for that, I suppose.

Much of why had to do with Roger's father, Abbott Archibald Bigelow number two, named for his grandfather, who had been a notable Luminist painter. Number one's self-portrait, which hung above the piano, could have been of Roger's father if he'd had a goatee and high-collared shirt. He had a walrusy mustache instead, and a polka-dot bow tie that was always askew.

He was called A.A. and I loved him as I never loved either of my parents, because, of course, he wasn't my parent, but also because he was the strangest, best person I knew. Certainly, at the age of eight I'd never encountered anyone the least bit like him. I didn't know then that I never would. I remember in my twenties overhearing my mother say, Oh, A.A. is the most extraordinary person I know. This surprised me, since I'd thought he was my discovery and since what I loved him for when I was so young were mostly things I didn't think would matter to my mother.

One wonderful thing about him was that though he was quite tall, an inch or two above six feet, he was bendable and foldy and could in a second telescope himself into a size compatible with an eight-year-old's. Another was that he didn't change his tone or his bearing when he got down to child level. His voice was a low, soft rumble, chatty and relaxed, and his speech was punctuated with lots of *mmm*s and *hmm*s, a comforting bass line of encouragement.

Roger, frustrated with something in the new chemistry set or a different kind of airplane, would say, "Papa, I can't *do* it."

"Hmm," A.A. would say. "Let's see. Okay, I think I understand. It's like this. Yes. That way. Okay. Mmm."

He also said *Mmm* and *Hmm* when we did dumb or even quite bad things, like empty out all the cabinets under the kitchen counter so as to use them as hiding places. This got him in trouble—as if he were a child too—with his wife, Ingrid.

"But why didn't you stop them?" she said. "Why?"

"Mmm," said A.A. "They were having fun."

"But it's a mess."

"Well, nothing broke."

Roger must have inherited his love of puttering from his father, because A.A. was always coming up with a new craft for us to try. One year it was enameling. He bought a small kiln and a kit with glass sticks in dozens of colors and stacks of metal bowls and beakers for us to enamel. We—I, really, since Roger always preferred airplanes—spent hours in the basement enameling things. The Bigelow ashtray collection increased threefold, and my mother had to devote a shelf in the broom closet to hiding the enameled objects I brought home every week. Then it was mosaics. A.A. worked on his masterpiece, a mosaic coffee-table top, while I grouted larger-size, more manageable tiles into trays and trivets.

We did decoupage and collage too, and then A.A. got excited by furniture-making. Table-making, mostly. He especially loved casters and put them on all the tables he made, which were low and square and had cubbies for storage. He'd paint them black, add casters, and sometimes tile the tops. He made a table for the television and a table for the record player and many tables to hold all the equipment that was necessary for enameling, decoupage, collage, tiling, and furniture-making in the basement.

My idea of heaven was to sit in the basement on a winter afternoon, warmed by the big black tanks of the furnace and the water heater churning beside us, with the air tinged by one of A.A.'s many cigarettes and the nip of Roger's glue. Sometimes Ingrid was running the washing machine, which added a cozy, moist vibration that stirred up all the inherent basement smells of chill and heat and dust and leftover paint and enamel. A.A. often tuned the radio to the broadcast of the previous night's opera at the Metropolitan in New York, so we tiled to *Tosca* and *Don Giovanni.*

Toward the middle of January, when the ice was firm, A.A. would take us skating on Spy Pond in Arlington. His skating outfit was a full-length black wool coat with a fur collar, an Astrakhan hat, and black leather gloves. Roger and I were in our red (mine) and orange (his) ski parkas and the detestable snow pants that all children in the Northeast wore until suddenly, in about 1960, they vanished. They were puffy without being warm, they were always dark blue, a color I hated, and they severely impeded movement, which wasn't good for skating. The padding was good for falling on, though, as we often did because of the clumsiness enforced by the pants. If we went early enough in the season we'd skate on virgin ice, sometimes powdered with a skim of snow so fine and dry that just the breeze of skating toward it would blow it out of the way. Whirls of snow made a kind of paisley pattern around the edges of the pond, where the rushes and catkins had frozen into strange sidelong postures.

Like a black swan, A.A. circled us on the ice, hovering over our many tumbles. Even his skates were black—old cracked leather lace-ups inherited from his father, Eustace, along with the coat and the hat. His father had been a doctor, as was A.A. In fact, with the exception of the Luminist anomaly, it was a medical family for generations. Eustace had been a general practitioner in Kansas City. Kansas City, Kansas, or Kansas City, Missouri? I loved the idea that a city could be in both places at once. (It was Missouri.) Even better was that Eustace had died from psittacosis, which he'd caught from either a patient or a parrot, depending on who was telling the story.

A.A. said he'd caught it from a patient.

Ingrid said, "He caught it from a *parrot*."

I pictured Eustace in the long black coat with green feathers peeping out, coughing and coughing until he dropped over dead.

"You can't catch it from a patient," Ingrid said.

She was a doctor too, so it was hard to know which version was true. Ingrid and A.A. were both doctors, but in almost every other way they were different. Ingrid was small and nervous. She was always saying, No, no, no. A.A. was from the center of America, from an old-time Tom Sawyer–ish place with big trees and a big river. Ingrid was from Sweden. Actually, Ingrid was Viennese. Well, not exactly; it was complicated.

Ingrid's family was even more medical than A.A.'s. Her father and her three brothers were all doctors. The family started out in Vienna and then things went badly after the First World War so they moved to Sweden, where Ingrid was born. Technically, she was Swedish. This turned out to be important. Maybe immigration quotas for Swedes were more generous than those for Austrians or maybe all the Austrians scrambling to escape history filled their quotas in a flash—whichever it was, Ingrid got into America because she was the only one in the family with a Swedish passport.

I loved it when she would tell the story.

She was nineteen. First she flew to London, where she was going to get another plane to Finland. Maybe the plane was going to Saint Petersburg? Was it called Petrograd then? Leningrad? How little I can remember it, this story that when I was eight and nine and ten seemed like a fairy tale because of all the mishaps and the happy ending. At any rate, in London she boarded the second plane, which seemed very full. There wasn't enough room for everyone to sit down. The steward stood near the cockpit and said: Is there anyone here who is not going to Berlin? This plane is going to Berlin and there are too many people on it.

"That was lucky!" Ingrid would say at this juncture in the story. "Suppose the plane hadn't been full. I would have gone to Berlin by mistake. That wouldn't have been any good."

Ingrid did not go into detail about just how not good it would have been for an Austrian-Swedish Jew to arrive in Berlin at that moment.

So she got off the plane and got onto the right plane and went to Finland or Russia or the Soviet Union and then she got onto the Trans-Siberian Railroad and went to Japan.

"And tell about the railroad," I'd say.

"The train had bunks," Ingrid would continue, "but it had three bunks, not just two. I was on the top, top bunk. All there was to eat was potatoes and sour cream. We were on the train for ages."

"How long, Ingrid?" I'd ask.

"At least a week. I think it was maybe for ten days. We had to keep stopping because of all the trains filled with soldiers heading to war, and we'd have to wait and not be in their way. Anyhow, everyone had diarrhea from eating sour cream three times a day. And I had to jump down from that top, top bunk with diarrhea all the time."

"But you got there, to Japan, right?"

"Oh, yes, eventually we got there. Then we got on a boat that was going to San Francisco. We had to go that way because of the German submarines in the Atlantic. It wasn't safe. That was why we were going on the Pacific. And then, two days out from Yokohama, the Japanese bombed Pearl Harbor."

"And then?"

"So then we didn't know if we would be allowed to land in America. Because it was an enemy ship now. So we waited, and waited, because maybe we were going to go back to Japan. But they worked something out, and we went to San Francisco.

"And that's how I came to America," she would say. She always concluded the story with those words.

One reason I loved this story was that I was crazy for sour cream, and eating it all the time sounded great. Also, it vouched for the story's authenticity. I knew that sour cream *was* Russia. My Russian grandmother gave it to me every morning, a bowl of blueberries suffocating in sour cream, in those summers when I'd been sent away from polio to spend two months with her in Atlantic City. Post-Salk, I no longer went there.

My Austro-Hungarian mother did not believe in sour cream. Cream, maybe, and after Italy, not much of that. But my father (the Russian side) loved it too. My mother kept a bottle in the refrigerator for him. My father and I sometimes stood in the kitchen together and ate sour cream with teaspoons straight from the jar, one of the few disorderly, uncouth activities he was willing to indulge either himself or me in.

They met during their residencies in San Francisco. After Eustace died from psittacosis, A.A.'s mother moved to the West Coast, and when A.A. graduated from Harvard he dutifully went out there for medical school. To find Ingrid, fresh off the enemy boat, speaking her singsong Swedish English. She was going to be a psychoanalyst. A.A. decided he was going to be one too.

So there they were at the top of our hill, two psychoanalysts, one semi-brother, and a house full of oddities. I could trot over there in less than two minutes on a winter day; pedaling the bike uphill in summer took longer.

Roger was good at being a student. Tests were fun, he said. He liked to memorize things, and he did it automatically. If you told Roger something, he'd remember it in exactly the words you'd used. He also remembered entire pages from books and where to find those pages in the books. I envied him. Almost everything I heard and read in school fell right out of my brain or bounced off it, as if my brain were the opposite kind of magnet from the information, the repellent kind. Roger loved arithmetic; I was still doing multiplication as addition—on my fingers. Third grade is long division, and doing long division on your fingers is a laborious process. I didn't like "arithmetic" in Cambridge any better than I'd liked "maths" in England.

A worse problem was that my classmates had begun to catch up to me in reading. I probably read more, and more difficult, books than they did, but it was no longer obvious that I was superior, because I wasn't.

I was a good speller. That wasn't much of a thrill. Also, the school was progressive enough to value spelling less than a regular school would. Content and comprehension: Those were the things. Spelling would follow, was their theory.

Theories were everywhere at that school, and they led to some pretty strange teaching. For instance, the Stick Man. He wasn't a regular teacher. He came in a few times a week with his new way of explaining arithmetic: colored sticks. Different lengths and colors for different numbers. It was hateful because it added one more dimension to remember—in my case, to forget—about the intractable, confusing realm of numbers.

A white stick an inch long was one, a red stick a bit longer was two, and so forth. They were made of fragile, splintery balsa wood like Roger's airplanes, and dyed with colors that leached out over the course of the year. The weightlessness of the wood bothered me. I wanted three to feel heavier than two, but they were indistinguishable.

This synesthetic theory had a name, now lost to me, that sounded like Cuisinart, though it must have been something else. Its proponent the Stick Man was cheerful, and we liked to see him appear at the door to the classroom. Nobody (except the teachers, of course) thought these sticks were helpful in any way, but his presence enlivened things.

I liked the Stick Man enough to confide in him, one day after class, that I detested arithmetic.

"It makes my head hurt," I explained.

"That's why sticks are good!" he said. "Sticks make the numbers visible."

"Not to me," I said. "Sticks are just a new way to feel mixed up."

"Oh, no," he said. "That's terrible."

He sounded so concerned that I started to cry.

What upset me was the feeling that he cared about my being mixed up. I didn't think anybody cared—or I told myself that nobody cared. And once I'd started heaving and sobbing, I couldn't stop. A big hot backlog of feeling sorry for myself and misunderstood and unappreciated and incompetent began to slither out of me.

Poor guy! He patted my eight-year-old shoulder and said, "There, there," and probably felt put upon. He wasn't a child psychologist or even a grade-school teacher, he was just a guy preaching the gospel of the stick.

"Let's spend some time together working on this," he said.

I could tell that he meant working on sticks, not working on how miserable I was.

So we did that for an hour in the dusty, deserted classroom. He was a nice, kind person. The only stick I liked at all was the number six, an intense blue-green wand. I held it tight in my sweaty, teary hand while he tried to soothe and engage me. My index finger was tinted a pale version of that green when we finished. But, as usual, nothing else stayed with me.

In addition to spelling, I had a talent for braiding hair. I spent a lot of the fall semester braiding the hair of the girl who sat in front of me. Her name was Meg and she had lovely, water-smooth light-brown hair down to her shoulder blades, the kind that slides shinily out of the braid as soon as you make it, even if you tie it at the bottom, which meant I had an excuse for braiding it again. My involvement with Meg's hair gave me the idea that we could be friends. Face-to-face, though, we had nothing to say to each other. Better to stick to the braiding relationship. And then the teacher decided I was too distracted by Meg and her hair and moved my seat. In Purgatory, sitting near the door, I looked down the empty hall and squinted toward the future I could almost see, when the last bell would ring and it would be time to go home.

Being confined in school, in a classroom, in a particular seat, listening to a teacher, made me stir-crazy. It wasn't that I couldn't sit still; I could sit still for hours watching my ants tramp along the paths I made for them by pressing the grass down with my hand, or lie without budging on my stomach until I was completely numb reading the *Narnia* books. But I couldn't sit still for all the school stuff. And beyond my physical restlessness was a more profound disquiet, which was: What is the point of all this?

I kept asking my father.

"What's the point of all this arithmetic? Why do I have to know this? I don't like this."

"You need it in life," he said.

"Why? What's it for?"

"It's like being able to read. It's being able to read numbers. You must be able to read numbers as well as words."

That made a little bit of sense. Just a little.

Then we started studying the Revolutionary War. We had to draw diagrams of battles. We had to learn lists of generals.

"I don't care about this," I said to my father. I never said these sorts of things to my mother. "I don't want to know these things."

"They're interesting," my father said. "The Revolution is interesting. And a lot of it happened right here."

"I don't care. I'm not interested."

"You don't give it a chance," he said. "You get all riled up about it before you even try. Calm down."

That sounded like something my mother would say. They were in cahoots.

I began to understand that, at bottom, school was a way to get me out of my mother's hair for the day. Also, a way to break my spirit. It was meant to grind me down, bore me into submission, and lure me into accepting its values until all I wanted was to be the best at reciting lists of generals and battles of the Revolutionary War.

Roger was interested in learning new things just because they were new. A little anti-intellectual, I kept asking about utility with my What's the point question. Nobody would address this question, which made me all the more intent on it. My father always put it back on me, telling me to relax and pay attention. Roger was worse than my father with his cheery "It's fun!" and his game mentality, in which everything he encountered was a puzzle to be worked out and seemed (as far as I could tell) to have no emotional content. I didn't even bother asking the teachers. I assumed they were totally brainwashed about how important all the stuff they were teaching was.

The only person with any sympathy for my position was A.A.

Sometimes when I ate dinner at the Bigelows' (which I did two or three times a week), Ingrid would start chastising me.

"You don't pay attention at school," she'd say. "Why don't you pay any attention?"

This would cause me to wriggle around on my chair as if I were in school at that moment and mumble, "I'm not good at it."

"It's not that hard," she'd say. "And you won't even try. Your parents are worried about you."

This information perked me up. It made me feel powerful.

One night A.A. came to my defense, in his languid way. When Ingrid told me it wasn't that hard to pay attention and I told her it was, A.A. asked me why, exactly, it was.

"I can't concentrate because it's boring," I said. "I don't see the point of it all."

"That does make it hard to listen," he said.

"No, no, no," said Ingrid. "You're encouraging her." She was a bit screechy, which was how she sounded when she was nervous or mad.

"Why not?" said A.A. "If she's bored, she's bored."

"That's no good to say!" Ingrid was really squeaky now.

"Oh, I don't know." A.A. turned to me again. "You might feel different someday. Things can change." He paused. "Of course, sometimes they don't."

I did feel encouraged, enough to say, "I don't want to know anything about that Revolution."

This made A.A. laugh. "I never found it very interesting either," he said.

"But you don't get to just pick and choose," said Ingrid.

"I like the Revolution," Roger put in.

I glared at him. "You like everything."

A.A. lit a cigarette and chewed on the smoke for a while. "It's really just a question of time. Waiting it out. There has to be the right thing, something that feels so interesting you want to know all about it. Then things will change. I'm sure. No point worrying."

"*You* don't have to worry," Ingrid said. "She's not your kid."

"It'll be fine," he said.

A.A. always thought things would be fine, and Ingrid always thought things would get worse. They disagreed constantly, which was yet another fascinating aspect of Bigelow life. My parents mostly disagreed in private. They liked to present a united, impenetrable front, and that made me feel they were ganging up on me.

This must have been in the fall, because as the weather got colder, the one interesting thing—which, when A.A. talked of it, sounded impossible to me—appeared at school. The one interesting thing was diagramming sentences. I was crazy for it.

I liked the way the dependent clauses and the phrases hooked off the main line, how almost every part of speech could have a little bracketed appendage to modify it, and how the skeleton of the sentence stood out bold and obvious while the extra parts thrummed along beneath it. The diagrammed sentence looked a bit like a long-division problem, and I liked that too, as if it conferred on words the seriousness and truth that had been reserved for numbers. I liked the nouns and their subcategories: the common noun, the proper noun, the collective noun, the abstract noun. Most of all I liked that what I took for granted—talking, reading, writing—could be rationalized and made scientific, and thereby be made real.

And so I was seduced into accepting the school's values.

All that I had done perfectly and loved without thinking I now loved for corrupt reasons. Language, which had been my secret music, became a branch of knowledge—one at which I excelled. Now I could tell myself I wasn't a dunce. Even the teachers could see I was good at it.

I didn't have to learn the rules of grammar because I already knew them; the rules were just articulations of patterns and structures I'd already felt and enjoyed. In a way it was a relief to find out that other people, the ones who had codified these rules, had also detected these patterns. It made me feel less strange. The teacher kept saying, "You already know how to do this," to the class. "You speak correctly without thinking about it," she'd say. But it wasn't true. Many of them didn't speak correctly, and even those who did, didn't hear what they were saying. They didn't hear the way the language was made and how it fitted together.

So I became the good girl. I understood everything right away and could spout it back with no mistakes. I looked forward to English class as if it were a movie or a trip to the beach. A warm, jittery, zingy feeling would come over me, sitting in my hateful chair near the door and waiting for the teacher to begin. My hand was always up in class.

"I know! I know!" I'd say.

At first the teacher was delighted that at last I knew something. Soon, though, my enthusiasm began to irritate.

"Let's give someone else a chance," she'd say.

Sometimes she'd say, "I'm sure *you* know. Let's see what everybody else knows."

Even this felt like a compliment. It went without saying that I, the Queen of Language, would know whatever it was. But after a while, she wasn't calling on me anymore. And my abilities didn't impress my classmates. By spring, I was back to my old position: No Good.

When I think about it now, I wonder if I had excelled at numbers, some special arrangement would have been specially arranged for me—tutorials, advanced classes, something to congratulate me on my intelligence and to certify that I was ahead of the game. A talent to be nurtured, in the charmless parlance of pedagogy.

But my talent for words was discrete. It didn't extend to my other capacities in any way. Still using my fingers for adding and subtracting at the end of the year, still not listening to the Revolutionary drivel, I had crept back underground. Just as well. I was immune to the seductions of achievement—or so I thought. I could tell myself that. I could claim outsider status, still, unsullied by my brief touch of success with dangling participles and complex sentences. I could keep growing and thinking and reading in secret, in my dark, sorry-for-myself basement of failure and neglect, like a little rat.

In Which, Vishwa

It was April before Frederika came over from Sweden. The trees had put out small leaves the color of lettuce, and the baby was walking around without help. My mother went into a whirl of repainting and refurnishing for Frederika's room, which was next to mine on the top floor. It had been a staging area for cast-off clothes and boxes of books destined for the sale basement of the Harvard Book Store, rather Bigelow-like in its disorganization. Transforming it took her only a week. She loaded the car with boxes and piles, drove off, and returned with new boxes and piles. Black deck paint for the chipped, eroded pine floor, lengths of white curtain fabric with geometric cutouts, a butterfly chair with a black leather seat, a long red-and-white-and-black-striped cotton rug from India, a tiny octagonal bedside table from Morocco made of mahogany and mother-of-pearl. Some bookshelves—she'd need those, wouldn't she? It would be nice to paint them red. No. Better black, and all along the low wall under the eaves. There. Done.

"Is it too much black?" she asked.

Frederika stood in the doorway with a suitcase (bulging, I was happy to see; she intended to stay a long time) at each ankle and started to sniffle.

"Nobody has ever done a thing like this for me," she said.

I'd forgotten Frederika's funny Swedish way of talking. "Nobody hass effer," she said. Ingrid had lost her Swedish accent by now; her voice tipped up at the end of words and sentences, but that was all. Frederika still sounded like a singing crow, especially talking through tears.

My mother had been waiting for a compliment on her decor, not her kindness. I could tell she felt let down.

My mother was complicated, and she came from a complicated family. Her mother, Leah, was the eldest daughter of an anarchist agitator who spent a lot of time in jail, though he was at liberty enough to father an additional seven daughters. Then Leah's mother, my great-grandmother, died young and left Leah in charge. This probably explains why my mother was an only child. There were many aunts for Leah to keep track of, some still children when my mother was born. My grandfather's side was also a muddle—like the brother nobody would talk to because he was a communist and they were socialists; you had to go to the other side of the street if you saw him coming. (This political dynamic turned up again later in my mother's life, since my father had been raised as a communist.) And somewhere along a cousinly branch of my maternal grandfather's family was our notable artist: Richard Neutra, the modernist architect. He'd left Vienna in the twenties and passed through Philadelphia on his way to Taliesin (that didn't work out) and then to Schindler in Los Angeles, leaving a deep impression of arrogance and a single snapshot in my grandmother's desk drawer in which his eyebrows rivaled those of Edward Teller. Maybe there was something about Hungarians (even if they were only Austro-Hungarians) that made for eyebrow growth. My mother inherited them, along with the talent for design. My grandmother Leah sniffed when his name came up in conversation. "Richard," she'd say. "Huh." Nobody heard a peep out of him between 1924 and the early sixties, when my father was in the news for being on the diplomatic team that negotiated the first test ban treaty with the Soviet Union. Famous! Richard called. Could he stop by for lunch when he was next in Washington?

My mother had several thwarted or perhaps renounced ambitions. Maybe they were not ambitions, only talents. To say *only,* to call them *talents,* is entirely to misrepresent her and her abilities.

Renounced, in the case of the piano. She wouldn't have studied for fifteen years and applied to conservatory if she'd had no ambition. When she was accepted, her mother the pragmatic anarchist had said, "Where's that going to get you? You think you're Horowitz?" My father had already proposed marriage, and my grandmother thought that was the way to go. "What else are you going to do with your life?" Leah said. Cruel, but a clear-eyed assessment of women's prospects in America between the wars.

Yet my grandmother had paid for all those lessons, twice a week when it became clear how very good my mother was. She'd leased an upright, she'd leased a better upright, she'd bought one, in the end, on their strained budget. When we made our semiannual pilgrimages to Philadelphia (Christmas vacation, summer vacation), my mother would walk into her childhood home and go straight to the piano, open the keyboard, and bang out some Scarlatti. Black, tinny, usually out of tune, it was a far cry from the baby grand crackle-finish chestnut-colored Baldwin that had its own room in our house.

My mother had a story that I liked as much as I liked Ingrid's Trans-Siberian story. It was the story of Herschel.

Herschel was a high school classmate and suitor of my mother's. She had many. My father was the main and perpetual suitor; he'd been on the job since second grade. Now and then he was supplanted. He'd wait, it would blow over, and he'd be back at the head of the line. They were all about sixteen. Herschel had been having a fair amount of success with my mother, enough to worry Herschel's violin teacher and probably my father as well. The violin teacher was always scolding Herschel: You're going to ruin your bow arm if you keep necking with that girl! Herschel had the brilliant idea to take my mother to his lesson so she could play something on the teacher's Steinway. She played a Bach partita with a Chopin chaser. The violin teacher rescinded his objections.

"And what about Daddy?" I asked.

"Well, in the end . . ." My mother would never finish that sentence.

They'd married a month after graduating from Penn. A photo of my mother in her mortarboard stood next to a photo of my newlywed mother and father on the upright in Philadelphia. They moved to New York and then the war started, and then and then. A photo of my father in uniform with a cocked triangular cap completed the piano-top album.

My mother's talent for the decoration of houses didn't need practice. It was innate. When something needed to change at home, or when she got in the mood for a change, she changed things and it was always right. She had aesthetic perfect pitch. It was a very specific aesthetic. Richard Neutra had become famous as the architect who domesticated the International Style, putting Bauhaus ideas into private houses rather than public buildings. He learned that from my mother.

The piano was a different story. It demanded a great deal of attention—more than I did, or perhaps its demands were louder. Every day by one o'clock, after the shopping and the minimal housecleaning, after feeding me some sort of lunch if I was home sick or on vacation, my mother sat down at the piano. She put her coffee cup and her ashtray next to the music on the ridged shelf above the keyboard, lit a cigarette she was going to forget to smoke, and got to work. Two hours, three hours, four hours: Often she was still at it when my father came home in the evening. In the delicious interludes of illness when I had a not-too-terrible stomachache or a scratchy throat but no fever and had cajoled her into letting me skip school, I spent my dreamy day off reading to the accompaniment of the Beethoven sonata she was working on or the syncopations of Debussy's "Golliwog's Cakewalk." Brahms, Ravel, the *Mikrokosmos* of Bartók, the Schubert Impromptus, miles of Mozart, the wrenching Partita in E Minor, one of her favorites, which she played with a frightening attack: I had a lifetime subscription to Carnegie Hall. So much for my grandmother's dismissal of my mother as no Horowitz fifteen years earlier.

But it was practice, not a seamless, straight-through performance. Circle back, start again from measure ten, take it from the repeat, too fast, too slow, with more feeling, less *legato,* missed that phrase, missed that transition, take it from the beginning.

And that was maddening if I was truly sick, which now and then I was. My fever rose with each repetition, and the hammer blows of the piano nailed my head at each stroke, until I was in a noisy nightmare of a phrase repeated over and over. The fever was the same as—maybe the result of—my mother's dissatisfaction with her playing. Edgy and hot, tangled in my dank sheets, I'd get stuck in the moment, convinced the rest of my life would be a repetition of now, right now, this phrase banged out again and again in my hot head and trembly pulse. In my fever-state I'd believe that if only she would play the thing all the way through, I would get better.

I never felt this way about the practice aspect when I was just malingering with my "tummy ache."

Some evenings she gave a concert for my father. He would lean into the sofa and conduct the back cushions with one arm, singing along in his atonal way. It was remarkable that a man of such musical ineptitude could be married to a woman of such ability. He couldn't keep time, he couldn't carry a tune, he didn't seem even to realize when a phrase had ended, but none of this diminished his pleasure in her playing. He knew her repertoire as well as she did. *Dum* dum, dah dum, dum, dum, *dum* dum, dada dum dum, he'd squawk as she launched into the *Italian Concerto,* and he'd croak and sigh in a sort of unison with the long, sad, sweeping measures of Opus 109, the Beethoven sonata to which my mother devoted more than three years of constant study. She wanted to get it right. She did. I have never heard a performance better than those she gave for the neighborhood cats and sparrows every afternoon while first one then another cigarette burned down to a ghostly black tube in the ashtray beside the music she didn't need to read anymore.

A bit of this talent passed on to me. I could sing a melody after hearing it once. I could also pick it out, with my middle and index fingers, on the piano. Therefore I was sent to solfège on Saturday mornings down the street at the Longy School of Music. As usual, I hated it. And I wasn't good at it either. Roger was there too, and as usual, he excelled. He could sight-sing with all the correct syllables, do re do fa, whatever it was. But since he didn't have much feeling for music, he didn't sing the tune right. He didn't care; he was having fun. My objection to solfège was predictable: Why did I have to say these foolish syllables? These syllables weren't really part of music. Nobody used these stupid syllables to play music with. My mother was willing to grant that the note names were just a convenience (inconvenience, I muttered), but, like my father insisting on the utility of arithmetic, she insisted that sight-reading was fundamental and that if I couldn't or wouldn't learn to do it, I couldn't learn music.

My ear was good enough for me to sneak my way through several months of music school relying on my ability to mimic what I heard. But I couldn't read worth a damn. I never got the note names straight. And, having decided that the bass clef was sinister, I refused to learn it.

So the evidence of my talent was spotty. Nevertheless, my

mother was determined to teach me to play the piano. Once a week we sat together on the bench. It never ended well, and sometimes it went badly from the start. One terrible fight was over the word *impromptu*.

The fight was really about practicing, something I didn't do much. This was in part because my mother was usually occupying the piano bench when I got home from school. Also, I didn't want her—my teacher—to hear just how badly I played. In the tradition of piano students the world over, I practiced the night before my lesson and only then.

Probably it was a little Bach piece. Possibly it was a Chopin prelude, though that seems a bit advanced for an eight-year-old of my meager abilities. I liked it, whatever it was, and walked around humming it all week. I could hum it up and down, treble *and* bass. What I couldn't do was play it on a piano.

My technique was to stumble through again and again in an unmusical manner, trying to memorize hand positions that would make the noises I heard in my head. I hoped if I did that enough times I'd get it into my fingers. I had no concept of structure, movement, variations or elaborations of themes. I was trying to produce an effect, not to learn a piece of music.

My mother couldn't help pointing this out.

"You don't understand it," she said. "You wouldn't make those mistakes if you thought about it. That chord couldn't possibly come next—it just doesn't make sense."

"I know that," I said. "I can hear it."

"Just because you can hear it doesn't mean you can play it."

That was stating the obvious. "Why not?" I asked. "I don't see why not."

"One thing you're not doing," she said, "is paying attention to the key. It's E minor, right? So there can't be an E-sharp unless it's marked."

I sighed, a dramatic, long-suffering child-sigh.

"I want to be able to sit down and just play it, the way I can sing it," I said. "Like, like . . ." I fumbled around for a moment. "Like those Schubert things you play, the one that goes"—and here I burst into a pretty good rendition of the descending glissando opening of the Impromptu No. 2 in E-flat Major. "An impromptu," I finished, pleased that I had remembered the name.

"Hah," said my mother. "You think Schubert just sat down and wrote that thing? That's what you think, isn't it? You think because it's called an impromptu, he didn't have to think about it or work on it."

"That's *not* what I think." It was exactly what I thought. Why else had he called it an impromptu?

"It's exactly what you think," said my mother. She always knew what I was thinking. "Well, you're wrong."

"I don't care what you say," I said.

Then she did the thing I hated most.

"This is how it goes," she said, and she played it, my Bach or my Chopin, beautifully, even better than I could hear it in my head.

That was a specially bad day, but they were all bad. What drove me crazy was I couldn't play as well as she did. It was absurd to think I could, and yet I did think that. Instead of being an example to me or even a spur, she was an impediment. She made me feel hopeless. Even though I knew the only way to become like her was to practice—even though I heard her practice every day—I felt she had a magic capacity to transform squiggles on a stave into glory out of a keyboard, and that I didn't have that magic and never would.

I gave up. I would sit at the piano and do nothing.

"Aren't you going to practice?" she'd ask.

"I am practicing," I'd say. And I'd keep sitting there with my hands in my lap.

I'd gone on strike, my inevitable reaction to defeat or any kind of setback.

Sometimes, in order to drive her crazy, I'd play one measure over and over, imitating her, but, unlike her, never getting it right.

"Move on," she'd say, emerging from the kitchen looking grim.

"I don't have it yet," I'd say, and torture the piano some more.

It took a few months to convince my mother to retire as my piano teacher. She didn't say she was retiring. She said things like, "Let's skip the lesson this week," and, "I don't think there's any point, since you haven't been practicing." When she said these things, part of me would curl up into a furious, rejected, desperate ball that wanted only to please her and was tight with regret and worry, while another part puffed itself into an equally furious, gleeful, flailing, shapeless enormousness, amazed at its ability to inflict the pain I saw in her face.

All this went on during the terrible third grade fall in which school was also no good. Then, diagramming sentences appeared, and piano lessons disappeared. Solfège went away too. I could spend chilly November Saturday mornings on my bike while Roger sang sol la ti sol at Longy. I'd ride past the school, a sprawling brownstone on Garden Street, and feel happy and free. A little needle of worry jabbed me now and then: Why had my mother given up on me so easily? How come she'd decided I was a lost cause? I made her do it, I'd remind myself, asserting my power. But feeling the power also made me feel uneasy. In the natural order of things, the parents had the power. Which would circle me back to Why had she given up on me so easily.

Winter: no more bike, no more music. Spring: Frederika.

Shortly after Frederika arrived, Vishwa arrived. Vishwa was supposed to be the solution to my music problem.

Vishwa was a small person, about five feet five, in his early twenties. His arms and ankles were bony and stringy and brown. He was brown in a caramel way, like bull's-eye candy—the perfect simile because his eyes, bright white, popped out of his head a little too far, giving the impression that he was fascinated and astonished by everything you (meaning me) said. He had very peculiar hair. It was coarse and thin, partly curly and partly straight. It looked like a wig. He had big hands with long, flat fingers and beautiful tapered nails. The flesh beneath his nails was nearly purple and the little moons at the base were a lovely pale pink.

Frederika talked like a crow, and Vishwa talked like a sandpiper. In fact, Vishwa was a sandpiper, skittering about on his stringy legs and peeping when he spoke. He had the sandpiper ability to suddenly be somewhere else. He was here beside me at the piano, and then, without seeming to move, he was over there at the door, where he'd left his black legal-size briefcase full of music.

"I have it, I have it!" he'd say, brandishing the score he'd been talking about above his tufted head.

Vishwa was the greatest.

Another good thing about him was how he smelled. Special Indian oils must have gone onto his mysterious hair every day in an effort to rationalize it. He smelled of cedar or teak—some kind of wood that was dark and dry and resonant with sap.

Vishwa's approach to the piano was different from my mother's.

"I will teach you music," he said. He didn't mention the piano.

The piano was in a glassed-in annex off the living room, which had probably been a conservatory, in the botanical sense, when the house was in its Victorian prime. It shared the room with a couple of straggly geraniums and a rubber plant my mother had picked up in the Star Market for $1.99. The geraniums were pathetic, but the rubber plant was happy, and over the course of several years it had become a giant, flapping its big dusty leaves out to touch the top of the piano. My mother said it liked music; she said all plants liked music. This didn't account for the geraniums.

The record player was the instrument with which Vishwa began my music lessons. It lived on the bookshelf that filled one whole wall of the living room.

We sat on the sofa, where my father would lounge and listen to my mother play. It was not a place I spent much time. The sofa was for grownups.

"Brahms's Third," said Vishwa. He pulled a record and a score out of the briefcase, put the record on, and settled down beside me. "Let's listen," he said.

"What about the music?" I reached for the score.

"This *is* the music," said Vishwa.

We sat and listened to the symphony together. A lot of it was sad, I thought. When it was over, Vishwa asked, "What's your favorite part?"

"The swooping," I said. "About halfway in, where it starts swooping and dipping."

"The third movement," he said. He put that on again. When it was over, he asked, "Can you sing it?"

I did.

"Good," he said. "That's the theme. Can you remember any of the other parts?"

"Not really," I said.

"Let's listen again."

It was nice, sitting on the sofa together listening to the sad music.

"It's strange," I said. "Even though parts of it are going up and other parts are going down or maybe sideways, they're all doing the same thing, basically."

"That's true," said Vishwa.

"It fills my head up," I said. I wasn't used to orchestral music. I was used to the piano. Most of my mother's records were piano works as well, with a bit of chamber music thrown in. The density and complexity of an orchestra was almost too much for me.

"Poco allegretto," Vishwa said. "That means a little, little bit fast." He laughed. "That's funny, isn't it? I like all the ways to say how fast. They have one that says, Fast, but not *too* fast. *Allegro ma non troppo.*"

"How do you know how fast too fast is?"

"Exactly!" Vishwa said. "That's just the question, isn't it?"

"But how do you know?" I hadn't thought about it before.

"You have to decide. You decide how fast you like it—or maybe how fast you can play it."

"But what about when there are all those different people in an orchestra?"

"That's where I come in. The conductor decides." Vishwa looked happy.

"You're the conductor?" I looked at skinny Vishwa nestled beside me in the cushions. He'd taken off his shoes—penny loafers—and curled his sock feet up under himself just as I had; neither of us had legs long enough to reach the floor while sitting back on the sofa. "Do you have a conductor suit?"

"I do," he said. "It's a used one, though."

"Will you wear it next time you come?"

"No," said Vishwa.

"Oh," I said.

"It's for conducting," he explained.

"Would it be bad luck?"

He considered this. "The suit is like magic," he said. "I put it on, and I'm the conductor. I don't want to use up the magic if I'm not conducting."

That made sense to me. On the other hand, I wanted to see him in it. "Where do you conduct? Can I come?"

He put his head down and looked embarrassed. "So far, I don't have a spot for conducting," he said. "There's a tiny orchestra—it's only about fifteen people—at Kirkland House. You can't really call it an orchestra. Sometimes I conduct them."

"But can I come?"

"We'll see," said Vishwa.

This was the first time Vishwa had sounded like a regular grownup. I didn't like it.

"Let's go back to Brahms," he said, in his usual cheery voice.

This time when we listened to the symphony, Vishwa put the score on his lap so we could follow along.

"Don't worry about the notes," he said. "Just follow the different lines, all the instruments, each with a line, each doing its own song, and try to see the patterns. The horns are doing this, the strings are doing that. Try to feel it all at once, like a thick, thick forest."

Before we got to the third movement, Frederika came in.

"Oops," she said. "I didn't mean to be disturbing."

Vishwa hopped up from the sofa, trying to put his shoes on as he stood. Only one foot got in.

"Vishwa," he said, extending his beautiful hand.

Frederika had hold of the baby's arm with her right hand to make sure she didn't wander away. She put out her left.

"And I am Frederika," she said.

They stood there holding hands, Vishwa with one sock foot, Frederika nearly a head taller, while Brahms swooped and dived and sighed. I sat on the sofa with half the heavy score in my lap, watching.

"You are the nanny?" Vishwa asked.

Frederika looked as if she were going to get mad, then she smiled. "Not exactly. But, I suppose I am. And other things too."

"Other?" Vishwa inclined his head toward her.

"General helpfulness," she said.

"General helpfulness is . . ." Vishwa paused. "General helpfulness is, well, helpful." I could see that he thought he'd said a dumb thing. Frederika liked it, though. Her smile got bigger.

"I am trying," she said. "Okay, now." She got a better grip on the baby's soft arm. "Let's not disturb."

"It is a delight to meet you," said Vishwa.

"Okay, okay," said Frederika.

Okay, okay, was Frederika's normal exit line, but Vishwa didn't know that and looked put out.

"She always says that," I told him, after she'd left. "She says, Okay, okay, instead of Good-bye."

"Uh-huh," said Vishwa. He was staring off at nothing. The third movement kept dipping and soaring.

"Is she new, this nanny?" he asked.

"She was in England with us," I told him. "First she was in England, then she was in Italy, and now she's come here."

"Oh." He patted his funny hair a few times. "Well, now," he said, all brisk business. "Lesson finished." He grabbed the score and stuffed it into his briefcase. "I'll leave you the record. That way you can listen if you like."

"Thank you," I said. "What should I practice?"

"Practice?" Vishwa squinted at me with his neck extended

while putting on his other shoe. "You practice listening," he said. "Listen and sing."

"That's all?"

"That's a lot," he said. "To really listen: That's work. But you're a good listener, I can tell."

"I am?" I was amazed. "Why? How? How can you tell?"

"You let the music in," he said.

All week I sang the parts of the symphony that I could remember. I even took the liberty of using the record player once, while my mother was at the Star Market. Like the sofa, the record player was somehow off-limits. It wasn't forbidden, but it was a restricted area, not part of my world the way the backyard was. I sat on the floor to listen so as not to commit the double trespass of using the sofa and the record player simultaneously.

I forgot to turn it off, though, and my mother noticed.

"Were you listening to your Brahms?" she asked.

"Vishwa told me to," I said, ready to fight.

"That's good," was all she said.

I was excited that Tuesday was coming around again, bringing Vishwa and my next lesson.

"Hello, hello," he said. "Did you listen?"

I nodded.

"Can you sing some?"

I did.

"Good," he said. "Now let's try with the score."

We got on the sofa and he spread the score across our laps. "You like the *poco allegretto,*" he said, "so let's start there. Look." He pointed at the big block of strings, the violins first and the violas and cellos below. "Can you see the line of the music making the song?"

I looked, but it was just a tangle.

"Sing it," he said. "Sing it and watch the line."

I sang, and suddenly, I did see it. I saw the score making the movement of the sound. "I see it!" I said.

It seems amazing to me now that with all the solfège and piano lessons, with all the exposure that I'd had to it, written music had not until that moment added up to anything. Each note or chord had been a distinct, unique problem I couldn't solve. I knew that the notes were the alphabet of sound, but for me they were dots and lines. Maybe it was because Vishwa was so cozy, or because I'd sung the third movement of Brahms's symphony a hundred times. Something changed that day. I saw that the music on the page was the sentences, the paragraphs, the story of the symphony, and that it could be read the way I would read a book. For the space of several minutes, I had the sensation of reading it as I sang.

"There," said Vishwa. "You can read it. You saw the sound on the page."

Immediately I had a bad thought. "It's because I know how it goes," I said. "If I didn't know the melody, I wouldn't see it there."

"Hmm," he said. "I wonder if that's true. And even if it is, is that important?"

"It's not really reading," I said.

"Do you want to try a part you don't know?"

"No!" I wailed. "Suppose it isn't real?"

For a minute he didn't say anything. Sticky little tears made the edges of my eyes itch.

"Why is this a big problem?" Vishwa asked. He seemed to be making a general inquiry, not really asking me, and I didn't say anything. I didn't know why, anyhow. "You have so much feeling and understanding for the music. I don't see why you're worried. You'll learn to read eventually, if that's what you want. Do you want to?"

That was hard to answer. I wanted what I always wanted, to know how to do it already.

"I ought to know how," I said. "I ought to know already. I went to all that stupid solfège."

"Solfège is not helpful," said Vishwa.

"I didn't like it," I said.

"Nobody likes it! It murders music."

Romantic Vishwa, the Indian Liszt—though my mother probably would have told me that Liszt practiced his finger exercises and went to solfège and I was kidding myself if I thought he hadn't.

While I was thinking about Liszt, Vishwa had done a sandpiper and was on the other side of the room rummaging in the briefcase.

"I brought another record," he said. "We can listen to a new thing. Not to read, just to hear something nice. There's a song for it too."

He put on the record.

"This is, the symphony, that Schubert wrote and never finished," he sang along with it. It was very beautiful. For the second line, which went higher and seemed to have changed key, he sang the same words, and then, a little extra downward turn in the music, "Never finished, never finished."

"Why didn't he finish it?" I asked.

"Didn't get around to it," Vishwa said. "Then, died."

We sat and listened together. Vishwa did a bit of surreptitious conducting, moving his right hand back and forth near his knee. I relaxed.

My mother came in. "This is, the symphony, that Schubert wrote and never finished," she sang.

"Does everybody know this?" I asked.

"I think so," said Vishwa. "Even people who don't know

much about music. Unlike you," he said, tilting his head toward my mother.

My mother nodded, agreeing with this assessment.

"And now you know it too," Vishwa told me.

"Sorry to interrupt," my mother said.

"No, no, we're done for today," said Vishwa.

"I wondered—Frederika and I wondered—if you would like to stay for dinner."

Frederika and I wondered, I thought. Why was Frederika part of the wondering?

An agonized look sprang onto Vishwa's face.

"I cannot stay tonight," he said. "I cannot. How I wish I could. Oh, dear."

"Is there a rehearsal?"

Vishwa shook his head, but didn't say why.

"Another time, then." My mother turned to go.

"Next week!" Vishwa was standing up to emphasize that next week would be good. "I could stay next week. Or even"—he looked at the floor—"tomorrow or the day after that."

"Next week," said my mother. "Stay after the next lesson. That will be nice."

"It will be wonderful. Thank you. Thank you very much." Vishwa bowed a little at my mother's back. When he turned toward me again, to collect the score from the sofa, he was smiling so fiercely I thought his lips might crack. He tried to resume a normal face to say good-bye, but he couldn't. I watched him failing to get a grip on his smile. "See you next week," he said, beaming.

Some Dinner Parties

Vishwa came Tuesdays. Wednesday there was a big planning session. Frederika and my mother holed up in the kitchen with cookbooks and notepads, toys for the baby so they could keep her distracted, lots of cigarettes for my mother, and lots of cups of tea for Frederika. Almost immediately they ran into a cultural complication.

"Is Vishwa a Hindu?" my mother asked. "That must be a Hindu name."

"I have no idea," said Frederika.

"Carl will know because of Jagdeesh. I'd better call."

"Who's Jagdeesh?" I asked. I had claimed a stomachache and been allowed to stay home and participate. My job was to boil water for Frederika's tea.

"Vishwa's brother," my mother said. "He's an economist with Daddy. That's why we have Vishwa."

She got on the phone.

"They're Hindu, aren't they?" she asked. "But what about being religious? I mean food." Pause. "Well, you have to find out!" Pause. "But suppose he doesn't eat beef? Suppose he's a vegetarian? We have to know." Another pause while my father gave a disquisition on something. "That's just impossible," my mother said. "I can't even—that can't be true. He would never have accepted the invitation." She hung up and stared out the kitchen window.

"What is it? What is it?" asked Frederika.

"Wait a minute," my mother said. She called my father back. "Do you think we should invite Jagdeesh too?" Pause. "No, I don't want to. What I'm asking is whether you think we ought to." Pause. "Fine. We won't invite him. But call back as soon as you talk to him." She hung up.

"He says if they're Brahmans, Vishwa won't eat any food prepared by us. That's part of being a Brahman. It's hopeless."

"But he wouldn't have accepted," Frederika said. "Just as you said. He wouldn't have said yes."

"Maybe to be polite? Maybe to see *you*?" My mother lit a cigarette. She had one going already.

"You have one," Frederika pointed out.

The phone rang. My mother grabbed it. "Okay." She nodded. "Okay. Good. Great! Bye."

"So?" Frederika leaned across the kitchen table.

"He will eat anything, even beef. But he prefers no beef. And they are Brahmans. But they're not religious anymore."

"Why can't we prepare the food?" I asked.

"We can!" said Frederika.

"Jagdeesh is pleased because he's been worrying about Vishwa. He wants to see Vishwa settle down," my mother said.

"But why did you say we couldn't prepare it?" I asked.

"Don't worry about it," my mother told me. "It's a system, an arrangement they have in India about who does what in society. It's very complicated and I can't explain it and anyhow it doesn't matter. I mean, to our dinner." She turned to Frederika. "Coq au vin? We could have polenta first. You remember that way they make it, cook it first on the stove, then cut it up and put it under the broiler with a little cheese on top. That's good. Polenta and chicken and then—I don't know what."

"Pickled things," suggested Frederika. She was a good pickler.

"Hot things, maybe? Indian food is hot," my mother said. "But we're not trying to give him Indian food, are we."

"I could make gravlax," said Frederika.

"Mmm," said my mother. "That's confusing, though, isn't it? Gravlax, then polenta, then chicken?"

"It's international," said Frederika.

"It's that," my mother agreed.

"I could make the cardamom cake," Frederika said.

"That," my mother said, "is precisely what you should make. Cardamom is Indian but cardamom cake is Swedish. It's perfect."

"No gravlax?" Frederika sounded disappointed.

"Let's see what develops with the rest of dinner," my mother said.

"Is cardamom from India?" I asked.

"I'm not sure," my mother said, "but they like it there."

I went into the living room and took down the big dictionary, the one I could barely lift off the shelf, to look up cardamom. "An East Indian plant," it said. "It *is* Indian," I called into the kitchen, but nobody responded. I sat on the sofa and hummed my Brahms. Then I hummed the symphony that Schubert wrote and never finished. Then I went back into the kitchen, where my mother was having a new idea.

"If he'll eat beef," she said, "we could have a kind of musical menu. Tournedos Rossini, Mozart cake. There's some kind of Something Verdi, but I can't remember what it is."

"But he doesn't like to eat the beef," Frederika said. "What other music foods are there?"

" 'If music be the food of love,' " my mother said. " 'Play on,' " she added.

"I'm going for a bike ride," I said.

"I thought you had a stomachache," said my mother. She was a stickler about that. I could stay home with my fake illness, but I had to pretend to have it all day.

Frederika clinked her teacup against her saucer. "I need more tea." She winked at me. She was being sweet, trying to make me feel important. "I can't think without tea."

My mother had been standing at the stove considering the dinner possibilities and looking at the burners as if she were imagining each thing cooking there. Suddenly she said, "We're making too much of this. We should just have dinner the way we always do. It's not a party. We want him to feel he's part of the family."

"Spaghetti?" Frederika asked. She sounded alarmed.

"Why not? Or a nice cozy roast chicken."

"With a bit of polenta and a cardamom cake?" Frederika had my mother's number.

My mother laughed. Then she pointed at Frederika. "This is your future we're talking about."

"I think you are jumping at a conclusion," Frederika said. Her face was pink.

"Jumping *to,*" said my mother. "I'm just trying to arrive at a conclusion. A successful conclusion for you."

"But we haven't even started," said Frederika.

"That's about to change." My mother went back to the pile of cookbooks and opened one. "Broiled swordfish?"

"I think swordfishes are ugly-looking," said Frederika.

I went upstairs to read.

Thursday, when I got home from school, it was coq au vin again. Friday, it was sole baked in sour cream and tarragon. Saturday, Frederika had a little fit.

"Maybe this is all a mistake," she said. "Maybe he only says he's coming for politeness. Because he can't say no he's not coming if we invite him!"

"Let's just have spaghetti," my mother said. This was meant to be comforting, but it didn't work.

"No!" Frederika was near tears. "Spaghetti is too poverty."

"Spaghetti doesn't have to be that way, Freddy," my mother said. "Freddy" was only for when Frederika was very upset, like when she got homesick. "How about a nice cozy chicken," my mother intoned. "Roasty, all crispy, who wouldn't like that?"

"Yah, yah, okay, okay," said Frederika, calming down. "And I do make cardamom cake sometimes. It's not so damnable special-occasion."

"It's damnable good," said my mother. *Damnable* was a locution of Frederika's that we had taken up.

Meanwhile, we had meat loaf for dinner. My father objected.

"Annette," he said. "Meat loaf?"

"I'm too busy with the Vishwa event to worry about making something complicated for us too," she said. "Anyhow, it's pretty good."

"Beets will be next," he said.

My father was permitted to indulge his multi-vegetable phobia. The only cooked vegetables he would eat were the expensive ones: artichokes and asparagus. Later in the century it turned out he liked fennel too, but that didn't help in the fifties, when nobody in America, including my mother, had heard of it yet. Potatoes were okay, but according to my mother, they were not a vegetable. Carrots and beets in particular were anathema. They were some sort of pollutant, and if they appeared on my father's plate, he couldn't eat dinner. Succotash was also taboo. By the age of eight I'd figured out that this phobia was about his mother, a great overcooker of carrots and beets and succotash—and cabbage and broccoli and squash. I liked these Russian mushes; they presented hundreds of opportunities to apply sour cream.

We ate a lot of salad. Some nights we sat at the table chewing wads of watercress like a herd of cows. My mother tried sneaking in peas, for instance, or celery. They were always discovered and abominated. Lettuce, all varieties, was okay, tomatoes were okay, endive was okay. Spinach, green beans, kale, chard: all not okay. It was a kosherlike insanity with not even as much logic as Leviticus.

That night we had roasted potatoes and a salad of endive and blanched asparagus with the meat loaf, so my father did not have much grounds for complaint. His real complaint was my mother's distraction. Dinner was when he told about his day. If my mother did not give the appearance of being focused on him—a performance that included making a marvelous, mostly vegetable-free dinner—he got irritated.

"Vishwa," my father said. "He might as well be the King of Siam for all the trouble he's causing."

My mother raised her eyebrows at Frederika in an Oh, men! signal. "It's just for this first time," she told my father.

"Is he coming to dinner every week?" my father asked.

"If things go well," my mother said.

"You're joking!"

"You don't even know him," my mother said. "He's very charming and intelligent, and of course, a musical genius."

"I want to have dinner with my family. I don't want all these hangers-on . . ." My father realized this could be insulting and stopped. "I do not mean *you,* Frederika."

Frederika tried to smile.

"I poached some pears," my mother intervened. "Let's have them."

Another thing Frederika was worrying about was the nature of the engagement that had made Vishwa unable to come the week before and unwilling to specify why.

"He already has a girlfriend," she said after dinner, when I was clearing the table and she and my mother were loading the dishwasher. "That's why. That's why he didn't say."

"He might have had a private lesson. Or a doctor's appointment," my mother said.

"At dinnertime?"

"Maybe some Hindu thing?" I could tell my mother thought

this was pretty feeble, because she backtracked right away. "I guess not," she said. "They're not religious. Whatever that means."

Frederika started up with Just Coming to Be Polite again. "And also, I'm sure that he has a girlfriend."

"But he was happy about dinner," I said. "He was smiling a lot, Frederika. He was smiling very hard." This was my first substantive contribution to the Vishwa effort, apart from boiling water for tea.

My mother looked at me. "He was, was he?" She seemed impressed, I hoped with me, not just with the information. "If he has a girlfriend," she told Frederika, "he won't have her by the end of the week, I promise you."

Tuesday was breezy, dry, sunny, one of those days that exemplify the idea of spring in New England but which actually occur only two or three times a year. I was more distracted than usual at school. The windows were open, and I could smell the spent, oversweet lilacs, the honey-vanilla early peonies, the bright new grass dotted with clover puffs. It was impossible to pay attention to anything other than the drama of growth. Add in my music lesson and then dinner with Vishwa, and I was barely able to stay in my seat.

The house was quiet when I got home. I'd been expecting bustle and worry. Instead the door was unlocked and there was a note on the kitchen table that read: NAPPING. Succinct and anonymous, it didn't explain whether this applied only to my mother or if it included Frederika.

I curled up with *The Count of Monte Cristo* in the living room window seat that looked onto the street to wait for Vishwa. After about half an hour I saw him coming down the block. He'd added a bulky tweed jacket to his usual ensemble of khakis and a white shirt. This was the full Cambridge uniform. Technically correct, it looked like a costume on him, probably because he was small and thin and dark and it had been invented by and for tall, well-fed fair people.

"Do I look nice?" he asked the moment I opened the door. "I brought a tie too." He pulled a fistful of magenta paisley out of his pocket. "I brought two ties," he said, when I widened my eyes at the red swirls. The second one had blue-and-white stripes. "Which?" he asked, a tie draped on each hand.

"Red," I said. "The other one is boring."

"Jagdeesh insisted," said Vishwa. "He made me take this horrible itchy coat and he made me take this stupid tie for a banker. I said, I have to have that red tie, it's so cheerful and excited. He said I needed a backup calm tie." He stuck the boring tie in the pocket of his itchy coat.

"My father doesn't wear a tie at dinner," I said.

"Then neither will I," said Vishwa. He put the red tie in the other pocket.

"He doesn't wear a jacket either," I said.

"Thank god," said Vishwa. He took it off and dropped it on the back of the sofa.

I picked up the jacket and took it to the closet under the stairs. "He doesn't like mess," I explained.

"What else doesn't he like?"

"Vegetables," I said.

"Hmm," said Vishwa. He took his loafers off and lined them up at the end of the sofa. "Is this mess?"

I hesitated. "When he gets home, it will be."

"I'll put them back on later," said Vishwa. "I'll remember. Now let's have your lesson."

"What are we going to listen to?" I asked.

"Today, we'll visit the piano."

This made me nervous. "I liked listening," I said.

"It'll be fun," Vishwa said. "You remember the part of the Brahms you liked so much? We'll play that." He sat down at the piano and patted the bench beside him. "Come and sit down."

I didn't move.

"You remember it," he told me.

"It's too complicated," I said.

"The *melody,*" he said. He patted the bench again. "I'm just talking about the melody."

I sat down, but I didn't put my hands on the keyboard. "I don't know where to start it," I said.

"Anywhere," said Vishwa. "That's part of what I want to show you."

"Okay," I said, but I didn't lift my hands.

"You're afraid of the piano," Vishwa said.

"I hate the piano," I whispered. "I hate it, I hate it."

Vishwa put his hands on the keys and played a big chord. Then he put his hands back in his lap.

"You don't hate it," he said. "What you hate is that you can't play it yet."

"Yet," I said. "Yet!"

"*I* can't play it," he said. "I'll never really play it."

"That's not true!"

"I'm adequate," Vishwa said. "I don't sing through it, the way your mother does. That's why I'm a conductor. I need a whole orchestra. I can't do it alone."

"I don't think I'll ever—" I stopped. "I don't think I want to—" I stopped again.

"Maybe it's something else? You need something else to sing through?"

I started crying, as usual.

"Have you ever tried a violin?" Vishwa asked.

I put my elbows on the keyboard with a dissonant *clong* and put my head down in my hands. A few tears fell onto the ivory.

"Oh, dear," said Vishwa. He didn't sound alarmed, though.

"Why is it always music?" I asked.

"You're good at it."

"Not good enough," I said.

"I'm not ready to give up on you yet," said Vishwa. "It takes time and practice to be able to say what you want with music."

I raised my head and looked at him. "But it's not what I want to say. It's what *they* want to say."

"They?"

"Brahms. Or Chopin. Or Bach. It's not what *I* want to say."

"Whatever you want to say, someone has written it. They talk about everything. You can always find the music of what you feel."

"It's not the same! It's like somebody's putting words in my mouth."

"Oh," said Vishwa. "Well, I think I understand. But they aren't words. That's what's wonderful about music."

He looked so happy that I didn't dare say what I thought: That was precisely what was not wonderful about music. It wasn't words. I sat on the piano bench, tense and slack at the same time, waiting for whatever was going to happen next.

"Here," he said. "This is something fun. Play the Brahms theme. You'll be able to do it—it isn't hard. Start at middle C."

It took me a while to figure it out, but he was right. It wasn't as hard as I thought.

"Perfect," said Vishwa. "That's perfect. Now, do it again, but start one note up, at D."

Immediately, I got confused.

"It's all different," I said. "I can't hear it. It's like my ears got stuck the first way."

"Hum it," he said. "Play the D and then hum from there."

Humming helped. But when I played it, every other note was a black key and it was harder to see the melody, somehow.

"You've got it," Vishwa said. "You see it now."

"Sort of," I said. I didn't feel confident at all.

"Now start at E."

It didn't work again. I tried humming. "Why does humming help?"

"I think you're right when you say that your ears get stuck. It resets your ears. Try again."

E was even more confusing than D had been.

"Vishwa, I can't!"

"Relax," he said. "It's always the same, no matter where you start it. I want you to understand the pattern of the melody."

"You mean three notes up and three notes down?"

"Exactly." He nodded. "And you can start those three notes anywhere you want. It's the relationship that's important."

I tried again. This time it worked better, at least for the first few phrases.

"It's like a translation," I said. "It's saying the same thing with different tones."

Vishwa smiled. "It's called transposition, and you're right. Translation and transposition are the same sort of thing."

Vishwa had said, "You're right," or, "That's good," at least three times since we'd sat down at the piano. He made me feel safe. I leaned against him, pushing my shoulder into his arm. He made an answering lean, so our bodies were propped together, like two playing cards starting to make a house.

"Better?" he asked. "Not so scary?"

"Yes," I said. I started to relax, but relaxing let me feel how scared I was. Listening to music was wonderful; trying to play it—being forced to play it—made me nervous. It felt like a test, one I always failed.

"I'm going to bring a violin to the lesson sometime," he said. "A piano is too big. It's at least ten times bigger than you are. I think that's scary. A violin is nice. It's light. It smells good. You'll like it."

"But I can't learn to play the piano on a violin," I said.

"It's all the same." Vishwa stretched out his arms to encompass every instrument in the world. "All one big thing."

I heard my mother walking around upstairs. She would not agree that it was all one big thing. There was the creak of her closet door opening and the rustle of her dresses. There was the *thunk* her bureau made because the drawer was swollen on one side. Some bracelets jingled. It was piano, piano, piano from her point of view. Once I'd heard her express some admiration for the cello, but fundamentally, the piano *was* music.

"My mother says the piano contains the whole orchestra," I told Vishwa.

"That's pretty much true," he said.

"So why isn't she a conductor?"

"Because she is such a very good pianist. If I could play the piano, or the oboe or the violin, like that . . ." He trailed off.

"You said you sing through the orchestra."

"Yes, I do," said Vishwa. "I feel it isn't quite as direct. Not quite the same as having your hands on an instrument."

"Don't underrate yourself," my mother said from the doorway. "An orchestra without a conductor is dead. It isn't anything. The conductor makes it alive."

"A symbiotic relationship, perhaps," Vishwa said. He rose from the piano and made the little bow he always gave my mother. "After all, I need the orchestra as much as they need me."

"We sound like we're in a French movie," my mother said. "A bad one. Would you like a drink? Do you drink?"

"And smoke too," said Vishwa.

"What a relief!" My mother pulled her Camels out of the pocket of her dress and offered him the pack. "I was worried that you would disapprove of these Western habits."

"Everyone in India smokes," said Vishwa.

But he had a funny way of smoking. He held the cigarette between his thumb and forefinger, as if it were a pencil, and took rapid little puffs. He looked so awkward that I thought he might be smoking just to be polite. He had none of my mother's debonair smoking tricks: breathing the smoke back up her nose so she looked like a dragon, blowing smoke rings, leaving the cigarette at the edge of her mouth with the smoke making clouds around her face while she talked.

"Scotch?" my mother asked Vishwa.

"Is that what you have?"

"I have bourbon."

"This is an American specialty?"

"Very," said my mother. "It's like Scotch, only more so. It's Southern Scotch."

"I'll try," said Vishwa.

"Go upstairs," my mother told me, "and see what's keeping Frederika."

Frederika was sitting on her bed beside a pile of clothes.

"Mummy says time to come down," I told her.

"I'm not ready," Frederika said. "I'm not dressed."

She was wearing my favorite Frederika thing, her red-and-white-striped shirtwaist with a full skirt that had rickrack around the hem. Unlike most of her clothes, it was store-bought, something she and my mother had found in Filene's Basement, French, reduced from $80 to $10.99. They had cooed over the whopping reduction and the delicate workmanship: silk pockets tucked in at the sides, buttons hidden in a placket, hand-stitched collar.

"I love that dress," I said.

"It's not right," Frederika intoned.

"Vishwa doesn't look special," I said. "He came with all sorts of extra stuff, like a tie, but he isn't wearing it."

"No?" Frederika looked up for a moment. "And your mother?"

I couldn't remember. "Something green?"

Frederika grabbed me and tickled my neck. Though I hated to be tickled, I would let Frederika do it. "Which green thing?" she asked.

"A green thing," I said.

"You are not the right age to care," said Frederika.

"I care!"

"Pfui," she said. "Look what you're wearing."

I was wearing overall shorts and a purple T-shirt that was too small and had a hole in front but it didn't show when I wore it with the overall shorts. That was what I wore every day (varying the T-shirt) from May to September.

"Vishwa isn't staying for dinner to see me," I said. "It doesn't matter what I wear."

"This is the problem," said Frederika.

"Frederika, you look nice. You look special-occasion nice."

"Yah?" Frederika sounded ready to be convinced.

"Let's go," I said. "Mummy will get mad soon."

Needless worry. My mother and Vishwa were lounging on the sofa chatting about Brahms while the ice in their bourbon settled with little chinks. Vishwa had forgotten to put his shoes back on (my father would get mad). One of my mother's black sling-backs lay sideways, asleep on the floor, and the other dangled from her toes. The combination of the late, pale spring light and the drift of cigarette smoke made the air alive with dust that outlined sunbeams to create a Blakean atmosphere akin to the print that hung in my bedroom of Adam and Eve perpetually being exiled from Paradise, just like me.

For the moment, though, I was in a kind of paradise. The insertion of the novel (Vishwa) into the routine (dinner) was the recipe for a heavenly evening. My mother had dressed up for it—odd I hadn't noticed when I first saw her. She wasn't wearing green at all but burnt-orange shantung with an amber necklace of her mother's. Also, one of the dark perfumes she specialized in, which were bitter and smelled brown in the way a cello sounds brown.

Vishwa stood up and made an obeisance to Frederika, putting his hands together and bending his head over them as if in prayer. My mother had never provoked such a gesture; for her, only a Westernized half-bow. Frederika, standing with her hand extended in a hearty, we're-all-equals Swedish attitude, looked perplexed. My mother flipped her shoe back on her heel, dug the other one off the floor, and grabbed hold of my arm.

"Let's go check on dinner," she said, and hustled me out.

The coq au vin was simmering at the back of the stove. Someone had set the table (my usual job) already. A pot of water was at a low boil and the two-cup measure full of rice stood waiting nearby. The salad was in its teak bowl, and the asparagus, washed and trimmed of its little horns the way my father liked it, lay in a green fan on the counter. There did not seem to be much to check on.

My mother lifted the lid on the chicken. "Smells okay," she

said. She peeked into the oven, and a waft of cardamom came out. "That smells okay too," she said. She stuck a fork on the edge of the oven rack and pulled. Then she percussed the top of the cake a few times. "Not quite," she announced. "Olives?" she asked me.

I didn't like olives. "No," I said.

"Olives," she decided.

There was a black bowl especially for them, because, as my mother had said when she brought it home, the black of the bowl was nearly the same as the black of the olives, but not quite, and that made it nice. My father liked Kalamata olives only. There was a white bowl, half the size of the black bowl, for the pits. And then the pistachios. "Not the red ones!" my mother cautioned as I groped for the bag in the cabinet beside the refrigerator. "They dye your hands. I don't know why he got them." "He" (my father) went every other week to the Armenian stores two miles away in Watertown to get olives and pistachios and the huge flat bread we called Syrian bread, though the Armenians surely considered it Armenian, like the Greeks at the Acropolis restaurant on Massachusetts Avenue who bristled when you asked for Turkish coffee. I thought of how nobody had ever heard of English muffins in England.

Waiting for my mother to set up the hors d'oeuvres tray, I began to compile a list of foreign foods that might be nonsensical in their native countries: French toast, Belgian waffles, Danish pastry. I could ask Frederika about that one. Maybe they called it Swedish pastry in Sweden. It was interesting that, aside from Turkish coffee, all these things were bread-based.

"Do they have French toast in France?" I asked.

My mother squinted at me. "What do you care?" she said.

"They didn't have English muffins in England, see, so I'm trying to figure it out. If they have French toast, do they call it French toast or do they just call it toast since they're already French?"

"I really don't know," said my mother. "Here. Take this in." She put the tray in my hands.

Bang, crunch, bang, clunk. My father was home.

Open the door and bang it into the table in the hall, crunch the doormat somehow (nobody else in the family ever did this) with the bottom edge of the door while closing it, bang the door shut, drop the briefcase with a clunk: a theme with no variations.

"Yum," said my father, taking an olive as he passed by me on his way down the hall to the kitchen.

I hesitated at the living room threshold. Suppose Frederika and Vishwa were already hugging? I poked my head in to see.

They were not hugging. Vishwa was sitting upright on the sofa (I was relieved to see that he'd put his shoes on again) and Frederika was sitting in the chair my father called the Cat Chair because it had a hole in the back "for the cat's tail." Pinch never sat in it. It didn't have the squishy, forbidden allure of the sofa. Frederika was perched askew, turned toward Vishwa, her legs crossed high and zigzagged with the red rickrack.

"Olives?" I asked in my best hostess manner.

They were not interested in olives. I put the tray on the coffee table and went back to the kitchen.

My father was leaning against the refrigerator drinking his Scotch and telling about his day. My mother was all over the kitchen, decanting things onto platters and into bowls, beating lemon juice with olive oil, while either listening or pretending to listen to my father.

"And so I invited him for dessert," my father concluded.

"Okay," said my mother. "Fine." She banged the oven door shut to show that it was not fine.

"At around eight," he said.

My mother nodded. She coaxed the cake onto a cooling rack, pushed my father out of her way with her shoulder, and stuck her head into the refrigerator. "Damn," she said. "No cream."

"Shall I go get some?" My father looked forlorn and guilty.

"Too late now," my mother said.

"I could call Jagdeesh and ask him to bring some."

My mother cocked her head. "That's a good idea. Tell him to whip it while he's at it."

"Really, Annette," my father said. "It's not any more work for you, if he comes. Dinner's made, after all."

My mother looked at my father, then at me, and said, "Never mind. Just never mind. Let's relax and have fun."

I didn't think that was likely. My mother had got into a huff of some sort, which meant she would pretend to be cheerful and pleasant to everyone except my father, to whom she would speak—if she spoke—with an icy formality. This drove him around the bend. He'd apologize and apologize, but she could stay frozen far longer than he could stay apologetic, so he'd end up angry. That only prolonged her huff. First he'd mistreated her, now he was mad at her too. They could get stuck like this for days.

I backed out into the hall and stood there for a minute. I didn't want to be in the kitchen, but I didn't want to go into the living room either. Grownup mysteries surrounded me. I tiptoed to the front door and opened it. There was Pinch, waiting for someone to let her in. I wanted to pick her up and put my face into her speckly back and smell her fresh, outside fur, but she dashed between my feet and scooted upstairs before I could grab her. Nobody loved me.

I stood looking at the street, wondering what to do. I could go to my room and sulk. I could walk up the hill to the Bigelows' and have goulash with them. I could get on my bike and ride to—where? England? Gray Gardens East, where I could do some al fresco sulking? It was getting dark and had become chilly, for a spring night. They'd be sorry when I froze to death two blocks away, a pathetic little creature with only my bicycle for a friend.

"Hey," my mother said, startling me. "Shut the door. The cat will get out."

"She just came in," I said.

"Dinner's ready." She went into the living room. "Come, come," she said in her icily cheerful, completely phony voice.

My father's technique for getting to know someone was to conduct an intensive interview. Birthplace, secondary education, undergraduate major, mentors in graduate school, first job: grill, grill, grill. The answers established qualifications, the manner of response established character. Vishwa was an uncooperative subject.

"You are how many years younger than Jagdeesh?"

"Many," Vishwa said.

"How many?"

"Twelve."

"And you were brought up in Calcutta?"

"No, no, no," said Vishwa.

My father waited.

"A child died in between," said Vishwa. "Most tragic."

My father wasn't asking about family tragedy. "You were brought up—where?" he said, his tone suggesting that Vishwa had said where, but that my father hadn't quite heard him.

"In the country." Vishwa waved his hand at the hinterlands of India.

My mother pushed the tureen of coq au vin toward Frederika and motioned her to pass it to Vishwa.

"I still have plenty, thank you," he said.

"More sauce, maybe," my mother said.

"Where in the country? You went to a country school?" my father asked.

"Well, yes, in a manner of speaking."

"And why did your father decide to send you to a country school?"

"It might have been your mother who decided," my mother said to Vishwa. "Right?"

"Shantiniketan," Vishwa said.

"Excuse me," my father said.

"It was Tagore's school," said Vishwa. "That's where I went."

"Socialist," said my father. "World peace, wasn't it?"

"Mmm," said Vishwa.

"Jagdeesh went there too?" My father seemed put out by the idea that Jagdeesh had gone there without letting him know.

"Only a little while. It didn't suit him."

"But it suited you." This was a statement. Vishwa did not contradict it.

"What a marvelous dinner," he said to my mother. "Delicious." He turned toward Frederika, who, like the rest of us, had said barely a word since we'd sat down. "And did you also go to a country school when you were a small girl?"

"No, I was always raised in Stockholm," she said.

My father was refueling, and the ensuing dinner-silence—knives and forks clicking on plates—gave me a moment to consider the wonderful things Frederika said. "I was always raised in Stockholm" was not hard to understand, but it was not anything an English-speaking person would say either.

My father pushed the chicken bones to one side and got going again. "So, you followed Jagdeesh to Cambridge?"

"It did help that someone was established here already," said Vishwa. "A beachhead," he added.

"I meant England," said my father. He was getting addled. "I meant, did you go to Cambridge like Jagdeesh?"

"Oh, no," said Vishwa.

If my parents had not been having a fight, my mother would have stopped this inquisition by now. Carl, she would have said, Enough already. Because she wasn't speaking to him, all she could do was try to get the rest of us to talk to one another. But my father was as persistent as a mosquito.

"So where did you go to university?" he asked.

"I didn't, exactly," said Vishwa.

My mother got up from the table in protest. "Vishwa," she said, heading to the kitchen, "wouldn't you like some more rice?"

"Yes, I would," said Vishwa.

"What exactly did you do, then?" asked my father.

"I was in Paris," Vishwa said, rather dreamily. "In Paris."

My mother could no longer restrain herself. "At the Conservatory," she said. She put a nice big spoonful of rice on Vishwa's plate.

The Paris Conservatory was out of my father's range of knowledge. "Aha," he said. He didn't look happy.

"I am envious of you," Frederika piped up. "I always want to go to Paris, but not yet."

Vishwa widened his eyes. "I go twice a year," he said. "We could meet."

Frederika ducked her head. My mother smiled, a real smile.

"Why?" my father asked. "Why do you go so often?"

"To visit my teacher. He's very old now, and he's failing. He was my father in the West, so it's important that I visit him. His wife died two years ago. Very sad. Tragic." Vishwa bowed his head at the sadness of life, the tragedies. This was the second tragedy in half an hour.

"Of course," he went on, "there isn't much I can do. I sit with him, and we talk about the good times. We drink some nice wine. I go to concerts and tell him about it."

"Oh, Paris," my mother said. Then she said, "That's so good of you."

"He was a father," Vishwa said. "Now, only a few years later, more of a grandfather."

"But that's expensive," my father pointed out. What he meant was, How can you afford to go to Paris on your income, which is how much, exactly?

"Hah, hah," said Vishwa.

I didn't understand why he was laughing. Maybe he flew to Paris by flapping his arms, or maybe he'd harnessed sleep-flying so he could do it when he was awake.

"I hop on the freighter," he said. "I take my scores. I take books. There's good food—especially on the Swedish freighter." He nodded at Frederika. "Nice fresh fish."

My father scowled. "Where do you get this freighter?"

"Sometimes in New Bedford. Sometimes in Gloucester. Once I had to go to New Jersey."

My mother liked the idea of the freighter. "How did you find out about it?" she asked.

"In *The New York Times,*" Vishwa said. "*The New York Times* is a marvelous newspaper. Every day it lists what ships are arriving all over the East Coast, and where they are going. Then you go to the dock and ask, May I travel with you? Usually they say yes."

"For free?" My father was astounded.

"How did you get the idea to do that in the first place?" my mother asked.

"You pay a little," Vishwa told my father. "Maybe about twenty-five dollars. Or you can work. You can be a waiter for dinner. Once I was a deck cleaner. Waiter is better."

"But how—" my mother repeated.

"It's the subcontinental pipeline," said Vishwa. "We have special information. We need a lot of special information because everything is far away and difficult."

"You're saying you can take a freighter from America to India for next to nothing," my father said.

"You have to have a few months to spare for that trip," Vishwa said. "To Europe, maybe ten days. Maybe less. Depends if they have to make a stop here first. Like New Jersey." Vishwa pursed his lips. "I did not like New Jersey."

"It smells horrible there," I said. I was happy to have something to contribute. "The smelly refineries. When we drive past them, I get sick."

My mother shook her head at me. Not at dinner.

"Like eggs," Vishwa agreed. "Bad ones."

"What are they refining?" Frederika asked.

"Eggs!" Vishwa started laughing.

"Petroleum," my father said.

"And they shoot fire and they look scary," I went on.

" 'Dark Satanic mills,' " my father said to me. He turned back to Vishwa. "So you weren't educated in England at all?"

"I went to Oxford for a little while," Vishwa admitted. "Have you seen those calling cards—usually it's Indians who have them—M.A. OXON., FAILED."

"You didn't finish your degree?"

"I was accepted at the Conservatory, and that was the important thing. I went there."

My mother caught my eye. "Salad," she said.

I got up and began to clear the plates. Vishwa hopped out of his seat too. "Let me help," he said.

My father's large hand descended on Vishwa's arm as it connected to a plate. "No," my father instructed. Vishwa dropped back into his chair.

Clear from the left, serve from the right. Do not stack dishes at the table. There were a lot of table rules, the most important being No bottles on the table. If there was mustard, the mustard had to be put in a small bowl with a spoon of its own. No bottle of milk, no jar of sour cream, no impregnable red tower of ketchup. Turn the blade of the knife in when you set the places. Do not scrape food from one plate to another (this was a subheading of Do not stack dishes at the table). Napkin rings are déclassé. A cooking vessel must not appear on the table; this rule ensured that every night my mother had to hand-wash either the serving platters or the pots, since she couldn't fit them all into the dishwasher. Where did he get all these rules? Had he made them up, the way he'd made up the vegetable rules? My father's one-man dinner cult. Lunch didn't have rules. It was a weekend free-for-all of salami and mayonnaise and old, buckled waxed-paper packages of lox that my mother wanted to throw away and that my father ate while she said, "You'll get sick." But for all his fussing about food, he never got sick from eating. Last week's rubbery pot roast from the back of the fridge, cheese that smelled diseased, Chinese menu entries that turned out to be turtle or ferret—he had an iron stomach. Later, when he worked at the White House and traveled to strange places on fact-finding missions, he ate monkey, he ate boa constrictor. Anything but a carrot.

I was setting out the salad plates—from the right—when the doorbell rang.

My father scrambled up from the table and down the hall.

"What is it?" Vishwa asked my mother.

"It's Jagdeesh," she said.

"Oh, dear." Vishwa looked at me. "The tie! Where is the tie?"

"In the closet, in the pocket of the jacket."

"Don't worry about the tie," my mother said.

"I don't care," said Frederika. "I like you without a tie."

Vishwa looked at his plate. He seemed to be blushing, but because of his toasty color, I couldn't be sure.

"Look who I've found," my father said, ushering Jagdeesh into the room.

Jagdeesh was tall and willowy. He had large tipped-up eyes that appeared to be lined with mascara because his lashes were so dark and profuse. His nose was a sculpted beak, big but delicate. The most striking difference between him and Vishwa was his hair. Jagdeesh had movie-star hair, thick, black, swept back to show off his high, shiny forehead. About the only thing he and Vishwa had in common was their creamy caramel skin. He was wearing a blue blazer tailored snugly to his long torso, a blinding white shirt (with cuff links, I noticed during dessert when he reached for seconds), black loafers like the ones my mother had bought my father in Italy, and a dark-purple, glistening, embossed silk scarf wrapped casually (perhaps) around his elegant neck. There were two rings of very yellow gold, one with a red stone, one with a green enameled disc, on his left hand.

I disliked him immediately.

My father, however, was in love with him.

"Sit down, sit down," he said, pulling the extra chair from the living room to the table. "We're so happy you could come and join us. We're eating salad. Would you like some salad?" He gestured to me: Bring a plate. Bring forks and knives and napkins for Jagdeesh!

To demonstrate to Vishwa that I loved him best, I served Jagdeesh from the left.

My mother had seated Vishwa beside me and across from Frederika, "So they can look at each other," she said in the kitchen before dinner. That left only one spot for Jagdeesh: between my father and Frederika. I wondered if she would be captivated by his Errol Flynn–ish aura. Vishwa seemed to be wondering something along those lines as well. He jiggled in his chair and cleared his throat several times. But Jagdeesh was focused on my mother.

"Your house is beautiful—of course," he said. "It's exactly as I imagined it would be. Perfect. I am not surprised. When I met you first—last year, wasn't it? At the department party? Yes, that's correct. You wore an Indian shawl, do you remember? It was green silk, very fine, embroidered in gold. Most striking on you. And I said to myself, I would expect no less from Carl's wife."

My mother did not seem to know what to say to all this.

Jagdeesh looked, briefly, at Frederika. "We must credit you for providing the occasion," he said.

Frederika nodded.

Swiveling his head back to my mother, Jagdeesh said, "It's the unusual combination of austerity with comfort. A certain Japanese influence?"

"Not really," my mother said. She did not sound pleased.

"Ah, you don't like the Japanese way? In truth, neither do I. It seems to me—how to say it—so minimal as to be almost not there at all. In Calcutta, for instance, there is so much vivacity on display, the colors and shapes and the ferment of the street, which carry on inside as well. My point is that the Far Eastern approach to space and form feels, to this Indian, at any rate, inert. Yes, that's the word, inert."

My mother lit a cigarette.

"Salad?" My father offered the bowl to Jagdeesh.

"Perfect," said Jagdeesh. "But may I?" He turned to Frederika. "You will have some?"

"Go ahead," she said. She did not seem captivated at all.

"After you," insisted Jagdeesh.

"Just *take* some," my mother said.

Frederika obeyed.

Salad precluded conversation. Heaps of tart watercress required everyone's full attention for several minutes. Jagdeesh, with his beautiful big white teeth, finished chewing first.

"Am I correct in thinking that you have an ancestor who was a great architect?"

My mother, delayed by her cigarette, was still deep in the watercress. She swallowed. "Ancestor isn't quite right, since he's alive. But yes."

"Talent will out," said Jagdeesh.

"Not always." My mother didn't look at me but I knew she was talking about me.

"For instance," he continued, "one of our grandfathers was a notable artist of the sitar, and this explains Vishwa, I have always said."

"But the other grandfather wasn't a notable economist," my father said, smiling at his own joke.

Vishwa laughed. Jagdeesh did not.

"We have some princes back there," Vishwa said. "Medieval robber-baron sorts. Maybe they were good at finance."

"Economics encompasses far more than finance," Jagdeesh told Vishwa.

"Oh, don't bother," my father said. "Nobody wants to know anything about economics. I suggest you stop trying."

"I have," said Jagdeesh.

"You haven't," said Vishwa.

"You don't have a grandfather who was a notable economist either," my mother said, addressing my father for the first time since her huff had started. "Do you?" She wasn't being friendly, but she was speaking to him.

"Hardly," said my father.

"I know nothing of your antecedents," said Jagdeesh.

"Standard," said my father. "The story of every Russian Jew."

"But what is this story?" Jagdeesh persisted. "This is not a story I know."

My father put his fork down. "One grandfather was a poor farmer in a village hundreds of miles from anywhere, the other was a peddler in a city."

"With a cart?" I asked. I hadn't known about that. "Grandma's or grandpa's?"

"My father's," said my father. "In Odessa, like everyone else."

"What did he sell on his cart?" I asked.

My father looked at me. "I don't know," he said. "My father never talked about it."

"Let's ask him!" I was excited.

"Piano, piano," my father said, dampening my enthusiasm with a downturned hand. He often "conducted" my behavior in this way. Maybe he was trying to participate more fully in the musical aspect of our family. The only direction he ever gave me, though, was *piano, piano,* with a rare *lento, lento* thrown in.

"The peddler is the economist in embryo," said Jagdeesh.

"Dessert," my mother said. "After all, we invited Jagdeesh for dessert, not watercress." She stood up.

I cleared the table and got the dessert plates from my mother. Before I'd gone two steps, she hissed: "Dessert forks." So I took those too. As I was setting them out, my mother returned to the table with the beautiful disc of the cardamom cake centered on the Ginori plate spattered with birds and grasshoppers that Annemarie had given her when we left Italy: super special-occasion. It had to date appeared only for birthdays.

"Here's a Swedish specialty Frederika has made us," my mother said.

"Oooh," said Jagdeesh. "I am such a softy for sweets."

Vishwa was definitely blushing now. "This is a very handsome cake," he said to Frederika.

Frederika pushed her glasses up on her nose. "Ah," she said.

"It's supposed to have whipped cream," my mother said, glaring at my father, "but we ran out." She attacked the cake with a kitchen knife and in four swift chops cut it into eighths. "There," she said, handing the plate off to Frederika.

"It needs no whipped cream," Jagdeesh said. "It is superb." He took another bite. "Perfect," he declared.

Vishwa put his chin on his hand and looked at Frederika. "It tastes like home," he told her.

"That is odd," she said. "Because to me it also tastes like home."

"Maybe we come from the same place?" Vishwa smiled.

Frederika had no answer for that.

My father and Frederika sat at the table cutting slices of cake so thin they fell apart, as if pieces that small didn't count and therefore they weren't really eating more cake. My mother was having her nightly struggle with the dishwasher, determined to stuff everything into it and failing. At least once a week she—or the dishwasher, depending on your vantage point—broke something. She felt it was malevolent: "Damned dishwasher," she'd say. "You might have overfilled it," Frederika would observe. "No." My mother was adamant. "It's a dishwasher. It's supposed to wash the dishes, not break them."

It was past eleven. I should have gone to bed, but nobody had told me to, so I was snuggled into a dining room chair, uncomfortable and happy. What my mother called the "debriefing" was a process I usually missed or, hidden halfway up the stairs, overheard only in snatches.

"Aren't they different," said my mother.

"Amazingly," said Frederika.

"You still like him, though, don't you?" My mother sounded a bit worried.

"He's a little . . ." My father searched for the adjective that would sum up without insulting. "Vague, maybe? Unfocused?"

"He certainly doesn't have Jagdeesh's self-confidence." My mother made that quality sound suspicious.

"He does not have the same basis for being self-confident," my father said.

"It's just another personality sort is my guess," said Frederika.

"Artistic," said my mother, clanging a pot on top of a lot of glasses.

"That's right." Frederika sounded relieved. "Also, maybe because the brother is so looking-good?"

"Good-looking," my father said. "It's a bit much, I agree. Scarf and all that. Rings. It doesn't matter, though. If he wants to wear rings, let him."

"You wouldn't say that if Vishwa were wearing those rings," my mother pointed out. "Then it would be, Too many rings!"

"Look," my father said. "Jagdeesh is really exceptional."

"So is Vishwa," said my mother.

"I predict Jagdeesh will get a Nobel. I'm sure of it," my father said.

"He's only thirty-five," my mother said. "Kind of young for that."

"Twenty years from now." My father considered for a moment. "Or maybe thirty. By 1985, he'll have one."

He was off by a bit—it was in the nineties—but his prediction was right.

"I really like him," Frederika said, looking out onto the backyard, addressing the night sky.

"Thank god, Freddy," said my mother. "I think he's the one for you."

"I'll have to learn more about music," Frederika said.

"Don't think about that." My mother closed the dishwasher with a bang. "All that having-things-in-common stuff is just rot. Anyhow, you like music."

"How do you know if someone is the one for you?" I asked.

"Haven't you gone to bed?" My mother came around the table to pry me out of the chair. "Go to bed." She rubbed my head, roughly but in a friendly way. "Bed, bed, bed."

"But how do you know?"

"You don't need to worry about that yet," she said. "My little chicklet."

My mother called me her little chicklet only when she was feeling very affectionate. She refused to explain what it meant. Was it a baby chicken, or was it the tiny sugar-coated squares of gum that rattled in their green-and-white box? "That's for me to know and you to find out," she would say when I asked. "How am I going to find out," I'd say, "if you don't tell me?"

"You'll be singing a different song in a few years," she'd answer. "You won't think I know everything then."

Another correct prediction.

For the moment, though, the little chicklet was content to go to bed, along with everyone else, all yawning, each privately pleased. Dinner had been a success; my father's banishment to the doghouse had been brief; Frederika could see a sketch, a hint of her future—shimmering, unclear, but wonderful, perhaps even more wonderful for its lack of detail.

The dishwasher, left alone at last, began to chew up a salad plate.

The trouble with Jagdeesh was he wanted to please everyone. Since he had several girlfriends, this wasn't possible. He started coming to my mother for advice. While Vishwa cooed in the kitchen with Frederika, Jagdeesh sat on the sofa with my mother and described his scrambles to clear evidence of his second girlfriend before the arrival of his first. Luckily, the first one, Delilah, lived in England and couldn't get over much. But Lucy, the second girlfriend, was snoopy and suspicious, probably because she was married herself and alert for infidelity in others.

They would arrive together of an afternoon, Vishwa rumply and smelling of balsam or myrrh, Jagdeesh suited up and redolent of lime aftershave or perhaps the gin-and-tonic necessary to sustaining his complicated life.

"It's going to come to a bad end," he said.

My mother had to agree.

"It happened quite naturally," he said. "I didn't intend to hurt anyone, really."

"It's always like that," my mother assured him.

"Delilah is so stubborn about staying in Cambridge. She won't even consider a half-and-half appointment. That's where the trouble started, you see. When I came to Harvard."

"You felt rebuffed," my mother suggested.

"Not that there was an offer for her," Jagdeesh went on. "But surely something could be arranged, no?"

"Did you ask Carl?"

Jagdeesh was uncharacteristically silent. Finally, he said, "Well, it isn't exactly his department."

He meant that literally. Delilah was a philosopher, not an economist.

"You hesitate to embroil him in private matters?" my mother asked.

Jagdeesh nodded.

My mother was what is called a good listener. She knew what people were really thinking and would encourage them by articulating the things they weren't saying to show she understood. I didn't like it. Everyone else who knew her adored it.

"With Lucy, it was a sudden passion—you know the sort of thing." Jagdeesh sighed. It was clear that sort of thing had happened to him more than once. "But now . . ." He stopped.

"Maybe that's all she's interested in," my mother said.

"I'm afraid not." Jagdeesh fiddled around with his cuff link. "She has told Ed."

My mother widened her eyes. "Hmm," she said.

"Hmm, indeed," said Jagdeesh. "I really don't know what to do."

"When is Delilah's next visit?"

"This weekend." He put his hands into his luxuriant hair and pulled it. "It will be the showdown at the Not O.K. Corral, I fear."

"Can you take Delilah out of town?"

"She arrives in New York, thank god," Jagdeesh said. "I will go there to meet her. But we can't stay there forever. I have a class to teach on Tuesday."

"I wonder why Lucy told Ed," my mother said. "Do you think she wants to marry you?"

"They both want to marry me," Jagdeesh wailed.

"And Lucy has no idea about Delilah?"

"Delilah antedates her, therefore she is aware of her existence. She thinks . . ." Jagdeesh paused. "I gave her reason to think that Delilah and I parted several years ago. Because we did." He nodded vigorously. "We did. Except we didn't."

"How about Delilah?" my mother asked. "She doesn't know about Lucy, does she?"

"That," said Jagdeesh, "would be curtains."

"Do you want to marry either of them?" my mother asked.

Jagdeesh grinned.

"I don't feel the need for a wife at the moment," he said.

"I'll bet you don't," said my mother.

In the kitchen, Vishwa was studying a score and Frederika was making a Bolognese sauce. I was being the babysitter, balancing my sister in my lap while she tried to grab Vishwa's pages. She was heavy now and almost too big for me to hold.

"All set," said Frederika, putting the lid on the pot and turning the flame down low. She held her arms out for the baby. "Oof! You're getting big," she said, and put her in a chair.

"I am a big girl now," said my sister. "I'm big."

The front door opened and closed. Jagdeesh had left. Soon, but not quite yet, the *bang, crunch, bang, clunk* of my father's return.

As always, my mother's solution was to invite them for dinner. "That way," she explained to Frederika, "I can get a feel for Delilah."

"What about this person Lucy?" Frederika asked.

"I don't think Lucy is a contender, somehow," my mother said.

"Have you met her?" Vishwa asked.

My mother shook her head. "I met Ed a few times. He didn't seem too formidable."

"Whatever it means to be a contender," Vishwa said, "Lucy is one. She is not the sort of person you say no to."

"You don't like her," my mother said.

"I didn't say that," said Vishwa.

"What a diplomat!" My mother laughed. "Well, maybe if Ed is so mushy and Lucy is strong and really determined . . ." She trailed off. "What about Delilah?" she asked Vishwa.

"Ah," said Vishwa. "She is very nice."

Frederika frowned.

"Nice for Jagdeesh," Vishwa said to Frederika. "She is a good person. You would like her. Everybody would like her, I think." He thought for a moment. "She is very nervous," he added.

"Sounds as if she's got plenty of reasons to be nervous," my mother said. "Well, we'll see. They'll be here for dinner on Tuesday with you, Vishwa."

"Who? Now who?" my father said.

"You're home," my mother told him.

My father had come to accept Tuesday dinner with Vishwa, with only a few grumbles about "extraneous" people. But his family dinner position remained firm. My mother would have had people to dinner three nights a week if he'd let her, even though the preparations made her anxious. "Oh, I'm doing too much!" she would say, putting her hand to her forehead as if she were going into a Victorian swoon. "Too many people!" my father would crow, delighted. "It's not natural," he'd say. "You're not natural," my mother would retort. "You're a misanthrope."

He wasn't. He was much more sociable and pleasant in company than she was. He just wanted to have dinner with his family.

"I'm home," he said. "Who is it this time?"

"Jagdeesh," my mother said. "So you can't complain."

"You said *they,*" my father said.

"And his English girlfriend."

"I didn't know he had one of those." My father took off his tie and dropped it on top of Vishwa's score. "The department gossip is that he's running around with Ed Barkey's wife."

"The department is right," my mother said. "He's a ladykiller, that Jagdeesh."

"He kills them?" I asked.

"It's an expression," my mother said. "It means that girls like him, a lot."

"Does Barkey's wife know about the English girlfriend?" my father asked my mother.

"Suspicious," she said. "So don't mention it."

"You mean Ed knows what his wife is up to?"

"Apparently," said my mother.

"Can you be a mankiller?" I asked. "I mean, could a girl be one?"

"There are other words for that," my father said.

Vishwa slid his score out from under my father's tie, gently, deferentially, making an effort not to disturb it.

"Off I go," he announced. To Frederika, he said: "I'll be done by ten. Shall I come back then?"

"Okay, okay," said Frederika.

"Such night owls, the pair of you," my mother said.

They were, but we all were. None of us ever wanted to go to bed, including the baby, who lay in her cot talking to herself until ten-thirty and never woke up before nine the next day. This was lucky for my mother and Frederika. They could blaze away until one or two in the morning and still get almost enough sleep.

My father and I suffered. I had to be ready for Ingrid to pick me up by seven-forty-five each day, and my father had to wake me. He started at seven and, like a frenetic cuckoo clock, popped into my bedroom every five minutes until, at about seven-twenty, he just lifted me out of bed and stood me upright. I would pretend to eat a bowl of cereal while putting on my socks. Then the bell, the search for my shoes, my father sticking his head out the front door to say, "Almost ready!" In the backseat with Roger, I usually fell asleep again, or tried to. My father had several times offered to share what was incorrectly called carpooling with Ingrid, but she always said, "I'm on the way to the office anyhow, and I know you people stay up late." Ingrid pronounced *people* as if it were spelled *pipple*. "And also, there's that stupid one-way," she'd add, referring to our street, which ran one way down the hill from the Bigelows' house to ours. If my father had ever driven me and Roger to school, rather than merely telling Ingrid he'd be happy to do it, he would have had to go entirely around the block first to pick up Roger.

In her cranky, dismissive way, Ingrid was gracious to my father about being my chauffeur, but she often took advantage of the situation to register a complaint with me about what are now called parenting skills. "No mittens?" she'd ask, with disapproval. "Did you eat any breakfast?" was another frequent question. "I think you wore those clothes yesterday," she'd say. "Peeyew!" Roger would yelp. "Smelly old clothes!" Then I'd poke him in the soft part of his side and he'd pinch me right above the knee. "No, no, no!" Ingrid would inform us.

I knew, or at least I guessed, that it would be easier to pay attention at school if I'd had a good night's sleep and a real breakfast. But I didn't want to pay attention. I relied on my morning fog to protect me from the stupefaction I couldn't avoid in the afternoon. By lunchtime I'd woken up, and I had to experience the boredom I skipped in those half-conscious mornings. There wasn't any payoff in getting enough sleep. Anyhow, nothing at school could compete with the goings-on at home.

By the time my mother invited Jagdeesh and Delilah for dinner, Tuesdays with Vishwa had matured into Wednesdays also with Vishwa. My father hadn't complained until the week Vishwa came Tuesday, Wednesday, and Thursday. The next week reverted to Tuesday only in a peacekeeping effort. But my mother felt things got "crowded" when dinner followed my music lesson.

"They really don't have time to visit," she said to my father.

"They see each other every night!" he said.

That was what kept me up.

After dinner, while my mother tangled with the dishwasher, Frederika put the baby to bed. The bath, the pajamas, the tucking-in, the Swedish lullaby. My mother made a ceremonial nursery appearance, like the lady of a well-run British manor house, for a goodnight kiss. By then it was nine o'clock. If I kept a low enough profile, reading in the window seat, for instance, I could stay in the living room until about quarter to ten, when one of my parents would register my presence and shoo me to bed.

Frederika was already up there on the third floor, primping. Sometimes she was lying in the tub, her hair in a seaweedish fan around her face and a strategic sponge floating on top of her other hair. Her half-submerged breasts looked like saucers—tidy little saucers with eyes on them. Other times she tried out hair-dos. I was the arbiter for these.

"Braids?" She turned toward me with braids pinned up on her head.

"Too Heidi," I said.

"How about braids, but down?"

"Farmer-y."

"Up on top in a pouf that comes downward?"

I liked this one: Frederika the fountain-head. "Yes!" I said.

She moved her head back and forth, and the explosive hair swung this way and that. "But maybe it's too much of a fireworks?" she asked.

She usually ended up where she started: bun.

There were also experiments with makeup. My mother bought a lot of makeup that she'd use once and reject: too dark, too light, not for her complexion, and so forth. She passed the little pots and tubes on to Frederika. With her intense eyebrows and dark eyes and interestingly sallow skin, my mother didn't need makeup—more accurate to say that no makeup was going to impart the pink, creamy face of the fifties she was aiming for. Frederika seemed a bit more likely to achieve that. She was pale, almost monochromatic: a blank canvas. She had a wonderful nose with a bump on the bridge and high, knobby cheekbones. It was an entirely un-American face, all structure, no color.

Mascara, a swipe of red lipstick, and a dab of rouge could transform Frederika into a monster in two minutes. It was terrifying. She looked like a clown, she looked demented, she looked truly awful. We were both fascinated by this. Even a toned-down version (Rose Blush lipstick, light-brown eyeliner) was bad. When I tried—which I always did, synchronizing my strokes with hers as we leaned over the sink in our shared bathroom—I looked ready for Halloween, which was less scary. On me, it looked like the joke it was. Something about Frederika's bony, pale face made the makeup look purposefully outlandish.

We needed a lot of cold cream to remove the makeup, and our bathroom smelled of it, fresh gasoline larded with lanolin. I loved cold cream; it reminded me of sour cream. When I brushed my teeth after our makeup sessions, the cold cream deliquesced on my hands and the toothbrush slithered from my fingers.

And then it was time for bed. "Ten-thirty!" Frederika would say, surprised every night by how late it was. "Too late for you."

In bed I could hear the muffled clatter of my parents unloading the dishwasher, their late-night ritual and one of the few domestic chores in which my father participated. Things were beginning to blur in my head. I had to fight off sleep for a second, then for three seconds, a minute. I was waiting for the doorbell. *Ping,* there it was, there was Vishwa's light, cheerful voice, my father's heavy tread on the stairs, going up to the second floor and leaving the field to the ladies.

Much later I'd wake for a moment to the creak of the third-floor staircase: Vishwa and Frederika, finally by themselves. Whatever they were up to next door to me—my idea of it was still a bunch of hugging—they were quiet about it. They murmured, they padded about on the black-painted floor in their socks, somebody dropped a book, somebody laughed. It was comforting. They were happy, and I could let myself go back to sleep.

My mother did not permit Vishwa to spend the night.

"Why?" Frederika asked.

"I don't want the neighbors to know our business," said my mother.

"You don't usually care about any neighbors." Frederika was sulky.

"In this case, I care."

It was rare that they had a serious disagreement. Neither of them knew what to do.

"What is it you care?" Frederika demanded.

"Just." My mother crossed her arms.

"It is charades," said Frederika.

"There have to be some limits," my mother said.

"Why? Why do there have to be limits?"

"I'm not going to have a philosophical discussion, Freddy."

Mollified by "Freddy," Frederika dropped the topic. Sometime between one and four in the morning, Vishwa would tiptoe downstairs and go home.

Vishwa lived in the maid's quarters of Jagdeesh's house at the juncture of Concord Avenue and Garden Street, five blocks away. The house had a magnificent, two-story, arched, mullioned window almost as wide as the street façade, with a view of the rundown Hotel Continental across the road. Vishwa's rooms faced the back, where there was a tangle of unpruned lilacs and self-seeded maples. He had a little bedroom and a little living room made smaller by the baby grand piano jammed in a corner. The rest of the room was mostly taken up by stacks of records. There was a lumpy brown plaid loveseat where we sat together to listen on the occasional day when the lesson took place at his house rather than ours.

"Next week at my house," he'd tell me. "I have wonderful new records."

After *Das Lied von Der Erde,* or *The Rite of Spring,* or *Come, Ye Sons of Art,* or the Mozart clarinet concerto, we'd walk back together to our house for dinner. My lessons consisted of listening and singing along the second time we listened. The piano was untouched in the corner, which was fine with me. The violin had not yet materialized.

Vishwa used the fire escape as his front stairs. It was only a half-flight up. The door opened onto a hall so tiny it could barely contain me and Vishwa at the same time. "It keeps the privacy to come this way," he told me. "I don't want to wander through Jagdeesh's library or what-have-you three times a day."

I wanted to see, though.

I still didn't like Jagdeesh, but because he turned up at our house so much, I was getting used to him. And I was getting curious about him too. After all, he was Vishwa's brother, so there had to be something worthwhile about him. I thought if

I could get a look at where he lived, I might be able to see what it was.

Several times I asked Vishwa if we could go into Jagdeesh's part of the house, but he always said no. He was—for Vishwa—surprisingly firm about it.

"That's his house. This is my house," he said.

"But it's the same house!"

"We don't pokety-poke in each other's places."

"Just to peek," I pleaded.

"You'd have to ask *him,*" said Vishwa.

Maybe I could ask when he and Delilah came for dinner.

This time my mother went all out. Half a salmon poached in court bouillon. Asparagus vinaigrette. Sliced potatoes in cream and butter, first baked, then crusted under the broiler. And the super-special-occasion chocolate roll, a thin sheet of dark-chocolate sponge cake impastoed with coffee-and-chocolate mousse, rolled up into a log, dusted with cocoa powder (the real stuff, bitter as dirt), and put into the refrigerator to cook.

"Montefiore as in Moses?" asked my father, shaking Delilah's hand.

"I'm afraid so," she said.

"That's an illustrious heritage."

"Mmm," said Delilah. "One can hardly live up," she added.

Delilah was almost as tall as my father and very thin. Her skin was translucent; several pinkish-greenish blood vessels quivered in her forehead. My mother and Frederika were wearing bright, smooth party dresses. Delilah was wearing a shambly tweed ensemble with a hairy skirt and a short jacket. Her slip was showing. This gave me a feeling of solidarity. She probably didn't like getting dressed up any more than I did—obvious, because she wasn't dressed up. I was. My mother had insisted I wear the middy blouse and blue pleated skirt combo that I hated most of all things I hated to wear. We'd argued for ten minutes over my red Keds. I won. Delilah's footgear was also peculiar: rubber-soled boots with canvas tops. She looked ready for a hunting party, not a dinner party.

"Drinks?" My father hovered at the living room entrance, ready to pop into the kitchen and do everyone's bidding.

"Scotch with a touch of water," said Jagdeesh.

My father ignored him: Ladies first. "Delilah?"

"Do you happen to have any Campari?"

He was delighted. "We do! Ice? Lemon?"

"A bit of each."

"Now for Jagdeesh." He turned toward him. "Ice?"

"Only water," said Jagdeesh, his arm outstretched to ban ice.

I saw Vishwa glance at Frederika. They were sitting side by side on the window seat, looking a little provisional, as if they didn't intend to stay.

"You two?" my father asked them.

"I would like some of the wonderful bourbon *with* ice," Vishwa said.

"I'll help you, Carl," said Frederika.

"No need." He waved her back. "You," he said, beckoning me. "You can get the olives."

The doorbell rang.

My father revised his plan. "You can get the door," he said.

"But who is it?" I asked him. He'd gone into the kitchen.

It was A.A. and Ingrid.

"Hello, hello," said A.A., his voice rising in welcome, as if he were the host.

"I didn't know you were coming," I said.

"Here we are," said Ingrid. She zipped straight over to Frederika.

"Where's Roger?" I asked. I didn't really want Roger. If he were there, my parents would banish both of us from the table as soon as we'd eaten.

"He's got a cold, so we left him home with Mrs. Foley," said A.A. "Sorry."

Pleased, I went into the kitchen for the olives.

My mother was puzzling over the seating. The only fixed point was my father at the head of the table.

"Ingrid and Freddy want to talk Swedish," she said, "so I'll put them opposite. And I have to be near the kitchen, but that means sitting next to You." She turned to my father. "Well, so what. Jagdeesh at the other end?" she asked. My father said nothing. "He'd like that," she told herself. My father continued to spoon olives into the black bowl. "I suppose Delilah goes at Your right. That puts A.A. and Vishwa across from each other. That could be good."

"What about me?" I asked.

"Oh, I guess I'll stick you beside Delilah."

"I want to be beside Vishwa."

"You will be," she said. "Right between them. I'm not sure Jagdeesh enjoys Frederika, or vice versa," she said.

"Don't worry," said my father. "He won't talk to her."

"Can you write little cards?" my mother asked me. "Nice little cards."

"Déclassé," grumbled my father.

"Christ!" said my mother. "It's too confusing otherwise." She handed me the notepad for shopping lists. "We're eight," she said. "Oops, I guess we're nine."

"Did you forget me again?" I asked.

"Probably I forgot myself," she said. "You always forget yourself when you're doing this kind of thing."

"Tear them in half," my father said.

"Or fold them," my mother suggested.

"So they can stand up?" I liked that idea.

"I'll write the names for you," my mother said. "Carl, how do you spell 'Jagdeesh'?"

"Two *e*'s," said my father.

Either because she was a woman or because she was a Montefiore, Delilah had been exempted from my father's usual interview. Exempted as well from his attention, which was focused on Jagdeesh. They had to toss their conversation overhand down the whole length of the table. But the rest of the pairings were working well. Ingrid and Frederika were gargling away in Swedish, and A.A. turned out to have a passion for Indian flute music. He leaned across the table to hear Vishwa tell the history, explain raga forms, and list the best players. A.A. took his place card and scribbled the names on the back.

"What a stroke of luck!" he said. "I've been operating in the dark. This is really wonderful."

"You may have some trouble finding the recordings," Vishwa said. "I have some, of course, and I could lend—"

"I wouldn't dream of—"

"It would be my pleasure—"

I could see that they liked each other. Another thing I saw was that they were alike, which was surprising, since they couldn't have looked less alike. A.A. was about half a foot taller than Vishwa and his mustache had more hair in it than Vishwa had on his whole head. But they were both polite, even formal, and they were both mumbly and soft, and they were the opposite of what my mother, referring to Jagdeesh, called self-promoting. Because Vishwa was small, I'd never been surprised that his presence didn't take up a lot of room. Now that I saw him with A.A., though, I realized that A.A. had the same sort of presence—a presence that left enough air and space for other people. It was why I'd always liked to spend time with him.

"In fact," A.A. was saying, "I have a tape recorder and what we could do, you could bring some records, and I could record."

"What a good idea!"

"We could make several copies, if there were other people who'd enjoy them."

"Perhaps for Frederika." Vishwa looked over at her. "But I don't think she has a tape player." He turned to me. "Does she?"

"We don't have one," I said. "I don't think she has one either."

"They're cumbersome and expensive," A.A. said. "But they do come in handy. So that's settled. How about dinner this Sunday, with Frederika, of course."

"I'll have to check to be sure she can," said Vishwa. "But it would be lovely, thank you."

"You want to come too?" A.A. asked me.

"Yes," I said.

"Good. Roger will be over his cold by then, I'm sure. But I wonder if you'll like the music."

"Of course she will." Vishwa put his hand on my shoulder. "She is a very discriminating listener."

"Really? Am I special?"

"Specially what?" my mother asked.

"We were speaking of Susanna's talent for listening," said Vishwa.

"To what she wants to hear," my mother said.

"Mummy, Vishwa and Frederika and I are going to the Bigelows' on Sunday for Vishwa's Indian records."

"We'll see," said my mother.

"It's okay," I said. "They asked us."

"We have a department party." My mother looked at Delilah. "You'll be there, won't you?"

Delilah looked puzzled. "Jagdeesh didn't mention it."

"Anyhow," my mother told me, "we need Freddy at home with the baby."

"Oh, she can bring the baby to our house," said A.A. "We'll park her in the guest room, and she can go to sleep. It'll be fine."

"We'll see," my mother said, again.

We'll see usually meant no.

Beside me, Delilah was looking at her lap and holding her fork, with a sliver of salmon on it, at a strange angle that pointed—accusatorily?—at Jagdeesh enthroned at the foot of the table. I'd been aware of my mother talking to her during the Indian-music powwow. I hadn't heard Delilah saying much in response. Now she seemed frozen.

"More potatoes?" my mother asked her.

Delilah pulled out of her trance. "I will," she said. "I have the British weakness for potatoes, and these are particularly good."

"They're French is why," said my mother. They both laughed. "Has the food improved at all since we were there?"

"That was two years ago?" Delilah asked.

"Not quite. Nothing but mutton and parsnips."

"Now it's lamb. And there are carrots. I suppose that might be considered an improvement. One must still cross the Channel for a decent supper."

"I don't get it," said my mother. "There was a war in France too, but they've managed to resume normal life."

"We're burdened with our Making Do ethic." Suddenly, Delilah became animated. She waved her fork. "It's frightful! The rooms at Cambridge are cold and dank, the food is dreadful, though the wines are good—which of course is an abomination in itself, because why waste these wines on ghastly meals." She shook her head. "I think we must prefer hardship, that's the only explanation for it. Everything's pinched and stringent, it's all fundamentally against any sort of delight."

"Maybe you should consider relocating," said my mother.

Bam, bam, bam: checkmate. I was impressed.

So was Delilah. Her mouth was open, only a little, but still.

"One can't just pick up . . ." She didn't finish.

"No, no, I understand. Arrangements," my mother said. "But maybe you should make a few. Arrangements. You don't seem to be content there."

"It's home. Though that doesn't necessarily recommend it." Delilah had enough good humor to smile.

"Anything we can do to help?"

Delilah didn't even respond to that. She ate some potatoes. Then she said, "Mustn't complain. Mustn't grumble."

"That's certainly the majority view, at least in England," said my mother. "Here, in this family, at any rate, we like to complain."

Delilah laughed. "It's one of those American characteristics I so enjoy."

"You like American things?" I asked. "What other American things do you like?"

"Hot dogs," Delilah said. "Maybe it's because of the name. I love that name, hot dog." She thought for a minute. "I like the way things aren't fixed here. It's a cliché, I suppose, but one does feel that anything could happen. Do you understand?" She looked intently at me.

"Yes," I said. "When we were in England, every day was the same day."

"Did you like England at all?" she asked.

"I liked the candy," I said. "I didn't like my school."

"And now? Do you like your school?"

I took a big breath. "I don't think I like going to school," I said.

"She's a little anarchist," my mother said.

"I also hated going to school," Delilah told me. "And look, now I'm a don at Cambridge—so don't worry," she said to my mother.

"Why did you hate it?" I asked.

"First off, I was sent to Switzerland, far from home. And then, just the sorts of things, I'm sure, that you don't like. The regimentation, the uniform, being bored by classes. That school was very keen on proper behavior, and your school probably isn't as concerned with that aspect of life."

"They want you to sit still," I said.

Delilah smiled at me. "I think all schools want you to sit still. I mean things like the correct way to serve tea. We had posture class: walking around with two books on your head. I don't imagine you have to do that."

"No. We have to play dodgeball."

"Is that so terrible?" She was surprised.

"It's stupid," I said. "I hate dodgeball. But I guess it isn't any more stupid than the math class with the stupid sticks."

My mother was glaring at me. She mouthed, Enough.

"What sticks?" Delilah asked.

My mother stood up before I could answer. "Frederika," she said, "will you help us clear?"

With me, my mother, and Frederika all absent from the table, Delilah at one end and Ingrid at the other were adrift in a small sea of men, none of whom was paying attention to either of them. Delilah was absorbed by her lap again and didn't seem to care, but Ingrid looked put out. Though I didn't like to give him credit for it, Jagdeesh was the person who noticed this situation.

"Annette tells me you are both psychoanalysts," he said to Ingrid.

"Yah," said Ingrid. It wasn't an encouraging answer.

Jagdeesh fiddled with one of his rings. "Have you different, ah, specialties?"

"I trained as an analyst, but my first job was at a school for mixed-up children," Ingrid said. She appeared to have made a decision to be friendlier.

"Not now?" Jagdeesh persisted.

"It's tough to psychoanalyze children, and I realized I was more interested in the problems of the parents," she said. "After I was a parent too. Then that was the side I was on, you see."

"Aha," said Jagdeesh. "I didn't know you could take sides in psychoanalysis."

"Oh, sure," said Ingrid. "Like sometimes you just hate a patient. That's no good!"

"What happens then?"

"Don't take them," said Ingrid.

"And if you already did take them?"

"Nah," she said. "You know right away about people." As usual, she said *pipple,* not *people*.

"If that's the case, it's rather an argument against the practice of psychoanalysis, isn't it?" Jagdeesh looked pleased with his idea.

"But you don't know *why*. And they don't know why either. Why they're bothersome. So, you could have a lot to talk about. Still, better not to take them."

I was lurking behind Frederika's empty chair with a dirty plate in each hand, listening to them. I'd never heard Ingrid say things about work before, and I was interested.

"What are people trying to do with psychoanalysis?" I asked her.

"A very important question," said Jagdeesh.

I wondered if he was giving me a compliment, then decided he wasn't.

"Just to understand themselves better," Ingrid told me. "So they don't feel so nervous and jumpy with themselves."

"How does it work?" I asked.

Jagdeesh nodded. "Another important question."

"Everybody likes to talk about themselves," Ingrid said. "If you get to do that for a couple of years, you feel better. You might even get bored with yourself—that's the best."

"You're watering this down considerably for her benefit, aren't you?" said Jagdeesh.

Ingrid shrugged. "It's basically true. Neurotic narcissists feel better when they get a lot of attention. So give them some!"

"I want to do psychoanalysis," I said.

Ingrid squinted at me. "You don't need it," she said. "You misbehave and then you get the attention you want."

"But I want nice attention."

She shook her head. "Who says psychoanalysis is nice attention? You're just assuming it's nice."

"You refer to the labor of achieving insight?" Jagdeesh asked.

"Hunh?" Ingrid was now squinting at him.

Frederika appeared beside me and whispered, "Your mother wants you in the kitchen."

My mother didn't even look at me. "Set these dessert plates," she said. "And don't interrupt grownups."

"I wasn't interrupting," I protested.

"Set those dessert plates." She pointed at them.

"I wanted to know—"

"Plates."

I set them. Jagdeesh and Ingrid had come to a standstill on psychoanalysis, but my father and Delilah were talking—rather, he was talking and she was looking at him, at least, and not at her lap. I set my plate last and sat down beside her. Her leg was jiggling; it made my chair jiggle too.

"Why don't I put out a few feelers," he was saying. "Just to get a sense of the situation."

"Please, don't go to any trouble," Delilah mumbled.

"It's no trouble at all," said my father. "Anything I can do. Because, you know how much we treasure Jagdeesh."

"That's the problem, you see," Delilah cut in. "It's the whiff of—'nepotism' is incorrect, but you get my drift."

"No, no," said my father. "I don't think that's right. I think that's absurd, really." He leaned back in his chair.

Delilah winced. In her fascinating lap, her right hand clenched. "I believe that Jagdeesh has already spoken to someone, and I think it's rather a no-go."

"Who?" my father demanded.

"Was it Quine?" Delilah asked the air.

"Quine's no good," my father said.

Delilah raised an eyebrow. "He's awfully good," she said.

"For this," said my father. "He's not the one for this. Dreben, I think. Dreben would be the one to talk to."

Delilah stopped twitching and clenching and jiggling. "I appreciate your concern, truly. It's extremely kind of you to bother with this. But it's far better for me to pursue this on my own. It just would not do, otherwise. It wouldn't look right. It wouldn't be right."

"Would look or wouldn't be?" My father smiled. "I think

you're overpunctilious. But, as you wish. I certainly don't mean to press you. If you change your mind, though, I'd be delighted to help."

"You're ever so kind," Delilah said. "Thank you."

If Jagdeesh had said, You're ever so kind, I wouldn't have believed one word. Delilah seemed to mean it. She seemed also to be done in by this conversation, paler than ever, slumped, too tired to wriggle or jiggle.

I wanted to say something nice to her, to cheer her up a bit.

"You like that Other Cambridge?" I asked her.

This wasn't the right thing to say. She quivered.

"Because when I went there, I didn't really like it," I went on, blundering and smashing around as if I were my father coming in the front door. Unable to stop, I said, "It looked funny to me. You know? I thought it was going to look just like home. It looked nice enough, I guess, I mean if you liked it. But it wasn't . . ." I petered out. I stared down at my empty dessert plate. I felt very bad.

Delilah put one of her strange, long, chilly hands on my arm. "You're right," she said. "That's my Cambridge, and this is your Cambridge, and they're not the same."

The chocolate roll had been eaten down to a dark stub now melting on the Ginori plate. That "softy for sweets" Jagdeesh had taken two pieces. The coffee cups were empty and stuck to their saucers, the ashtrays were filling up, and the atmosphere was gritty and acrid from smoke and chocolate.

This was the moment I liked best at a dinner party, though I was not often up late enough to see it. It was when the structure of grownup life began to falter and the grownups became different, as if they were all Cinderellas turning into pumpkins at midnight. Except they turned into real people—people I could make some sense of.

They'd drifted back to their original partners, Vishwa beside Frederika, A.A. in Vishwa's old seat beside Ingrid. Jagdeesh had taken his chair from one end of the table and parked it at the other between my father and Delilah to assert his oversight of them both. He had his arm around her shoulder, and now and then dipped his hand down into her fuzzy jacket to stroke her sharp white collarbone. Even my mother had loosed her hold on the proceedings. She'd propped her feet in my father's lap and stretched back in her chair, smoking and pursuing the question of Delilah's future, single-handedly, for the most part, since Delilah wasn't contributing much.

"Fall semester there, spring here," my mother was saying. "Or maybe the other way around, so you can avoid the snow."

"Mmm," said Delilah.

"You could try a year, to see how you like it."

Delilah looked down at Jagdeesh's hand, which was on its way into her jacket again. "We would have to discuss it," she said.

"I know Jagdeesh wants you to come," my mother said.

Delilah looked up. "You do?"

"Don't you know that?"

Delilah shook her head. "I find it difficult to know what Jagdeesh wants, in any given situation."

"What's this?" Jagdeesh asked, leaning over toward my mother. "I hear my name."

"Annette is trying to convince me to come here, maybe on a fellowship year," Delilah told him. "I doubt they'd have me."

"Oh, they'd have you," Jagdeesh said.

My mother and Delilah looked at him, waiting for a further comment. But he made none. Delilah sighed and glanced at my mother.

“You should bring Delilah to the department party on Sunday,” she said to Jagdeesh. “Give her a taste of Harvard life.”

“Ah, yes, the party,” he said. “I’d forgotten.”

My mother made a face.

“You hadn’t mentioned it to me,” Delilah said to him.

“I thought it would be a bore for you, darling,” said Jagdeesh. “I thought I would just pop in and out.”

“I see,” said Delilah. She looked grief-stricken.

“I think you would enjoy it,” my mother said. Turning to Jagdeesh, she said, “I hope to see you both there.”

I wanted to remind my mother about Indian records at the Bigelows’ on Sunday, which I was looking forward to, but I knew this wasn’t the moment. These sorts of situations were tricky. If I asked, or reminded, at the wrong time, she was likely to say no, but if I left it too late, too near the event, she would say that I hadn’t told her, that I couldn’t just expect to go off and do whatever I wanted whenever I wanted. Another reason to say nothing (at this moment) was to avoid attention, nice or not, because attention might result in her telling me to go to bed.

I didn’t want to go to bed. I wanted to figure out what was going on. Jagdeesh was lying—I could see that, and so could my mother and Delilah. He hadn’t forgotten about the party at all. It was the Lucy person, I supposed. She would be there. What I didn’t understand was my mother’s plan. She was up to something, but it was mysterious.

“We might give it a miss,” said Jagdeesh. “After all, Delilah is here such a short time.”

“Oh?” My mother looked at her.

“I leave Tuesday,” she said. “It will have been ten days.”

“Eleven,” said Jagdeesh.

Delilah made a small throttled noise and slipped out from under Jagdeesh’s meandering hand. “But who’s counting?” she said, and then she laughed—at least, it was a stab at a laugh. She stood up. "The lavatory?" she asked my mother.

"First right upstairs," my mother said.

As soon as she'd left the room Jagdeesh leaned over to my mother: "This is making terrible trouble! I don't understand."

My mother took her legs out of my father's lap and sat up straight. "You think she doesn't know about Lucy? She knows. She knows." She jabbed her cigarette into the ashtray, killing it over and over.

Jagdeesh put his hands on the table. "You're wrong," he said.

My mother said, "Pshaw."

"Even if you're right," he said, "I don't see how this idea of going to the party helps anything."

"Throwing a little light on the situation," my mother said.

"But for whom?" Jagdeesh gripped the table. "If, as you assert, everybody knows, then who will be enlightened?"

"You, I imagine," said my mother.

To Fall in Love with Old Cape Cod

Third grade was finished. Now June and July stretched out ahead. I could loll in the creamy thick grass again and barrel around town on my bike. In August we were going to Cape Cod, to a cottage the Bigelows had found us down the road from the one they rented on the bay in Wellfleet. Frederika wasn't coming. She and Vishwa were going to drive across the country in a black Nash Rambler Vishwa had bought for a hundred dollars from Ed Barkey.

What my father referred to as the Enlightenment Crisis had produced mixed results. Delilah changed her ticket and went back early to England to avoid the Sunday-night party, seeming to forfeit the game. Then Jagdeesh stayed away from our house for many weeks. More than a month of unmitigated Lucy, though, had done him in, and he was back, complaining that he missed Delilah.

"We spoke on the telephone every week, you know," he said. "Like family."

"I didn't know," my mother said.

"And we wrote letters." Jagdeesh closed his eyes. "She's been part of my life for nearly fifteen years. It appears that she is necessary to my existence."

"Oh," said my mother.

"This is what you wanted, isn't it? This is why you muddied the waters, to prove that I am a cad."

My mother looked taken aback. "I think the waters were muddy already," she said. "And I don't think you're a cad—exactly."

"So exactly what do you think?" Jagdeesh asked.

"I think the situation wasn't tenable," said my mother.

"This is what's untenable!" Jagdeesh said. "Everything was fine." He considered that for a moment. "Well, it took some dexterity, but I managed."

"I don't think you can have them both," said my mother.

"I had them both," Jagdeesh pointed out. His tone was cool.

"That's true," my mother said, "but now you don't."

"Why did you do it?" Jagdeesh asked—not for the first time. His question was rhetorical, like asking God why he'd inflicted the flu on you. He didn't expect an answer.

It was a different story with my father. "What were you hoping to achieve? Were you hoping for any particular outcome or were you just fiddling around to amuse yourself?"

"Oh," said my mother, turning away, busying herself with something, anything.

"Because now it's a complete mess," my father went on.

My mother put her head into a cabinet. "Oh, gee, out of rice, I see," she said.

"It's irresponsible," said my father. "And I have to deal with it, not you." He stormed out of the kitchen.

Within thirty seconds he was back.

"You and your manipulations!" he said.

That was the day after the dinner. And he kept at it.

"Is it because you don't like Jagdeesh?"

"It's because I do like him," my mother said.

"Hah," said my father.

"You have an unconquerable need to meddle in other people's lives," he told her the day after that. "And I wish you wouldn't. Frederika, Vishwa"—he gestured toward the third floor, where all that Frederika and Vishwa business went on—"enjoy yourself. But this is different."

"Oh, I see," said my mother. "The department is sacred. *Your* stuff is sacred."

My father sputtered. "It's, it's different."

"How?"

"There are consequences."

"And at home there aren't any consequences? Or, I guess, those little domestic sorts of consequences aren't really important? Right?"

"You know what I mean," said my father.

"I certainly do," said my mother.

She stopped speaking to him. He didn't notice immediately, because he'd stopped speaking to her. It took him more than a day to realize that the usual had happened: He was angry with her, and therefore she wasn't talking to him.

They'd settled things by the time Jagdeesh started visiting again. The Cape Cod cottage was part of the reconciliation.

Villas in Italy were one thing, but we'd never had an American vacation. It was a real indulgence. What dollars could buy abroad was way beyond our means at home. Another factor at work was my mother's Filene's Basement Theory, according to which you had to get it because ordinarily it cost $500 but here it was for only $22.95. By this reasoning it was impossible to forgo a Florentine villa: You were there, it was there, and the exchange rate meant that renting it for the summer cost far less than one semester of my detested progressive school. But the Cape was expensive.

In the local dialect, the Cape was "down." I'm going down the Cape, people said, the way they said I'm going down cellar to mean they were getting the lawn chairs out of the basement. This was especially strange in the case of the Cape because it's an elbow bent back toward Boston. All the way "down," at Provincetown, is not even fifty miles across the bay from the city. The concept of the Cape as down meant that there was an Upper Cape and a Lower Cape. Upper was closer to Boston in road miles, but farther away geographically. It was where blueblood Yankees summered in towns named Dennis and Yarmouth. Lower was out, exposed to the ocean, wild and lumpy. Only fishermen and artsy riffraff lived there.

By the fifties a migration of psychiatrists, first wave from New York City, second wave from Boston and Cambridge, had changed the landscape of the Lower Cape. Inaccurate to put it that way. They adored the landscape—the puckered hills and boggy inlets and swaths of noisy, surfy beaches. What they changed was the economy. Playwrights were camped out in fish shacks in Truro, sculptors were living in garages in Wellfleet, painters were perched in the old boathouses on stilts that lined Provincetown's inner harbor, and psychiatrists would pay—they would pay!—to rent these places for the month of August. They paid enough to get the painters and sculptors and playwrights through much of the succeeding winter, back in their fish shacks and boathouses again. Where did they go in the interim? Maybe to New York (most of them had come from there to begin with) to house-sit for the psychiatrists in their Upper West Side apartments, or maybe they went to other fish shacks in places like New Bedford, where nobody, not even psychiatrists, would want to spend the summer.

There were also real houses built by cod kings and oyster barons. Some were Victorian piles with turrets and widows' walks plopped onto the Truro downs, where they looked odd. That kind of architecture generates a lot of outbuildings, and the Bigelows' cottage had been a caretaker's house. Our cottage was a fish shack. It was dark and grimy, the two bedrooms were only a bit bigger than the beds, the kitchen was an aluminum galley nailed into one corner, and the deck listed downward on creaky pilings. The bathroom was an off-the-shelf affair from the lumberyard in Orleans with a plastic shower stall and an unreliable toilet-and-sink unit. Everything was a bit stinky. Old fish, whiffs from the septic tank, a hint of the propane that fed the stove, and the nose-burning mildew that loves Cape Cod the best.

Those details—I don't actually remember all of them. But I know it was like that. That's the way Cape Cod cottages are. Like the view, they don't change. You're paying for the outside not the inside, and you really could not, cannot, and never would be able to put a price on that. It's beyond the realm of price. It doesn't exist in the world of price, and that is its value, that constitutes its pricelessness.

To wake up on a summer morning in Wellfleet and stand on a deck, however sloped and rotting, and breathe the exhalations of the bosomy landscape, all the breasted hills between the two faces of the ocean—the serene, almost brackish bay and the crazed Atlantic—and to smell the sweet marsh hay mixed with the fecal lowtide oozes and watch a tern snip little quarter-moons out of the sky and see the bay waters gray and flat or nearly white with froth but in any weather seeming, oddly, not to move because of being contained by the long curving arm at one end and Wellfleet Harbor at the other—well, that's something. A sort of something unlike any other thing.

The first visit: obscured by the many that followed later in my life. Except that every time was a kind of first time. Every time there was that moment on the bridge over the Cape Cod Canal when I felt the mainland sloughing off behind me and saw the last piece of American land, Provincetown, just visible from the midpoint of the span and bent toward me, drawing me on down. On the other side of the bridge the air was thin and pure, as if the Cape were a mountaintop rather than a salty spit. It was a different life down there, an alternate way to be, a way that, from the first, I wanted to be.

There are photographs of me and Roger on the beach at dusk, with the long, wiggly shadows of A.A. and my father in the distance beside the little bonfire where the hot dogs were cooking. They would make a ring of stones, fill it with eelgrass and driftwood, and place over that the grate from the rusted-out two-and-a-half-legged grill at the caretaker's cottage, which we carried down to the beach on a string every evening for this purpose. We needed a new piece of string the next evening because the fire burned it up each night. My mother smoking in the sunset, Ingrid fussing over the buns—"You're scorching them!"—and doling out the ketchup packets, which she kept in her beach bag along with never enough napkins. The baby making piles of clamshells and one-bucket sandcastles. The gulls hovering and yelling about how they wanted a handout. Sometimes a wiener (Roger loved to call them wieners; I thought it was a disgusting word) would fall through the grate and become a stiff, blackened tube, and Roger and I would fish it out with a stick accompanied by a lot of cautionary exclamations from the mothers: Watch out! Hey, be careful! Don't *do* that! Then we'd throw it toward the tide line, where a dozen birds could fight over it.

The birds were nonchalant about humans. Even the sandpipers, who darted away when we first walked onto the beach every evening, would be back within minutes of our arrival, poking their beaks in the surf. The gulls were the best. I loved their squawks and mutters and waddles and dances, and the way they'd bend their necks down and bark at the sand. They seemed to have a real language, a vast array of comments and warnings and, mostly, bragging. In my later Cape Cod life a gull once landed on my shoulder because he wanted the blueberry muffin I was eating. I was astonished by the weight of him, three pounds at least, and his rank fish-breath, and the power of his cold, nasty foot. His wing banged into my head. It was a hard, scratchy hinge, unlike anything mammalian. His feathers made a dry noise. I dropped my muffin on the beach. He was off me and on top of it in a moment, and stood with his big foot covering it, bragging, *Rrrrrra, rrrrrra,* to the summer sky.

On sultry days we went to the ocean, where there was always a breeze. This was a long journey, twenty minutes by car instead of the ten-minute walk from our smelly cottage to the bay. Many provisions and precautions were needed. Lunch in a padded plastic hamper, two coolers of iced tea, backup bathing suits, umbrella, white zinc in a crackled tube, a sweater for the chills after body surfing. A.A. had a little transistor in case there was a good concert; Ingrid brought knitting. Without Frederika, my mother was mostly occupied with watching over the baby and making sure she didn't wander into the water, but when she got a chance, she was reading Anthony Powell's latest volume, *The Acceptance World.* My father thought the whole Powell enterprise was middlebrow. "You're wrong," my mother said. "Anyhow, it's getting better and better with each book." Then she said, "I don't see how you can say that when you're not reading it. And look what you're reading!" He was reading Rex Stout. He'd brought six Nero Wolfes from Cambridge. "I'm on vacation," he said. "I'm on vacation too," she said. "Right," said my father. "Proving my point."

For Roger and me the ocean beach was heaven. There was nothing we could break or bang into, there was nothing sharp (the bay supported an enormous colony of razor clams, and their pointy corpses, hidden in the sand, really hurt when you stepped on them), however far away we went the parents could see us because the coast was quite straight (the bay had lots of curves and inlets), and, most important to me, there was almost never seaweed. I had a horror of seaweed. The worst was the big brownish fingers with bubbles on the end, but it was all terrible. The beautiful, frilled bright-green lettuce leaves were nearly as bad, and the stringy stuff, some green, some brown, which dried to a crispy dark nothingness the moment it washed up on the beach, was creepy because it got entangled in my legs like a spiderweb. But there wasn't any. If we wanted to pee we could do it right away where we stood in the water and the pee would just zip out toward Europe. At the bay we had the feeling that we were swimming in our pee for quite a while. We could even poop in the ocean. It was the ocean. What could one little poop do to it?

The wonderful noise, a monotony that was active and calming simultaneously. It was the same thing over and over again. A wave coming with a big roar and making a dark water stain on the slope of the sand, clearing away every mark Roger and I had put there. Then the wave sucking out, leaving air pockets that sizzled like pancake batter cooking. The moment between breaths, when the ocean sat there not doing anything; maybe five seconds of that? Then it gathered itself up again and bang, onto the sand. Water stain. Air pockets sizzling. Stasis. Bang. We could watch it for hours. We did. We stood knee-deep in the surf until we turned blue and our feet were scoured smooth by tumbling sand. Another good thing was to sit at the point where the tide hit the beach. Part of what made this good was that point kept changing. You could get two or three iterations of bang, water stain, sizzling, stasis, and bang before the tide shifted enough so your bottom detected it, by being either much wetter or dry. Also a good peeing position. The hot pee drilling a hole in the cold sand and all the evidence erased within moments by the next bang, stain, and sizzle.

Sometimes an analyst strolled over to chat with A.A. They called him Archie. I thought they were idiots. They didn't even know his name! Ingrid was the only woman analyst, and most of them seemed scared of her. I didn't blame them for that. If they came with wives, the wives tried to engage me and Roger in conversation, usually about where we went to school. Roger was friendly; I ignored them. My mother would scowl and growl at me to be polite, but I refused. I felt the beach was exempt from ordinary rules of behavior. After all, we were barely wearing clothes and we got to go to the bathroom whenever we felt like it. It wasn't regular life. And I wasn't going to waste my time with nervous wives.

The days went by, every day the same day, varied only by the morning decision: ocean or bay? We always finished up on the bay, with our bonfire and our wieners, because, as my father informed us every night, it was the only place on the Eastern Seaboard (with the exception of the Florida Keys) where you could see the sun setting into the sea. And therefore, we mustn't miss it, ever. After the hot dogs, the parents packed us into the car with books and blankets and took us to the Lighthouse in Wellfleet or the Lobster Hut in Truro or the Portuguese place on Commercial Street in Provincetown where they had the best kale soup and ate their own dinner. Once or twice, A.A. had tried adding four filets of sole to the grill on the beach, but they got stuck and then fell into the embers in the process of being removed. More for the gulls.

Skin cancer didn't matter. The inadvisability of a diet of hot dogs didn't matter. Dragging children around in a car way past their bedtime, letting them run wild on a beach fraternizing with seabirds and mollusks, didn't matter. Nobody worried about any of it. If you got a cut from those pesky razor clams, just put your foot in the ocean. The ocean cures everything. If it rained, play Monopoly and be quiet—the grownups are reading.

It was easy, being a child back then.

All of a sudden, summer was over. We woke up to see the quiet, murky, predictable bay banging itself against the shore in a fairly good imitation of the ocean. When we went to the real ocean the wind blew the sand all over us and into our ears and hair, stinging like sleet in January. We curled up under the umbrellas and wrapped ourselves in towels and tried to enjoy it, but in less than an hour we'd given up. "I guess that's it," said A.A. as we climbed up the dune to the parking lot.

There was a showy burst of heat for Labor Day, but it was untrustworthy. The sun was low and the sand wasn't hot. It had been almost too hot to walk on at the start of August. The top sand was still warm, but when I dug around with my toe, the sand underneath was cool and moist and a bit sticky. It clumped together, as if it were snow.

The gulls stood in a line looking out over the waves, guarding the water from our approach. It was their beach and they were reclaiming it right under our noses. Wind pushed their feathers out at odd angles. They looked messy and threatening. Tumbleweedy balls of eelgrass rolled around on the stiff, wind-starched sand. It wasn't inviting out there anymore. It wasn't ours.

On the last day, while the mothers were organizing and packing, A.A. took Roger and me to the Pilgrim Monument in Provincetown. We walked up a hundred pee-smelling stairs to the crenellated tower top. The whole Cape stretched out below us, looking more like a map of itself than a real place, looking small and perfectly colored, as if by hand: pale green with scallopy white edges floating in a blue-tending-toward-black sea.

"It really is an arm," Roger said.

"There's Hyannis at the elbow," A.A. told us.

"No, no, Papa, that's Chatham."

"Hmm," said A.A. "You could be right."

A.A. was so nice. Why was he so nice? Suddenly, I felt sad. Now it was all over, now we had to leave. We had to drive all the way up that arm and go back to the city.

As we walked down the hundred stairs I thought about how

I didn't like life. Life was always something new. I didn't like something new. I liked the same thing over and over. Even at that moment, I could see there was a logical flaw in this version of myself, since until I'd been on the Cape and had the bay-and-ocean thing over and over, it had been something new. That is, something I didn't like. And I thought as well of how England had been the same thing over and over, but I hadn't liked that.

"You know, I'm really looking forward to fourth grade," Roger said.

The Greeks

Miss Evie Ward looked like a wren. She was plump in the breast and had a tidy russet head that was stripey, like a wren's. Her hair was a mix of auburn and brown, thick, straight, and tucked neatly behind her ears. She was leaning against her desk, surveying us. "Let's rearrange the classroom," she said.

We all got up, clattering.

"Let's make a circle," she said. "I'll stay here near the blackboard, and you be all around me."

With more clattering, we made a horseshoe out of our desks and dragged our chairs into place.

"That's better," she said. "Now we're all together and I can see everyone and everyone can see me." She smiled. She had small teeth.

"This is the year of the Greeks," she said. "This is the year you're going to begin to understand the world, because everything that matters, the Greeks started it."

Roger put his hand up. "Miss Ward, what about the Chinese?"

"Aha!" she said. "What about them? And you can call me Miss Evie."

"Didn't they invent lots of important things? Didn't they invent paper and pottery and gunpowder?"

"Gunpowder," said Miss Evie. "They certainly invented that. And you might be right about paper. But I'm sure they didn't invent pottery. People all over the world invented pottery. I don't think the Chinese can take credit."

"Miss Evie!" Roger was wiggling his hand again.

She looked at her class list. "Are you Roger?" she asked.

Roger nodded. "But what I want to know is, didn't they invent pottery, really?"

Miss Evie tilted her head at Roger. "I bet you like to read the encyclopedia," she said.

"I do!" Roger was pleased.

"Look under Sumerians," she said. "That's S-U-M-"

"I know about the Sumerians," Roger interrupted.

"Okay. Then see what the encyclopedia has to say about Sumerian pottery. Then look under India—"

"So you're saying the Chinese didn't invent pottery?"

Miss Evie looked as if she'd gotten irritated and had then decided not to be irritated. That took a minute.

"Roger, how about this," she said. "You could look up pottery, and see when the Chinese started making it and when the Sumerians started making it, and the Indians and the Egyptians. You could make what's called a timeline and bring that in to class. Would you like to do that?"

Roger was, I could tell, weighing the hours it would take to do that against the hours he'd planned to spend in the basement with his model airplanes. The Chinese won, for the moment. "Yes," he said. "I can do that."

"That will be good for all of us," Miss Evie said. "Greek civilization didn't just come out of nowhere, and this will show us about that. But the Greeks were especially devoted to beauty, and they thought hard about the best and the most beautiful way to do all the things everyone around them was doing, like making pottery and writing poems and building temples. They had a special affinity for balance and perfection."

"Why?" I asked. It popped out. I hadn't planned to say anything.

"It's a mystery," said Miss Evie. "Now and then there are big upheavals and changes, and nobody really knows why. These days, some historians think it had to do with food. There were plenty of farmers growing lots of food, so people in the cities could stop worrying about getting enough to eat. And that gave them the time and energy to think—to think hard." She pointed at us. "So, if you want to be like the Greeks and think beautiful thoughts, eat a good breakfast, right?"

"Yes, Miss Evie," the class intoned.

During the neither-this-nor-that week between our return from the Cape and the start of school, A.A. had taken me and Roger to the Museum of Fine Arts. He'd pitched the outing to Roger as a visit to some Bigelows—and there were several ancestral landscapes hanging in a dim corridor between Colonial furniture and Colonial silver. I thought A.A. and Ingrid had better ones. They had a picture of the big Venetian piazza and a picture of Mount Etna and a nice big waterfall somewhere in the West. The museum ones were just a bunch of lakes and woods in upstate New York. Then we headed to the Egyptians, where Roger and I liked to scare ourselves in the replica of a tomb, a narrow, stony universe whose walls were covered with thousands of tiny hawks and tiny cows and tiny people all walking in the same direction. There was a special Egyptian-tomb smell in there that added to the scare; it smelled like dead stone. Roger invariably extended his hands in a zombie way and said, I am a mummy and I curse you, and that always gave me the shivers even though I knew he was going to do it.

But we took a wrong turn somewhere and ended up in the Far East.

"Gosh," said A.A., "I haven't been here in ages."

"Papa, the tomb," Roger objected.

"Well, let's just see," A.A. said, ambling down the hallway. "Look, that's pretty good." He stopped in front of a stone dragon on a pedestal. It was all curly, including its tongue, which was sticking out at us.

The next room was full of weapons: bronze semicircular axes

incised with twisty designs, and shields that were discs with points in the middle that looked like bosoms to me. There were cabinets stuffed with armor, interlocked chips of stone or metal to cover arms and legs and sheets of metal curved to fit a chest and helmets with nose slits. I thought it all looked like dismantled insects and I didn't like it.

"Wow," said Roger. "Why didn't we come here before?"

"I guess I forgot about it," said A.A. "It's been years since I ventured in here. Let's go farther. The earliest stuff is in the back."

We walked past a scroll that went on and on. I liked that. Part of what was interesting was thinking about the frame. It was as long as our living room.

"How did they make a frame like that?" I asked.

A.A. paused to look at it with me. "It's very long," he agreed. "What's it about?" He leaned closer. "Oh," he said suddenly, "what a great monkey."

I had to stand on tiptoe to see. It was quite a large monkey, with snow on its head. To the left, some mountains. To the right, some other mountains. Even though the scroll was dozens of feet long, nothing seemed to be happening. Snow, mountains, some little people, and the monkey.

"It isn't about anything," I told A.A.

"Usually it's about something," he said. "And this one's so long, it's got to have a story. Often it's the life of a philosopher."

"And the monkey?" I asked.

"Wasn't there a monkey king?" A.A. looked up at the ceiling, trying to remember. "Maybe I'm mixing it up with India."

"Papa," Roger called from ahead of us. "There's a bell in here that's bigger than you are."

We spent the afternoon with the huge bells and the infinite

scrolls and the other strange Chinese and Japanese things, and it was in these circumstances, rather than by reading the encyclopedia, that Roger had become fixated on them.

"Here's what I know about the Chinese," A.A. said as we leaned over glass cabinets filled with jade inkpots. "They invented paper and they invented gunpowder. And this is the best part—Roger, you'll like this. What they did with gunpowder was make fireworks. They loved fireworks."

"They didn't use it for guns?" Roger asked.

"They didn't even think of guns. It didn't occur to them to use it for anything but fireworks. It's like inventing glass but never thinking of making a window. Interesting, isn't it? War just wasn't on their minds that much."

Roger looked around at the weaponry. "All they thought about was war," he said. "Look at this stuff."

"Hmm," said A.A. "Well, I guess I meant something about categories of thought. Gunpowder was in the aesthetic category."

A.A. and Roger were having a better time with the Chinese than I was. I thought the things were fussy. There were too many curlicues and embellishments for me. When we got to the bowls and plates, though, my opinion changed.

"Hey," I said. "Look at this black-and-blue bowl." It wasn't very big, about the size of a cereal bowl. The black was on the lower part and then it oozed into being blue, and the blue went over into the inside.

"The Chinese invented porcelain," A.A. said. "I don't know how I could have forgotten that."

Hence Roger's contention, the following week, that the Chinese had invented pottery.

• • •

"Not pottery, porcelain," Ingrid said on the weekend. "Pfffh." She shook her head. Who couldn't distinguish between pottery and porcelain?

"What's the difference?" asked Roger.

"Big difference." Ingrid took a white Rosenthal dinner plate out of the draining board and held it up. "Look. It's so thin you can almost see through it." She put that down and grabbed a teacup out of the cupboard. "And this is old Meissen my mother brought from Vienna and you can see right through that. Look." She handed it to me.

It was painted with pink and blue morning glories and didn't weigh anything.

"Hold it up, hold it up," Ingrid told me.

I put it to my eye and looked toward the window.

"It's true! I can see the window," I said. The window looked pink and blue.

"Let me try," said Roger.

"Pottery is heavy and thick," said Ingrid. She looked around for some. "Here." She dumped the oranges out of the blue fruit bowl onto the *New York Times* that lay half read on the table. "See? Can't look through this. Breaks, too. Porcelain is strong."

"Like if I dropped it, it wouldn't break?" Roger asked, holding the teacup in a precarious, threatening manner with one finger.

Ingrid motioned him to give it back to her. When he did, she said, "Anything can break if you're not careful."

"Hey, Ingrid," I said. "Is that why it's called china?"

"What," said Ingrid.

"Is that why china is called china?"

"I don't know. Probably not," Ingrid said.

When I got home I looked it up. That was why. China the thing was named for China the place. I thought how funny that was. Suppose there was a thing called cambridge—forks, or bread, or a roof? I sat in the window seat pretending that a roof was called a cambridge. It just didn't seem workable. But it must have been strange at the beginning of calling porcelain china too.

Everybody loved fourth grade and Miss Evie except me, of course. I didn't hate it, but I had some objections. Miss Evie bothered me. She reminded me of my mother. She sneakily made me like her, but underneath I didn't actually like her. One reason was, I saw that she didn't like Roger, though she paid a lot of attention to him. Roger was strange, even I knew that. But I loved him. I loved his obsessive, whiny, persistent ways. He was like a nice fly. When he decided he wanted something, *buzz, buzz,* he would pester until he got it. And he was funny-looking. His head was too big and too thin in some way. It looked like a skull, not a head. Sometimes I'd look at him in class (he sat a few chairs away in the circle to my right) and see him as if he were someone new: pale, skinny arms, big head, fuzzy, long, thick, pale eyelashes. Miss Evie probably saw that, when she looked at him.

So Miss Evie was a sneak who didn't like Roger. Two bad things. Then there was the problem of the theme. It was like England, where we'd had to pretend we were living in caves because of early man. The Greeks were a thousand times more interesting than early man, but we were just as trapped. It was as if I'd been condemned to live in a world with only one color. Even if that color had been, say, green, my favorite color, I still would have missed the other colors.

And I had another problem. Parts of me seemed to be disappearing. I didn't understand what was happening. Something was happening—something was eating up my insides or chewing up my past. It was hard to know what it was. It was even hard to know what it felt like. That was part of what was terrible about it. Was I asleep? Was I dead? Was I sick? I seemed to be asleep, mainly. But it wasn't the sort of lively, hating sleep I'd had in second and third grade, when I'd slept because I felt school was a waste of my time. That had been intentional; this was out of my control. It came in waves, a death-wave of not-feeling, not-seeing, not-caring. Then I'd come back to life, but each time I felt I'd left something down there under the waves. I was getting smaller. I was getting quieter. I was getting—really, the only word for it was *boring*.

I'd come back from these death dives with a shred of a memory, like of my father putting me to bed when I was four. A little memory. He used to sing to me. He couldn't sing at all. It was croaking. Every night he groaned out "The Skye Boat Song." "Speed, bonnie boat, like a bird on the wing, Onward, the sailors cry. Carry the lad that's born to be king over the sea to Skye." When I was about five, my mother played this song for me on the piano and I learned its real tune, not my father's croak-tune. Then I could sing it with him when he put me to bed. He told me about the prince who'd been hidden in Scotland waiting to get on the throne of England. In the dark, with the bulk of my father's body making my narrow bed tilt to the side, I'd picture the island as blue and frothy, like its wonderful name. There was a line I specially liked: "Baffled, our foes stand on the shore, follow they will not dare." Why were they baffled? I asked. Because they couldn't navigate the waters, my father said. They weren't from Scotland and they didn't know how to get around in that part of the sea.

Now and then he sang a different one: "You'll take the high road and I'll take the low road, and I'll be in Scotland before you." Why? I asked. I guess the low road was quicker for some reason, my father said. Then soulfully, sadly, croakily, he'd conclude it: "But me and my true love, we'll never meet again, on the bonnie bonnie banks of Loch Lomond." Why? I asked. Why wouldn't they meet again? He didn't have an answer.

It was terribly sad. Even my father's atonal rendition couldn't disguise or subdue the sadness in that tune and those words, and sometimes I cried when he sang it. He didn't sing it often.

Thinking of these things now, in fourth grade, I felt they had happened to somebody else. I wasn't that person anymore. I could make myself teary by singing "You'll take the high road and I'll take the low road" to myself, and I would do that, to try to be once again the little girl in the bed, with the tuneless father sitting by. But it didn't work. I wasn't that little girl, and me and my father would never meet again on the bonnie bonnie banks of Loch Lomond.

Eventually I had to leave the Isle of Skye and Loch Lomond down at the bottom, under the waves I kept sinking into. Likewise the vivid pictures in *Struwwelpeter,* a book my father had adored when he was a child and had cajoled me into adoring as well, though it gave me nightmares. It frightened me, but I couldn't leave it alone. I wanted to see the bad boy with his electrified hair and talon-nails, and the one who wouldn't eat his dinner and turned into a stick, and the pair who were dipped in ink and became silhouettes. The very improbability of these stories, which offered some sort of protection, also made them scarier. That couldn't possibly happen, I'd tell myself. Nobody is going to come and cut off my thumbs. So I don't have to worry about that. Then I'd worry that because I was so sure it wouldn't happen, it was going to happen.

But now I knew it wasn't ever going to happen. If I thought of my thumbs being cut off, which I rarely did, I'd think: I used to be really afraid of that.

I'd been lots of things: scared and mad and curious, caught

up in patrolling Cambridge on my bike and eavesdropping on grownups trying to figure out what they were up to. All that was over.

I wasn't much of anything anymore. No matter how far down in myself I poked, I found empty, blank nobodyness. The worst part was the way the past seemed to have vanished. It hadn't really vanished—or so I hoped. But it felt foreign. There wasn't any continuity between now and what had gone before. I couldn't even get nostalgic about it. The most I could manage was a sniffle over a Scottish song.

Only one thing could break through my stupor and make me feel something: my mother. She had decided to study Ancient Greek. She was horning in on my Greek year. Why was she doing it? It was like the piano. She wanted to make me look bad. She wandered around the house practicing. Alpha, beta, gamma, delta, epsilon. She kept *The Iliad* in the kitchen and worked out lines while waiting for the water to come to a boil or the steak to be done. Zeta, eta, theta, iota. Her teacher was a dapper classics professor named Eli, with a dotted silk handkerchief in his sport coat breast pocket, who came Fridays. He had a devil-beard and green eyes and two-tone lace-up shoes. They sat on the sofa together and he read Pindar aloud and they laughed. Who did she think she was? Sometimes he stayed for dinner, just as Vishwa had in the old days.

But there was no more Vishwa. There was no more Frederika either. She'd gone back to Sweden. Their cross-country car trip in the Rambler had done them in, somehow. It had been a big September muddle. Frederika in tears, Jagdeesh coming over to discuss the situation, Vishwa not coming over. And now the house was quiet. I was alone on the third floor next to Frederika's abandoned, dusty room, with her leftover, hand-me-down makeup from my mother in the cabinet above the bathroom sink.

The lipstick dried up and got waxy and the powder solidified into a cracked cake, and I plodded through my days. I didn't care. It was easy to be dead. Now and then I got a jolt of hatred for my mother over the Greek competition, but that just encouraged me to enjoy my diminished self, because hating—and loving—took a lot of energy, and I didn't have much of that.

I couldn't understand what had happened between Frederika and Vishwa. I asked my mother about it, even though I didn't want to talk to her. But it didn't help. She couldn't explain it. Maybe she didn't know either. She had a lot of different versions of it.

"They are both stubborn," she said.

Another time—I kept going back to her, picking at it—she said, "He is a fatalist and she is an optimist."

"Am I a fatalist or an optimist?" I asked.

"You are more of a pessimist," my mother said.

"What's the difference?"

"A fatalist is cheerful. A fatalist believes that whatever happens was meant to happen and doesn't fight it. A fatalist is brave and calm." She looked at me with her intense eyebrows arched high. "You are not calm."

She was right. I was pretending to be calm. I'd thought I was doing a pretty good job.

"And what about a pessimist?" I wanted to know. "What's a pessimist like?"

"Just a disappointed optimist," she said. "An optimist who doesn't have enough backbone to stick to her beliefs."

That didn't sound good. I supposed she was talking about me.

"And that isn't Vishwa at all," she continued. "Which is why he's a fatalist. Happy and resigned, unflappable, really. He always makes the best of whatever comes. Whereas Frederika is a big improver of things."

Maybe she hadn't been talking about me. Maybe it was like when she was making the shopping list and she'd stare at me until I thought she was angry and about to say a mean thing, and all she was doing was trying to think of what to get for dinner.

"I still don't see what happened," I said.

"I bet she tried to improve him," my mother said.

The worst thing she said was, "What they love you for in the beginning is what they will hate you for in the end."

I couldn't get that out of my head.

It was a terrible idea, and I believed it. I had believed it before she said it, so hearing her say it was frightening because that made it true. I knew that inside me was an indigestible nastiness, which was bound to poke through and kill anything nice that had managed to grow between me and somebody else. I knew that my balkiness could be appealing at first. It made people want to help me, and plenty of people had tried: the man with the sticks in third grade, the solfège teacher, my mother at the piano bench. But one way or another, I defeated them all. I wore them down until they tired of me and my difficulty. My capacity for disappointing people was bigger than their capacity for putting up with me.

"Can you improve people?" I asked her.

My mother laughed. "You can bribe them to act better. Or try to scare them." She shook her head. "It doesn't work very well. Just look at you!"

What did she want from me? What was I supposed to be, that I so obviously wasn't? I didn't dare ask.

In late September I'd sat on Frederika's bed while she cried into her open suitcase. She folded her shirts and skirts and her sweet lace-edged slips and packed them into tidy tear-splotched stacks. She rolled her marvelous Swedish tights that were red or lilac or dark green—colors American tights never came in—and jammed them into the toes of her shoes and sniffed and coughed from crying.

"Why?" I kept asking. "Why do you have to go away? I know you're unhappy, but I could take care of you. Stay here."

On a normal day Frederika would have laughed and told me that it was her job to take care of me, but that day she didn't.

"I must go back home," she said. "It isn't really home, though, now." This started more crying. "I'm not sure where I belong now. Am I a Swedish person? Am I a sort of half-Indian, half-Swedish person? Am I an American person?"

"American," I said. "Anybody can be an American person. If you just stay here, you'll be American." This seemed like a good solution.

She shook her head.

"Did Vishwa do mean things?" I asked.

"Vishwa is never mean," said Frederika.

"I know," I said. "Then why do you have to leave?"

"It's time to go," said Frederika. "Every story has an end. It's time for the next story. This wonderful story is over now."

"But, Frederika," I wailed, "does it mean you don't love me anymore either?"

"Of course not! I always love you. Always and always." She sniffed. "And I always love Vishwa too."

"But what am I going to do without you?"

"You were fine without me," she said. "It's only a few years that you have me."

"You said you'd make another gingerbread house for Christmas. And little paper baskets for cookies to hang on the tree.

And I hate school so much! Please, please, Frederika." I suddenly had an idea. "I'll go talk to Vishwa. He'll listen to me. I'll tell him, Be nice! Don't be bad to Freddy."

"Don't you dare to," she said. "Don't you talk to him about me at all. Anyhow, he never did any bad things."

"Did you do some bad things?" I hadn't thought of that possibility before.

"Nobody did bad things." She sat down on the bed. "Sometimes love just dies, that's all." Then she sobbed, a huge sob that seemed to pull all the air in the room into her chest.

"How can love die?" I asked. "I don't understand. How does it die?"

"I don't understand either," said Frederika.

My father took her to the airport. My mother stayed home with me and the baby. The new regime had begun.

But at least, maybe, with Frederika gone, Vishwa could come back and we could listen to records again.

My mother said no. "Vishwa is very busy now," she said. "He's conducting the Harvard-Radcliffe Orchestra. It's a big job and he hasn't got time for lessons."

I didn't like Miss Evie but I had to admit that she understood some things about nine-year-olds. For instance, that we knew enough about hate and pride and envy to enjoy the story of the House of Atreus. It was one of the lead-ins to the Trojan War, but we could have studied the Trojan War without going all the way back to the cannibalism. However, that's where Miss Evie started: Tantalus serving the gods a dinner made of his son, Pelops, whom he'd killed and cooked. What was amazing was that then Pelops came back to life and had two sons, Atreus and

Thyestes, and the same thing happened again, only this time Atreus killed Thyestes's sons and served them to *him* for dinner.

I thought this was very good. I liked that the story was the same but not quite—gods replaced by a man, two sons instead of one, nephew-murder, not son-murder. But the same thing kept happening, and something about that was satisfying. The horribleness was also satisfying. The storytellers hadn't made even a gesture toward saying why. Tantalus cooked his son for dinner and that was that. Atreus had a bit of a motive. He was mad at Thyestes for stealing a ram with a golden fleece. But anyone could see that killing and cooking his children was an overreaction. It was clear that Atreus had to do what his grandfather had done. It was his fate, as the Greeks said. And it was the story's fate as well, to repeat itself.

I wondered about the golden fleece, and whether it was the same one that had sent Jason off on his voyage with the Argonauts. I hadn't liked that Jason story very much when I'd read it in *Gods and Heroes* during the early-man doldrums in England. I looked at it again now. The fleeces didn't seem to be connected. For starters, Atreus's fleece was still on the hoof. The fleece Jason was after had long before been stripped off its ram and nailed to a tree in Colchis, wherever that was. It wasn't in Greece. The story was full of how special the fleece was, how there wasn't anything like it anywhere else. But there was. There was a golden fleece in Greece too.

Poor Jason. He could have skipped the trip, I thought.

The further we went in the story of Atreus and his family, the more things happened twice. Or more than twice. First Aegisthus killed his uncle Atreus. Then Atreus's son Agamemnon killed his uncle Thyestes, who was Aegisthus's father. Later on, Aegisthus helped to kill his cousin Agamemnon. That was just the killings. There was also the sister and brother not recognizing each other. First Electra, Agamemnon's daughter, didn't recognize her brother, Orestes, when he came home (not surprisingly, he'd come home to kill his mother and cousin). Then Orestes didn't recognize his sister Iphegenia when he found her in Tauris.

Iphegenia was a surprise. We'd assumed she was dead. Agamemnon had sacrificed her to get a good wind for his trip to Troy. That was the trouble! That had been the start of the whole second round of killings—third round, if you began with the cannibalism. Clytemnestra and Aegisthus would never have killed Agamemnon when he got back from the war if they'd known he hadn't actually sacrificed Iphegenia. And if they hadn't killed Agamemnon, then Orestes wouldn't have had to come home and kill them. And all that mess could have been avoided.

But Iphegenia was fine. She was living as a priestess in Tauris. Artemis had saved her at the altar, right there, with her neck under the knife. A beautiful young hind had appeared to be sacrificed instead. That got my attention. Wasn't this the same thing that had happened when Abraham was about to sacrifice Isaac? Except maybe it had been a goat, or—this would be funny—a ram, maybe one with a golden fleece.

On my ninth birthday my father had given me a King James Bible. The family tradition was to give presents with cryptic clues on them. You had to guess what it was before you could open it. The rule might be waived for extremely difficult clues. The Bible's clue was: FROM JC TO THE JEWS. I didn't get it. I was allowed to open it, but even then I didn't get it.

"Who's JC?" I asked.

"Jesus Christ," my father said.

"But it's the whole thing," my mother pointed out.

"It's true," my father said. "Technically, it should have been only the New Testament. But the Old Testament is better."

"*We* think," my mother muttered.

"The stories are much better," my father said.

It was hard to read those stories. Every paragraph had a number, which was distracting. The names were dotted with squiggles and slashes and accents, which was also distracting. And it was somewhat repetitive. I hadn't made much progress.

I'd made enough, though, to get to the sacrifice of Isaac. I looked for it again. It had been a ram, caught in the thicket by its horns, said the Bible.

What did all these rams mean? I wondered. What did the sacrifice of children mean? Why did so many things happen twice?

I could have asked Miss Evie, but I didn't want to. I didn't think she would like my asking, and I was afraid she would tell me I was wrong—things weren't happening twice. As for my parents, I didn't ask them things like that anymore.

"You're very sulky," my mother told me often.

She was right. I was half dead and half sulky. But as the fall went on, I noticed that some of my deadness was being replaced by an intense feeling about the Greek stories and the Bible stories. They were similar. They were violent and arbitrary, and they didn't explain. There was something naked about these stories. Terrible things happened, and then some more terrible things happened. The Greek stories were a lot easier to read, but I plugged away at the Bible too. I'd found a child's illustrated Bible that I didn't even remember owning (forgotten down under the waves with everything else), which was a good trot. When I couldn't stand the numbers and the squiggles anymore, I'd leaf through the pictures of Daniel in the lion's den and read the potted version of Joseph and his brothers. Then I could make sense out of the King James because I already knew the story.

Unlike me, my mother was in a good mood. She was playing a lot of cheerful Scarlatti. No agonizing Beethoven or abstract

Bartók. Some days she'd try writing the shopping list in Greek, for practice. Kappa, lambda, mu, nu, xi. But, "No Greek word for cottage cheese," she said.

"Or vermouth," said my father. "We're out."

"Oh, omicron. I always forget that one," my mother said.

"Omicron and omega. Little *o* and big *o*. I am alpha and omega, the first and the last," said my father.

"What's that mean?" I asked.

"That's what Jesus said," he told me.

"Jesus spoke Greek?"

"No, he probably spoke Aramaic, which is a kind of Hebrew," said my father. "But the Bible was written in Greek, so in the Bible he says it that way."

That explained why the stories felt the same. "I didn't know the Greeks wrote the Bible too," I said.

"They didn't," said my father. "The people who collected the Bible spoke Greek, so they wrote it down in Greek. The New Testament."

"And the Old," my mother said. "Those seventy old Jews." She shook her head at my father. "What's the matter with you? Forgetting the seventy old Jews."

My father shrugged. "Dumb?" he suggested, smiling. "Just a big dope?"

They seemed to be getting along nicely.

"What seventy old Jews?" I was lost.

"The ones who collected the Old Testament."

"Was it lying around?" I asked.

"In a way, it was lying around," my father said. "There were lots of different versions in various languages, Hebrew and Aramaic, and probably some others. These old Jews were the editors. They took all the versions and collected them into one version in Greek."

"When did they do this?" I asked.

My mother and father looked at each other.

"Two hundred B.C.," my mother said, firmly.

"It might have been earlier," said my father. "It was before Christianity, anyhow."

"Why were there seventy Jews in Greece?" I asked.

"They were in Alexandria," said my father. "Have you gotten to Alexander the Great yet?"

"No," I said. "We're reading about the Atreus people and how they kill each other all the time."

"It's already November," my father said. "You've got a lot of history to pack into the rest of the year."

"And so what does it mean, 'I am alpha and omega'?"

"It means I am everything. I am the beginning and the end and everything in between," my father said.

I didn't see how one person could be everything. But I'd had enough of sitting in the kitchen with my parents, so I said, "Oh, okay."

Dapper-devil Eli was from Baghdad, like Aladdin in the fairy tale. My mother told me this in an effort to improve my Friday-night behavior. She also told me to address him as Professor Safar.

"He's very formal," she said. "He likes that."

He didn't seem very formal when he was sitting on the sofa guffawing with her all afternoon.

I didn't like it when Eli Professor Safar came for dinner. He was a poor substitute for Vishwa. The main problem was he paid no attention to me. My mother's instruction to address him by his title was needless; we almost never spoke to each other.

"You should be friendly to him," my mother went on. "He

hasn't had an easy time. After the war he had to leave Baghdad and go to Israel, and then his wife died, and now he's ended up here, where he doesn't know anyone."

"He doesn't like me," I said.

My mother tightened her mouth. "I'm sure he doesn't think about you," she said.

"Then why should I bother to be friendly?"

"To make him feel at home."

"If he doesn't know anyone, how does he know you?" I asked.

"Werner," my mother said. "I was looking for a Greek teacher, and Werner Jaeger recommended Eli—Professor Safar—who'd just joined the department. Do you remember Werner? He gave you your copy of *Gods and Heroes.* He wrote the introduction to the English translation. He thought you would enjoy the stories. But maybe you don't remember him. You were only about five when he gave it to you."

"Does he have a mustache?" I asked.

"Yes," said my mother.

"Like A.A.'s?"

"No. It's the thin kind, the proper German kind."

"Proper?"

"A certain kind of German professor has a thin mustache."

I didn't really care about mustaches. "How come all these people who teach Greek aren't Greeks?"

"It's too complicated to explain right now," said my mother.

I persisted. "Aren't there any Greek people to teach Greek?"

"It's not the same language anymore," she said. "What they speak in Greece now isn't what they spoke then. It isn't Ancient Greek."

"What happened to the old Greek?"

"It died," said my mother.

That was sobering. I hadn't known that a language, like a person, could die. "How—" I began.

"Enough," said my mother. "That's enough now."

We were in the kitchen. It was Friday, and Eli Professor Safar was returning for dinner at seven-thirty. My mother was salting the inside of a chicken and stuffing it with parsley and thyme, and then she was going to stab a shish-kebab skewer into its neck and close it up with a quick, nasty twist. Was Professor Eli Aegisthus? I didn't want to think about that idea.

My mother finished assassinating the chicken and put it in the oven. She washed her hands twice. "Chicken is poisonous," she told me. "Always wash your hands well after getting near chicken."

Her plan was to poison all of us? "If it's poisonous—"

"No. You *know* what I mean." She was really fed up with me. "Raw chicken. Now go get ready. Go take a bath or something."

I went upstairs and reread some of *Gods and Heroes* instead. I read the story about Zeus and Io, and how Zeus turned her into a cow. She knew she was a cow, and she didn't want to be one. It was sad and worrisome, especially the part where she spelled out her problem with her hoof in the dirt. Luckily, her father understood her. But he couldn't do anything. She was stuck. Eventually it worked out, but there were a lot of bad things first. The gadfly! What was a gadfly? It sounded terrible.

I had a vague memory of some other cow situation. I leafed through until I found it: Europa. Europa wasn't the cow this time—it was Zeus. Zeus turned himself into a bull. He was an extremely beautiful bull, just as Io had been an extremely beautiful cow. The difference was he could switch back whenever he felt like it.

I had never been close enough to a cow to determine if it was an especially beautiful one. A black-and-white group in a field as we drove to somewhere in Vermont was all I could remember, seen through the car window at forty miles an hour. "'I never saw a purple cow, I never hope to see one,'" my father would sometimes recite. "'But I can tell you, anyhow, I'd rather see than be one!'" Then he'd laugh. I didn't want to be one either. Purple wasn't the problem. I thought about Io trapped in the cow's body—but that wasn't quite right. That made it seem like Jonah eaten by the whale. This was worse. She was imprisoned in cowness. She was the cow but she wasn't; she was Io. The book talked about her piteous cries to be released.

If I were turned into a cow, I thought, I wouldn't be able to read, because I wouldn't have arms and I couldn't hold the book. Maybe I could use my hoof, like Io. But I'd have to stand up all the time. I wouldn't be able to talk and I would be enormous.

I looked around my room, with its sloping attic eaves all along the edge, under which I could still stand up. Frederika had been too tall to stand under her eaves next door. If I were a cow, how would I get up the stairs?

It wasn't worth worrying about. Nobody was going to turn me into a cow. I was just enjoying myself by pretending to be afraid of it.

Except something about it was real: not the cow part, the stuck part. I was stuck as myself. I wasn't going to turn into anybody else. Sometimes, when I was very angry or very happy, my feelings seemed to be bigger than I was, as if they were the size of giants, and I would have to break open, the way, I thought, I had been able to break open at the chest in England when I traveled at night back to Cambridge or up and down our grim, gray English street. But I didn't do that anymore. I didn't take those nighttime trips. Probably I was no longer able to. Whatever that had been, it was now underwater with the lullabies and the snipped-off thumbs. All that was left was making believe I might be turned into a cow while knowing it was never going to happen.

"Dinner," my mother called up the stairs. "Come and set the table."

I went down slowly. On the second floor, my father was sitting on the bed in my parents' room unlacing his shoes, and the baby was in her cot singing a lullaby to her favorite new toy, a stuffed owl.

"Did you get to Alexander the Great yet?" asked my father.

"No," I said. "It's all about the Trojan War. Too many battles."

"It picks up," he said. "Have they gone back for Philoctetes?"

"Is that the guy with the smelly foot?"

My father nodded.

"No. They left him on an island."

"Yes, but they go back for him. And then they win the war. Still, hundreds and hundreds of years are left to cover. I don't understand the organization of this program of study."

"Maybe Alexander isn't in it," I said.

"That's impossible," said my father.

"Hey!" my mother called. "What are you two doing? I need a hand here."

My father put on his black Italian loafers, once sleek, now cracked and curled from their émigré life in arctic Cambridge, and we went downstairs to help.

"Put the salad plates on top of the dinner plates," my mother said. "We're having artichokes first."

"Don't forget the little cups for butter," my father said.

"Ingrid always has mayonnaise," I said.

"Ingrid makes her own mayonnaise," my mother told me. "I'm not putting Hellmann's out in a little cup."

"Butter is better," said my father.

I thought mayonnaise was better. A.A. used sour cream. He was as crazy about sour cream as I was. I'd tried that, but it drowned out the artichoke. I loved artichoke because it made everything else taste sweet. The best was eating bread afterward; it tasted like cake.

"Why do artichokes make things taste sweet?" I asked my father.

"Do they? I don't think they do," he said.

"Maybe it's like asparagus pee," my mother said. "Not everyone has asparagus pee."

I hated asparagus pee. It made me think of mice or guinea pigs.

"That's not true," my father said. "Everyone has it, but not everyone can smell it. That's the difference."

"Those people are living in a fool's paradise," my mother said.

"Is that a good thing?" I asked.

"By definition," my father said, "you're a fool. That's no good."

"But if you're happy . . ." My mother didn't finish.

"Better to suffer and to know," said my father.

Artichokes with melted lemon-butter. Chicken roasted on a bed of endive and leeks. Rice with currants—"What's this?" my father asked.

"It's a Persian sort of thing," said my mother.

"Quite typical," Eli Professor Safar said. "We often have this."

"But Iraq—" my father began to object.

"Isn't Persia," Eli interrupted him. "But it's a general cuisine. General to the area of Iraq and Iran. Jewish cooking in the Middle East is much influenced by the Arabic and Persian penchant for sweet-and-sour."

"Like spareribs?" I asked.

"No," said Eli.

If I'd had a plate of spareribs, I would have dumped them on his head. I had a penchant for doing things like that.

"I wouldn't call this Jewish cooking," said my mother.

"Chicken?" Eli was surprised.

"Why is chicken Jewish?" I asked.

My mother mouthed, It's not, at me. To Eli she said: "I think chicken is universal."

"Oh?" said Eli. "The prevailing meat is lamb."

"There," my mother pointed out. "In the area of Iraq and Iran. Right?"

"Also goat," he went on. "In Greece as well, there is a great deal of goat. Some would say too much."

"Now, is goat stringy?" my father asked. "I don't think I've ever had goat."

"Unfortunately, yes. But then, often, so is the lamb. Poor grazing country," Eli concluded.

I was so bored my teeth itched. I banged my feet on the rung of my chair a few times. I knew if I looked up, my mother would scowl or shake her head, so I looked at my plate.

"You are studying Greece?" Eli was addressing me.

I nodded.

"Like your mother." He looked across the table at her.

"I was doing it first," I said.

"Greece is big enough for both of us," she told me. "Anyhow, I'm studying Greek and you're studying Greece."

"You don't study the language?" Eli asked.

"No," I said. "Trojan War, that kind of thing."

"There is no 'that kind of thing,'" Eli said. "Nothing is like the Trojan War." He smiled a scary, pinched smile. "You ought to be studying the language as well."

"She's only nine," my mother said.

"At nine, I was studying Greek and Hebrew," Eli said. He tucked his pointy beard into his neck like a pigeon.

If I'd said that, my mother would have told me not to brag. But to Eli she said, "Boy! That's impressive. And I suppose you spoke Arabic as well."

Boy was not one of her customary exclamations, so I decided she was just being polite.

"Of course," said Eli.

"And then your English is beautiful," my mother went on.

I wondered why she was making such a fuss.

He briefly pretended not to accept this compliment. "No, no, I merely stumble along." He ate a bite of bread. "But it is imperative, you know. Or maybe you don't really know."

My father put his fork down. Something he didn't know? "You mean a native speaker couldn't possibly appreciate the importance of English?"

"I suppose." Eli was willing to grant my father his version. Then he warmed up to the idea. "That is what I mean. It's a passport, you see, a ticket out of the East."

"I thought the East meant China," I said.

"The East begins in Greece," said Eli.

"Really?" My mother was genuinely surprised, not just pretending to be. "How can you say that, when we think of Greece as the foundation of the West? It *is* the foundation of the West."

"Bribery, corruption, inefficiency, the attitude of letting it go until tomorrow, a tomorrow that never arrives. Pah!" Eli pushed his plate away. "Unbearable."

"Greece?" my father said. "Hmm. But Israel wasn't like that, was it?"

"Different but worse," said Eli. "The—the—smugness, I believe you call it?"

"Probably," my mother said, "from what I've seen of them."

"But more efficient," my father put in cheerily.

Eli didn't say anything.

"So it was good to move here," my mother said.

"It has been a great relief," said Eli. "I must be a crypto-German. I like order. I like the rational. I even like the winter."

"It's only November," my mother said. "You haven't seen much winter yet. But maybe you are a touch German—I mean, perhaps you have German ancestors, and some sort of Jungian race-memory?"

"No. Safar, Sephardic. They came after the expulsion." He squinted at my mother. "Are you a disciple of Jung?"

"It was a joke," my mother said.

"Anti-Semite," Eli mumbled.

"The Spanish expulsion?" my father asked.

"Yes," said Eli. "We do not have an illustrious bloodline going back to the Babylonian Exile."

My mother stood up and pointed at me. Time to clear the table. "What would people like for dessert?" she asked. "We have chocolate ice cream or orange sherbet. Or, I suppose, you could have both."

"Sherbet, please," Eli said.

"Continuing in the Persian mode," said my mother. "Did you know that?" she said to me. "That the Persians invented sherbet?"

Standing in the kitchen stacking the plates beside the sink, I felt the chilly undertow, the tired, dim, muffled sinking into deadness coming over me. I didn't like Eli; he was fussy and mean. I didn't like the Trojan War. I didn't like finding out that almost everything in the world had been invented, one time or another. Things were better when they were unexplained. Watery, super-cold sherbet was more wonderful before it was

Persian. Before it was Persian, it was a miracle of nature. Now I had to imagine someone—and inevitably it was an Eli-like someone, with a pointed beard, pleased with himself—tinkering with fruit and water until—Bingo!—he'd invented sherbet.

Miss Evie had said that now we would begin to understand the world. I didn't enjoy understanding it. I preferred the mysteries. She'd been wrong about a lot of things, anyhow. She said the Greeks invented everything important, but it turned out they hadn't. They hadn't invented the Bible, for instance, and that was a lot more important than some of the other things they hadn't invented, like sherbet or porcelain.

"I'm tired," I said to my mother. "Can I go to bed?"

"Sure," she said. "You don't want any sherbet?"

"No."

"Okay. Say goodnight to Professor Safar. And take the dessert plates to the table."

I took them. I said goodnight. I tromped upstairs to my attic room, where I sat on the bed and stared at the wall. From up there I could hear an occasional tinkle and murmur as they ate their sherbet and chatted about how important Eli Professor Safar was and how difficult his life had been. I stared at the wall until my vision became peculiar, as if I were looking through a dark, throbbing funnel and could see only a small circle at the narrow end. My ears were buzzing. I felt swirly and horrid, and I liked it. I wanted to feel even more horrid. It was comforting to have a body to represent the mind or the soul or whatever it was inside me that hurt.

I'm just too tired to go on with all this, I said to the wall.

That made me feel better. I don't want to and I'm not going to, I said to the wall. Good-bye to the Trojan War and Chinese porcelain and people coming over to pay court to my mother and Alexander the Great and even to things I liked or had once liked—my bicycle, the blood-soaked House of Atreus, sour cream. I didn't have the energy for any of it.

I wasn't going to be transformed into a cow. I was going to turn myself into a kind of human seaweed that lived in the clammy dark where you don't want to put your foot. I would hide there, wafting back and forth, cold and unseen. Maybe someone would come looking for me. Probably not.

Along with the Bible and perhaps in compensation for the loss of Vishwa, my parents had got me my own record player for my birthday. It was red and black and had two boxy speakers that hooked onto the sides but could be detached and pulled out several feet to create a somewhat stereophonic experience. It came with a pack of needles and a yellow cloth for wiping the records. A.A. and Ingrid had added a sophisticated damp roller of the kind A.A. used to clean his records and a small bottle of intoxicating acetone-tinctured fluid. They also gave me two records that Roger and I listened to a lot at their house, *The Moldau* and *The Fountains of Rome and The Pines of Rome.* And my mother gave me *Petrushka.*

Soupy, melancholic Smetana and agitated, overstated Respighi were more enjoyable over at the Bigelows'. Their sounds were part of the whole Bigelow atmosphere, and when I listened to them in my bedroom, I didn't have the same sorts of feelings about them that I had in the crammed, dark Bigelow living room, where Roger and I would do what we called modern dancing to Smetana (Respighi was too unpredictable melodically for this). We'd whirl around, knocking into sofa arms and standing lamps and heaps of magazines and picture books while A.A. sat in his big black leather chair reading a psychoanalytic journal. Alone in my bedroom, listening to these records without using them as program music, I heard a cheesiness I hadn't noticed before. A.A. was well aware of it. When handing them to me the day after my birthday, he'd said to my mother: Nice whooshy garbage the kids like.

Petrushka was another thing entirely.

It was about me! The simple sad melodies, the hurdy-gurdy interludes broken into by yelling brasses, the skipping about among many different tempos and moods—its surprising shifts and turns reminded me of myself. It sounded the way it felt to be me. It was familiar before I'd finished hearing it for the first time.

This made me irritated with my mother. How had she known I would like it so much?

I also liked looking at the photograph of Stravinsky on the record sleeve. He looked a bit like Eli Professor Safar, which was bothersome, but his expression was different, sad, like the songs in *Petrushka,* and tired out. He had enormous bags under his eyes. I liked that as well. I too had bags under my eyes, inherited from my mother. Sometimes I stood at my bathroom mirror and pulled the edges of my eyes upward until I'd eliminated the bags. They popped back the moment I let go. Stravinsky's bags were so big and puffy that it looked as if he'd taken the opposite approach and decided to cultivate them.

Didn't I have some things to cultivate? Couldn't I find in myself some qualities that others might see as flaws but which I could make into the hallmarks of my specialness?

Winter. I'd sit in my room listening to *Petrushka* in the long dark that fell as soon as I got home from school. I knew it by heart and could sing it straight through; Vishwa would have been delighted with me.

The disappearing-underwater-seaweed act had been a bust. It had been too effective. As I'd feared, nobody noticed and nobody came looking for me. That clarified my goal: I didn't want to disappear, I wanted to disappoint. I'd listen to *Petrushka* and list all the things that were wrong with me so I could figure out how to make them worse. I was going to be a failure: That was clear. I wanted to be the biggest failure possible.

One of my major faults was I had no interests. Interests were things people liked to do even if they weren't good at them. Roger, for instance, liked to play the clarinet despite having little talent for it. He went to solfège and learned the names of the notes and didn't care if he sang off-key. Whereas I, the solfège dropout with excellent pitch, would freeze when I sat down at the piano, furious that I couldn't tear off a mazurka without practicing.

Another big fault was my attitude toward school. I didn't want to bother learning things I'd decided (on nearly no evidence) were boring, and if there were things I wanted to know about, I couldn't stand not knowing about them already. Trying to learn them in public humiliated me. The only way I could learn things was in secret, slowly building up knowledge by poking around in books with nobody watching or telling me what to read.

Sometimes I wondered what I would be like if I weren't this way. A cheery little girl who changed her T-shirt every day and played the violin and could recite the times table up to twelve? I didn't even want to know her, let alone be her. Other times I wondered how I'd gotten this way. But that was fruitless. I was this way, and I had to try to make some use of it.

What could I do, how could I parlay my incapacities and disinclinations into a successful position, an unassailable major badness that nobody could dispute or take away from me?

Even then, in the midst of this fourth-grade turmoil, I could see that my will to failure was an ambition, no different from the ambition that seethed in all the inhabitants of Cambridge, who dashed around me pursuing glory. I was just like them: determined not to be mediocre. I would stand out. I would, I would. My Nobel Prize—Worst Daughter, Worst Student, whatever it might be—awaited me.

Greece

Light everywhere, like a trumpet.

Stony headlands and sea fingers that pointed in between the spits. A high hissing—maybe crickets—in the hills above Piraeus. It was July. At the cement wharves, ferries and freighters and two-man dinghies and yachts with maroon sails strained and bobbed at their bollard lines on the tideless water, pursued by wind.

My father was involved in a big commotion. The other participants were a pair of guys with blue caps and black mustaches, our guide-friend-interpreter George, and the sideview mirror that had once been part of our Chevrolet, which was newly disembarked from the freighter that had sailed out of Providence, Rhode Island, six weeks earlier. Wounded, ignored, the car sat on the pier looking huge and American and lopsided, while my father brandished the evidence above his head.

"You broke this off!" he yelled.

George translated.

Both men in caps yelled things back.

"They say they didn't break it."

"But it's broken," my father yelled.

The men yelled. George translated.

"It was broken from the start, they say."

"Lies! Lies!" My father raised the amputated mirror, which flashed a frantic circle of light on the concrete where we stood. "It wasn't broken in America."

The men lifted their chins and sniffed.

"They say, 'Prove it,'" George translated.

"How can I prove a negative?" My father looked briefly defeated. Then he perked up. "Liars. You are liars and thieves."

George declined to translate. He put his hand on my father's shoulder. "You will not get anywhere with them. I have a wonderful mechanic in town. He will fix it for you."

"I want compensation," my father said. "I want a refund." He turned to the duo again. "Money," he said. He rubbed his fingers together in the universal money symbol.

The men conferred. Then one said an earnest long something.

"They say," said George, "that we will have a drink together. There." He pointed up the dock toward town.

My father shook his head.

"Yes," said George. To the men he said something more complicated than yes. "We will have a drink with them and we will go to my mechanic."

"It's eleven in the morning," said my father. "It's too early to have a drink." It was a stab at an objection.

We walked up the long shimmering jetty. "It is not satisfactory," my father said. I trailed behind the phalanx of men.

The bar was the size of a closet. A man who looked exactly like the two guys in caps uncorked a grubby bottle and poured four glasses of a clear spirit, then added several drops of water from a clay jug on the counter. The glasses clouded over, as though they'd been filled with smoke.

In chorus the sailors raised their glasses, said, *"Eeseeyeyensas,"* and drank them off in one gulp. My father and George drank too.

"America," one of them told my father.

He nodded.

"My brother, he Chicago," he said. "Many years." He began to sing. "Chicago, Chicago, That's my home town." He sang quite well. "You Chicago?" He pointed his glass at my father.

"Boston," my father said. To George, he said, "Let's get going."

But Chicago's brother had signaled another round. Now they both lifted their glasses toward my father.

"You Ess of Ahh, You Ess of Ahh," they said. "Very magnificent country," Chicago's brother added.

George poked my father in the side. My father raised his glass. "Hellas," he said. "To Hellas, also a magnificent country."

The non-Chicagoan said something to George, who nodded.

"They're going to bring your car down here, to you," he told my father.

Without the two guys, the bar was almost big enough for the three of us. I'd been leaning in the doorway; now I came in and sat on a stool at the counter. The proprietor lifted the bottle toward my father, who shook his head.

We waited for the powerful familiar grumble of the Chevrolet. George picked his teeth. I sniffed one of the empty glasses: licorice. A strange country! The barman began to whistle and clear his throat. Eventually, he tapped George on the arm and whispered to him.

"He wants to be paid," George said to my father.

"I am paying?" My father was astounded. "They invited us. It was my refund. They invited us!"

"They're getting the car," George explained.

"That's a refund? Driving the car four hundred yards? That's not a refund."

"He needs to be paid," George said.

"But *they* invited us!" My father could not accept this injustice.

"It's only a few drachmas."

"Liars," said my father. "Thieves and liars." He paid.

We followed George's Fiat back to Athens on the terrible twisting road. My father had calmed down by the time we arrived at our apartment building. To my mother he said only: "The side mirror broke off in transit. George's mechanic will fix it." No duplicitous seamen, no bar, no rage on the docks.

My mother was stretched out in a rattan deck chair on the balcony, drinking fresh orange juice and smoking her new favorite cigarettes, Papastratos Ena, with the Bauhaus packaging: white background, green circle inset with a red numeral, very chic. From our wraparound terrace you could see—almost—the Parthenon. You could see the Acropolis, at any rate. You had to go up three floors to the roof, where the maids hung the washing in the midday sun, and part the sheets and the double-D brassieres and the vast fluttering undershorts to get a real view of the temple: white and silent, self-contained, framed by laundry and unconcerned about it.

My mother was as chic as her cigarettes. This had happened in Italy too. She was a chameleon. She took on the prevailing look. In much of Greece, the prevailing look for women was a black shawl and premature age, but not in our neighborhood. Our seven-story apartment building on Kolonaki Square probably contained half the wealth in Athens. We constituted a large part of it. Our dollars made us millionaires. We had five bathrooms and six bedrooms and two kitchens, and crackled gilded mirrors built into the living room walls, and chandeliers that jingled in the breeze that blew in through the French doors open to the balcony in the mornings when Kula, the maid with a feathery touch of mustache, brought my father an orange carved into a lotus at the dining table that could seat twelve. On the street floor a café with a black-and-white-striped awning sold coffee and a sugared apricot dipped in honey and balanced on a spoon for ten times what it cost a few blocks away. Next door was a boutique so special you had to ring a bell to get in. Our first week in Greece, my mother rang the bell, went in, and bought a green suede jacket the color of an olive and a geometric-patterned, full-skirted linen dress in black and brown and a short, midriff-hugging sweater she called a shrug made of loosely knitted undyed silk yarn that she said would be perfect for an evening on a boat.

My mother at forty looked ten years younger than the other women her age who patronized that shop and whiled away their afternoons at the expensive café. Their hairdos were stiff and poufy, and their ankles were thick. They wore suits with tight, straight skirts and boxy jackets in horrid pastels, and extraordinary amounts of perfume and jewelry that clanked when they picked up their tiny cups of coffee. Here and there, though, strode her sole competition, or perhaps the look she was aiming for: a few slant-eyed beauties, Amazon-tall in their stiletto heels, often draped in a stifling, unnecessary fur wrap, wearing real pearls.

"You can tell," my mother said, "when they're real."

I couldn't. I couldn't figure out anything that had to do with clothing and adorning. I didn't think beyond loving my red sneakers or hating that middy blouse, and picking a T-shirt for my overalls-and-T-shirt ensemble. But the overalls didn't fit well anymore.

This probably was because disconcerting lumps were growing on my chest. They seemed like breasts, but I pretended they weren't anything. They were mushy and sometimes sore. Some days I had to admit that they might be breasts. Other days I'd wake and think: They're gone! They were never gone. I couldn't believe they were so persistent. I didn't need them. They complicated clothing. I wanted to wear things that squashed them down and made them invisible, but anything tight enough to squash them did the opposite of making them invisible.

Before we left Cambridge my mother had got me five cotton sundresses with flower prints in Filene's Basement. They were the kind of thing I hated. One of them was pink! There was a green one that was tolerable, but they all pulled under the arms, chafing, too tight for my new, mushy additions. To protect and disguise my breast-things, I hunched over, which made the underarm pulling and chafing worse. Also, then my mother would say, "Stand up straight."

I sacrificed one of my two pairs of blue jeans to the scissors and created a more grownup version of my traditional costume: blue-jean Bermuda shorts. Then all I had to do was find a few shirts that weren't too tight.

"You should tuck that in," my mother said.

"It's too hot," I said. I hoped this excuse would work.

"It's sloppy," she said. "Tuck it in. You'll look so much nicer."

That was typical of her. She'd tell me I would look nicer, but what she meant was, I like it better when you tuck it in. She thought she could make me do what she wanted by appealing to my vanity. She didn't understand that my vanity had been destroyed. It had been vanquished by what was happening to my body. If this was how I was going to look, I reasoned, I didn't want anyone to look at me. Sloppy shirttails and frayed denim edges were perfect for deflecting interest.

In the old days, at the few moments when I thought about it, I'd liked the way I looked. I was small and could fit nicely into little spaces. I was bony and quick, and my skin was a nice brownish color, though in winter it was a rather yellowish color. But on the whole I was fine. Now I was turning into a kind of monster who had to be disguised. My mother was forever giving me tips. "If you wear a belt, it will distract from the top." "The top" was her name for the eruptions on my chest. "Patterns are good," she'd tell me. I knew this was part of her plot to get me to wear the sundresses. "You have such a tiny waist," she'd say. "I wish my waist were still so small." She could have my damned waist. All it did was accentuate the breast-things. I would have given her my waist in a second if I could have got my old self back in return.

But I couldn't get that. I was on an inexorable march toward a new, unrecognizable me. Some nights I'd lie in bed and press them—the breasts—into my chest, hoping to push them back to wherever they'd come from. If I could get them to retreat, I'd wake up the way I'd been only a few months before, skinny and straight from top to bottom. But they had a will of their own. They wouldn't back down.

My father was my refuge. He didn't notice what was going on with me and my top because he was in a perpetual welter of enthusiasm. To the Agora! To lunch at the little taverna five blocks away to have kokoretsi! (I didn't want any: livers and hearts of unknown animals on a spit.) Let's go into this pottery store and see if there are any nice coffee cups. Then, turning to me: Is this a nice coffee cup? That meant, Would your mother like it? Neither of us was confident enough to risk her aesthetic disapproval, so we left the shop. Let's explore the Plaka (mostly prostitutes in 1959). Let's go to the top of Mount Lycabettus.

My mother declined all these explorations. Too hot, too much to do getting the apartment into a livable condition. The apartment was crowded with stuff in a Bigelovian manner, but the stuff wasn't interesting or nice to look at. Every gilded side table had its bronze shepherdess, every marble mantelpiece its curly tinkly clock, every corner its half-size plaster replica of a statue whose eternal original lived ten minutes away at the National Archaeological Museum. Lurid little rugs were scattered throughout, waiting to trip you. As in Italy, there was a superfluity of furniture, but in Italy that had been cozy (and the furniture had been beautiful) and here it was bothersome. And, as my mother said every day when my father proposed a trip—Let's go to Epidaurus—we were here for a year and she just couldn't live with it the way it was.

She wanted my father and me out of the house so that she could enlist Kula the maid with her peasant strength to help move at least half the furniture into one of the several unused bedrooms. My sister trotted around with them, chattering in Greek, which she'd learned in two weeks from sitting in the kitchen while Kula made lotuses out of oranges and soup out of lemons and seven-egg omelettes and all the other peculiar things she had to offer us, about which my mother said, "I've got to get a handle on Kula's menus, but that's the project after this one." In the mornings my father and I stood in the doorway, flanked by a miniature discus thrower on one side and a dwarfish Poseidon hurling an invisible spear on the other, and waited for our good-bye kisses, while the maddened female trio planned their attack for that day.

Our attacks on Athens were not so carefully planned. In an uncharacteristically relaxed decision, my father had declared the entire city—the entire country—to be a museum. Therefore, as long as he had his *Guide Bleu* to document our activities with, it didn't matter if we were meandering, dead-ending, or, often, totally lost. Wherever we were there was Something. That's the Church of the Haghii Assomati, not just a brown brick heap. Oh look! This confusing pile of rocks is the Pnyx. Usually we weren't looking for the thing we ended up standing in front of. It didn't matter. He would flutter the pages of the guide as I shifted from one hot foot to another, waiting to be instructed. His endurance was astonishing. He never needed to pee, he never needed to eat, he never got tired of the brick heaps or the toppled columns strewn among the cafés and the fruit markets and the cheesy souvenir stands. If we headed out to the Panathenaic Stadium and instead ended up watching the evzones lift their red slippers toward their noses in Syntagma Square, he didn't care.

Only one thing was stronger than my father: the heat.

We were both foolish. We thought we were tough because we

were used to the intemperate Cambridge climate, which ranged from arctic to a swampy Floridian humidity, and we'd weathered a summer in Italy. Athens in July at midday was intolerable. All the metaphors people used about summer—my brains are fried, it's an oven, it's an inferno—turned out to be plain description. Our brains fried. It was an oven. It was an inferno. There wasn't a Greek on the street between one and four. It was the kind of heat that could kill you. I could see why it had been personified as a golden chariot drawn by golden horses whipped on by a golden, molten god.

But like the sun itself my father pursued his daily rounds, dragging me, his satellite, along. He consented to an hour's break for lunch, but then it was back to the blaring pavement, the glittering ruins, the relief when we turned in to a shady street. The shade was as palpable as the sun, a musty, dry, stuccoed shade where I could almost manage a shiver.

And so passed our first several weeks, carless in Athens.

My father had postponed until some auspicious moment the conquest of the Acropolis.

One morning my mother said, "I've got to conclude the so-called redecoration by the end of tomorrow or I will go nuts."

"So will I," said my father.

The next day, the last day of my mother's frenzy, was the day he chose to go to the Parthenon. It was like all the other days. The delicate, rosy sun came up above the yellow city and by mid-morning had built heights of heat that you thought could not be surpassed, and which were surpassed every twenty minutes. We ate our oranges and toast with honey and were on our way by nine-thirty. In consideration of our adventure's scope, my father stopped in a café at the foot of the Acropolis, where he ordered me a fortifying baklava and lemonade. He had coffee—the tiny super-sweet Greek coffee that is half dregs and that leaves a thick residue in the cup and on the throat. Then we started up the long, already hot footpath.

There were the remnants of marble stairs, but mostly underfoot was rubble and dirt. Stunted, dry vegetation had attracted some dusty goats. We passed an antique man with a box camera on a wooden tripod, napping on his stool. In the clear, dry air we could hear snatches of German floating down from above us.

"Why are there always Germans?" I asked.

"Germans are mad for Greece," my father said. "Just like the English. But right now, the Germans can afford to come and the English can't."

It was too hot to ask why the Germans but not the English could afford to come.

We kept trudging upward.

It's in the nature of a steep-sided outcropping that the top isn't visible from the approaches, and for much of the climb I was too hot to look around or to look forward to where we were going. My father was a few steps ahead. His shirt was soaked, stretched wet across his back. A sudden gray-green lizard froze near my foot, looking up at me. We exchanged glances, then he vanished into a rock.

We reached the top.

A moment when the world unfolds: few of those, in life. Everything peeled back. I could hear it rolling away. This was the skeleton of humanity I was seeing, this colonnaded marble spine. And after the hiss of the shivering unrolling there was silence. It was an uncanny silence, indifferent and detached. Thousands of years of quiet floated in the hot, bright air.

We stood in the shadow of the Parthenon's broken pediment, between the columns where the sun had not yet heated the stone. My father raised his arm and pointed west.

"The plain of Attica," he said.

So this is reality, I thought. It's hot and bare and permanent, it's broken and chipped and huge, it will last forever, even in ruins, it will make you speechless.

We stood there for a while, until the sun invaded our recessed shade. Thick, black shimmering shadows made a Parthenon on the floor. We walked around the rim of the temple through these shadows and the light in between them. The difference in temperature was as sharp as a sound, as if we were walking on the black and white keys of a vast piano made of marble and daylight.

My father stopped again to point to a small building below.

"That's the Erechtheion," he said. "Look, look at the pillars."

"They're girls!" It was a relief to see something on a human scale, with a human face. Six girls standing on the edge of a temple, just as we were.

"Let's go down there," my father said.

It was a scramble. The way was littered with chunks and bits, sometimes fallen so I could see that this had been a column. Now it was a horizontal, dismantled column. Mostly, though, there were hunks and blocks of stone lying around in disarray.

"How come it's such a mess up here?" I asked. "It looks like it got blown up."

"It did," he said. "The Turks were using the Parthenon to store their ammunition in, and the Venetians attacked it. So the whole thing blew up."

"When was that?"

"About three hundred years ago," my father said. "Until then, it looked the same way it had when it was built."

"That's crazy! Why would the Turks put their ammunition in there?"

My father shook his head. "Well, it was big, and nobody was

doing anything else with it." Then he said, "They didn't think much of the Greeks."

"And the Greeks let them do that?"

"They didn't have any choice. The Turks owned Greece. It was part of their empire. And the Venetians were at war with the Turks. That's how it happened." He walked on a little bit. "Let's not think about it right now. All of that is sad."

My father rarely used the word *sad*.

From where we were, below it, the Parthenon was anything but sad. It was splendid. There was nothing to say about it, that's how wonderful it was to stand and look at it. As we picked our way over to the stone girls on their parapet, I wondered about what my father thought was so sad.

He must have meant the wrecking of the temple: For two thousand years it had been fine and then, boom, it was shattered. But it wasn't completely gone, and it looked correct anyhow. It looked just right to me. Whoever built it had planned it so well that it didn't matter if half of it got blown up, because it was perfect and so whatever was left was perfect too.

"Now these are the caryatids," my father said to me. "These girls." He seemed halfhearted about giving instruction, which was fine with me. He hadn't opened the guidebook since we'd started our walk up the Acropolis.

"I know that," I said. And I did know that, though I hadn't quite put it together that these statues were those caryatids. Seeing them in a picture was one thing; being with them was something so different as to have made me forget that I knew them already, sort of.

We looked up at them. They looked out over our heads, the way they'd been looking out for thousands of years. A couple of them had a tiny bit of a smile, more the idea of a smile than the real thing.

The day was getting hotter and there wasn't any shelter out in the rubble. Even though it didn't have a roof, the Parthenon had been better—all those long shadows to duck into. Also, the girls, in the end, were as disengaged and impassive as everything else. I'd been misled by their faces, by the fact that they had faces. I thought that would make them comforting because they would be like me in some way. They weren't. They weren't like anything except themselves. Nothing on the Acropolis was like anything anywhere else. That was what made all of it stark and immobile and unyielding and unbearable.

That's what it was: unbearable.

"It's getting a bit hot," my father said.

It must have been over 100 degrees.

"Let's go to the museum," he said. "They put a lot of the Parthenon sculptures in there to preserve them."

"In case somebody else tries to blow them up?" I asked.

He didn't laugh. "Things were eroding from pollution and weather. And people stole a lot of them. Like Lord Elgin. Do you remember the Elgin Marbles in London?"

I didn't.

"We saw them," he persisted. "Magnificent horses. You don't remember them?"

"I don't see how you could steal things this big," I said. "Even the broken things are huge."

"You get a crane and a crew. It takes a lot of organization."

"But why didn't the Greeks stop them? Why did they let people come here and steal stuff and blow it up? Could we just come here with a crane and take away a caryatid?"

"Not anymore," my father said. "But when you could, people did. It's because the Greeks were always part of some bigger empire, so they weren't strong enough to look out for their own interests. But, you know, this isn't the only country that got looted by empire builders. Napoleon took half of Egypt back to Paris. The Romans started it. They'd take obelisks and whatnot from cities they'd conquered and set them up around Rome."

"Bragging," I said.

"Exactly. And the early archaeologists, in the nineteenth century, took just as much as the Romans ever had. Nobody had the idea that an ancient site ought to be left intact, that it was more meaningful that way. Everything was a trophy."

"Where's the museum?" I asked. I was feeling woozy from the heat, and I wanted to interrupt my father's archaeology lecture.

"Of course," he went on, "it is wonderful to be able to go to the British Museum and see that winged lion from Nimrud—"

"Daddy," I said, "where is this museum up here?"

"Oh." He stopped and looked around. "It's over this way," he said. He didn't sound convinced, but he strode off, looking purposeful.

I followed. My parents often argued about where they were heading. My father did not have a good sense of direction, but he was determined and forceful, which meant we could go quite a ways into nowhere before he would agree that he'd been wrong. I was glad that didn't happen this time. Two hours outside was enough.

The museum was cool and dimly lit. The polished marble floor gleamed as if it were water, a refreshing effect. There was a tempting bench at the entry, but my father ignored it. "Elgin missed some friezes," he said, "and I want to see them. They're in here." He barreled on in.

I was more interested in the statues. Grownups liked bas-relief, I'd noticed. I didn't like it at all. It made me feel itchy and unsatisfied, whereas they—even A.A., whom I thought of as a better sort of grownup—would stand and Oooh at it for much too long. I wondered what they saw and why I didn't see it.

My father established himself in front of a long wall of friezes. I took a look and felt my usual urge to get away. Part of what I didn't like was that it was too busy, as if the sculptor felt he had to make up in surface activity what was missing in depth. These reliefs were blurry and blunted. I could see why they'd been put inside. Some parts looked as if they'd been sandblasted almost flat.

I left my father and went to see the many large figures that stood on plinths around the room. There were lots of stiff young women who looked like cousins of the caryatids, except their drapery was unrealistic and their smiles were more realistic. Still, something about their expressions was peculiar. Like the caryatids, they were staring out into oblivion in a way that said: I am ignoring you. They seemed happier about it than the caryatids were, though. There was a wonderful man with a little calf slung across the back of his neck. Both of them were smiling in that unfocused way. The man looked Egyptian to me. Maybe it was his stance, which was the same as the Egyptian gods in the long hallway at the museum in Boston: one foot forward, but both legs still embedded in stone, as if the figure were being born out of the marble, or trapped inside it.

Beside the man with the calf was a boy, standing straight with both arms by his sides. He too had one foot forward, but his legs were free. He'd escaped from the stone. He had a kind of Egyptian hairdo. Long, tight curls made a triangular frame around his face that reminded me of a pharaoh's headdress. And, like almost all the statues there, he had a half-smile that was benign yet chilling in some way.

I leaned closer to read his caption. KOUROS, it said.

Leaning, I felt a wave of buzzing. First a light, fuzzy feeling, then an effervescent spinning, then a deep, thick blackness that swooped over me. And then, nothing.

Nothing and nothing. A half-smile floating. A smooth, clean shiny pillow for my head.

I was lying on the marble floor. I was still buzzing, but not as loudly, and a number of faces were hanging above me, saying, "Water," and *"Wasser,"* and *"Nero, nero"*—Greek for water, one of the few words I knew.

My father was cradling my head so I could drink from the cup held by a small old woman in black. She was talking excitedly in Greek. A German said, "It's too hot for a child today." One of my ears felt very sore.

People helped me to stand.

"Are you okay?" my father asked. "You can stand, right?"

I nodded. I looked down at where I'd fallen and saw a few drops of blood, maybe five or six.

"I cut my ear," I said. It was scratched and still bleeding, inside, in the shell. "On him," I added, pointing.

The *kouros* kept smiling. It must have been his toe, on the foot that was forward. I must have scraped into it on my way down.

The old woman put the hem of her black skirt into the cup of water and cleaned the blood off my ear with it. Then she patted me on the shoulder and said something to me with a big smile.

The German who had objected to my being out in the heat translated: "She is saying the gods love you," he said.

My father looked displeased with that idea and with all the fuss. "All right," he said. "I think we'd better go home now."

"Why?" I asked the German. "Can you ask her why she says that?"

The German asked her, but she didn't answer.

Another German came over with a present for me: his newspaper, which he'd folded into a hat. "This is for the prevention of sunlight," he said.

My father thanked him in German, and they had a stuttery-sounding conversation for a few minutes. The first German joined in. Now that he saw my father could speak German, he was less disapproving. The three of them chatted while I stood still, holding my new hat and feeling around inside my ear. I kept my back to the *kouros*. I didn't want to look at him. I wasn't exactly afraid of him, but I felt it was better to avoid his enchantment—the whatever-it-was he'd exerted over me that had made me fall down.

The old woman in black had retreated to a three-legged stool in the corner near the friezes; she must have been a museum guard. As my father and the Germans began to conclude their conversation, she scuttled over to me again. She had an apricot she wanted me to take.

My father shook his head in the Greek manner, jerking it up and saying, *"Oxi, oxi."* "Thank you," he added, but he didn't look very grateful.

She jabbed her hand at me and said something insistent.

"From her own garden," one of the Germans explained.

"Fine," said my father. He put his hand on my shoulder. "We'd better get you home for a rest."

Going down was easier, and the paper hat helped more than I'd thought it would. My father walked beside me, pausing a few times to ask me—to tell me, really—"You're okay, right?" And I was. I held on to the apricot, though I wasn't sure I wanted to eat it. It made me nervous, as if it might be part of the Acropolis spell.

"What does *kouros* mean?" I asked my father.

"Young man," he said. "A beautiful young man."

Then he said, "You'd better not eat that apricot."

"Why?"

"Fruit isn't safe," he said.

"We eat fruit all the time," I said.

"We eat oranges. You peel oranges. We don't eat fruit you can't peel, especially if you can't wash it."

"Why not?"

"You could get the runs," he said.

We walked on a little. "Those Germans were classics professors from Tübingen," he told me. "They were actually quite nice. We're going to have lunch with them in Kifissia someday soon."

We passed the photographer with his box camera. The trip was over. My father decided we should take a taxi home and walked off to the corner, where several Mercedes-Benzes idled in a diesel haze.

I took a bite of the apricot. Just one. It was very sweet and the juice ran down the side of my mouth. Then I put it on a chunk of a column that was lolling around at the foot of the hill.

"There," I said, to any *kouroi* or gods who were waiting for an offering.

The car was fixed and the apartment was rearranged to my mother's satisfaction or, "As good as it's going to get." Sunstroke and enchantment were behind me, and so were the long days of traipsing around with my father. My mother would not put up with that sort of rigorous program. Anyhow, now that we had the car, we could drive right up to what we wanted to see and afterward eat a two-hour lunch on a terrace under a grape arbor with a cat asleep in the corner and then spend some time in the little store beside the taverna looking at handwoven bags and shirts. Or, if we hadn't gone too far away, just go home and take a siesta like normal citizens.

My father, of course, wanted to go too far away immediately.

"Let's go to Mycenae," he said.

I perked up. I really wanted to go there.

My mother said no. "It's too far," she said. "It's too hot. And there are bandits."

"There aren't any bandits," said my father. "Honestly!"

"George says there are. He says the whole Peloponnese is riddled with them. He says he'll take us down there in the fall, when it's cooler."

My father frowned. "It's barely the Peloponnese," he said.

"George says we need an escort," my mother repeated.

"When was this, anyhow? When were you and George having this conversation?" my father asked.

My mother blew one of her special I-don't-care-what-you-think smoke rings.

"What do the bandits do?" I asked.

"Rob you, of course," said my father.

"Sometimes they take you hostage," said my mother.

"Annette!" My father dropped his hand on the vast mahogany dining table with a thud. "This is nonsense."

"Mmm," said my mother.

My father tried again. "Let's go to Meteora," he said.

"I think we should wait until, maybe, October." My mother finished her cigarette. "When it isn't as hot."

"It's in the mountains. It *is* the mountains," my father said. "Is there anywhere at all that you would be willing to go? Epidaurus? How about Epidaurus?"

"Epidaurus is in the Peloponnese," she said. "Sounion, that could be a nice trip."

My father was silent for a minute. Then he said: "Why can't you just come out with it? You could say, I want to go to Sounion, and forget all that guff about bandits. You could state at the outset what you want, and then I wouldn't have to guess."

My mother glared at him.

"I want to go to Sounion," she said. "Okay? Happy?"

"Okay," said my father. "We'll go to Sounion."

My mother got up from the table. "I'll call George," she said.

"What's George got to do with it?" my father asked. "It's not even fifty miles away. We don't need George."

My mother was already dialing. "We do need him," she said.

My father shook his head. "Pirates? Werewolves of Sounion? What's the problem?"

My mother and George fixed it for the day after.

"The roads are extremely bad, he says," she told my father. "He'll lead us."

"Every road in this country is bad," my father said. "Nothing special about that."

George and his solicitude were a gift from Doxiadis, the mysterious outfit where he and my father worked, though they never seemed to do any work. A few days a week, my father went there for an hour or two in the morning, came home for lunch, went back for another brief spell, and was home long before dinner. When I asked him what Doxiadis was, he said, "Urban planning." "What does that mean?" I asked. "Think tank," said my father. "They think big thoughts." "What do they think about?" I asked. "They think about how to bring Greece into the twentieth century," said my father. Then he laughed. "That will take a few centuries," he said, "so they'll never catch up."

Doxiadis was a person as well as the name of an institution. Once I saw him get out of a taxi at the entrance to our building, delivering my father home in the evening after an unusual day of real work. My view from the fourth-floor balcony was partial: bald head, long, lavish overcoat (it was December), graceful, gesticulating arms. From above he looked somewhat like a spider. Doxiadis—either the man or the company, or perhaps they couldn't be distinguished—had found the apartment for us, had arranged an end-of-the-summer cruise to Crete for us (this was the trip my mother had in mind when she said her "shrug" would be good for an evening on a boat), and had commissioned George to protect and guide us. Unlike George's office job, this required a lot of effort.

George was in his mid-thirties, several years younger than my parents. He was quite short, as if he'd been underfed in his youth, and probably he had been. He'd made up for that in the postwar decade. His thin arms, narrow shoulders, and stalky legs attached to a solid, round middle composed of baklava, octopus, and retsina. Mustache, aviator sunglasses, suit and tie on all occasions, and his otherworldly courtesy could not quite disguise the nervewracked, melancholy inner George.

I liked George, in part because he treated me with as much formality as he did my father. My mother elicited something quite different from him—love, possibly veneration. Another reason I liked him was that his hunger made for a lot of refueling stops. He was the opposite of my father. Going on a trip with George was more about eating something delicious than seeing something beautiful. Few of his country's monuments impressed him. Many Greeks were like that. George could eat moussaka sitting beside a rather well-preserved temple to Zeus and never turn his head to acknowledge it.

But Sounion: "This is my favorite spot," he said. "I am delighted we are going there. Also, on the road is an exceptionally good place for barbounia. The little red fish—I don't know their English name."

"We probably don't have them, so there isn't an English name," said my mother.

"Could be," said George. "Or possibly, you don't eat them. Poor countries are happy to eat what rich countries consider inedible."

"Oh, right. The tragedy of Greece." My mother always poked fun at George's gloom.

"But it's true," he said, smiling. Then, to my father: "I have taken the liberty of leaving the Fiat at home to spare it the trip. May I ride with you, in the American car?"

"Sure," said my father. "Anyhow, it's easier than trying to follow you."

George refused to ride in the front with my parents.

"I will direct you from the back," he said. He wedged himself into the worst spot, straddling the hump in the middle, between my sister hugging her stuffed owl and me staring out the window.

Rocks, goats, a donkey pushed onward by a woman dressed in black, dust from the terrible road: Excursions in Greece were predictable. There was never anything but rocks and goats and donkeys and dust on the way to a broken temple or amphitheater. The countryside was a wasteland. Athens was different. Athens was alive. So what if the wrecked Acropolis brooded above everything, trying to remind you that time was coming to eat you up? Below it people were rushing around and cars were honking and waiters were pouring out tiny cups of coffee in a hundred cafés. Out in the hinterland we might as well have been on the moon. It was hard for me to believe that the ancestors of the old woman poking her donkey with a stick had built the temple whose remaining columns rose out of a nest of lizards and bracken off the road to our left, a site so minor we weren't even stopping to look.

I didn't like the red fish at the restaurant.

"It has too many bones for you," George said.

I nodded.

Without looking up from his plate, George snapped his fingers. This was the Greek way of summoning a waiter. I always felt embarrassed on the waiter's behalf, though I could see that everyone thought it was fine. Our waiter came over and George barked at him. In a minute he was back with a bowl of boiled potatoes and a plate of feta pockmarked with olives. It wasn't a big improvement, but I ate it anyhow. I didn't want to spurn George's efforts.

Then it was back into the hot car, more dust and donkeys, all of us sleepy from food. The cicadas screamed so loud I could hear them through the rattle of the tires over the ruts and stones.

All of a sudden there wasn't any road. Also, the light had become even brighter and whiter. A salty wind whooshed into the open windows of the Chevrolet.

"We're here," George announced.

My father stopped the car. "We just leave it here?" he asked. "There isn't some sort of parking lot?"

"Not necessary," said George. "After all, no cars, right?"

"Maybe if there were a parking lot, more people—"

"Everybody know it's here," George interrupted my mother.

"*You* know," said my mother. "Some German tourist doesn't know."

Snorts from George. "So much the better," he said.

"My mistake. A stupid example. Let's say a French tourist," my mother said. "This is part of the trouble with Greece. It's all so haphazard and disorderly. It's unplanned."

"You think perhaps there should be a souvenir booth selling small plastic columns on key chains?" George was teasing my mother, wasn't he?

"I think a sign would be useful."

George extended his skinny arm. "This way for panoramic view of the Aegean, sacred to Poseidon."

"You can scoff, George," said my mother, "but this is what Greece has got. This past is your future, and it's foolish not to make intelligent use of it."

"It will come," said George. "The plastic-column key chains and the signs and the parking lots. And then"—he pointed at my mother—"you will be sad. You will be one of those who say, Oh, it was so wonderful before the parking lot and the sign. Won't you?"

My mother laughed. "Of course I will. You're right. But I'll get to say that I was here before all that stuff. Also, I'm right too, and you know it."

"Ah, life is impossible," said George.

"We can agree on that," said my father. "Do we go up this hill?" He took my sister's hand and led the way.

My mother and George walked together, and I lurked in the rear. Blood-colored flowers were everywhere, dipping in the wind. "Are these poppies?" I asked.

"Yes, they are," said George. "Don't lie down in them because you will be drugged and fall asleep."

"They're anemones," my mother said.

I wanted to lie down right away and go to sleep to prove my mother wrong. "Hurry up," she said. "You're dawdling."

"The temple isn't going away," I said, but I picked up my pace a little.

And there it was.

Greece is too much for me, I thought. Greece makes me scared about how long time is, and it's too hot and it's boring and there are too many bones in the fish and now *this.* Why did my parents keep dragging me around to see things that were too big for me to contain?

Because there was so much less of it than there was of the Parthenon, it was more frightening and more beautiful. Below, the sea was banging and banging. Whirly winds dashed around the last, leftover columns; the rest had dropped into the rocky surroundings. The marble floor slabs had been colonized by clumps of coarse grass. There was a sweet smell of salty vegetation.

"Look!" my father called. He was pressing his finger onto a column. "My God! Annette, come here! It's Byron's signature."

My mother ambled over to him. "Did he come here with a chisel?"

"You mean Byron the poet?" I thought this made things even worse. This made the arcade of time even longer and more cavernous—to think this had been a ruin when Byron came, which was so long ago that it was already history in itself. It made me both dizzy and mad.

"Yes, the poet Byron," said George. "I forgot to mention that, the famous signature. I wonder if he did indeed bring a chisel."

"Maybe someone came after him and improved it. A post-Byronic chiseler." My father laughed.

"It's the Romantic-era equivalent of a souvenir stand," my mother said. Then she too put her finger in the marble to trace the letters. " 'The isles of Greece!' " she said.

" 'Where burning Sappho loved and sung,' " my father responded. "It's really just Kilroy Was Here, though, isn't it?"

"It was the opportunism of the post-Byronic chiseler I was thinking about," my mother said. "If Byron didn't do it himself. Or even if he did, somebody must have gone over it afterward. It's quite deeply incised."

"You know, this is where Theseus's father jumped off," my father said to me. "I can't remember his name. What was his name, George?"

"King Aegeus. Hence, this sea. The Aegean."

"That was when Theseus forgot to change the sail from black to white? After he killed the Minotaur?" I was pleased to have remembered this.

"Right," said my father. He shook his head and muttered, "How could I forget that, Aegeus. It's ridiculous."

"George," I said, "was this temple here when King Aegeus jumped off the cliff?"

George made a torso-heaving Mediterranean shrug that expressed doubt about many more things than whether there'd been a temple here when Aegeus killed himself.

"Was there actually a King Aegeus?" He kicked the base of one of the columns, gently, so as not to hurt his foot. "There was a temple," he said. "We can see that. There was probably some sort of a king. The rest?"

My mother had sat down on a chunk of stone, with my sister curled up in the grass beside her. My sister was asleep, my mother nearly so. The owl lay in the dust with his cotton face turned up to the sky. The cicadas were still screaming on the hill, and the sun was beginning to lower itself toward the Aegean.

"Coffee?" said George. "And a little galaktoboureko? I know just the place."

"Do they have baklava?" I asked. Galaktoboureko was too creamy, a kind of wiggly junket jammed between phyllo sheets.

"There is always baklava," George assured me.

My mother decided that George should ride in the front on the return trip. "I'll just nap in the back with the girls," she said.

"No, no, no," said George.

"Really," my mother said. "Please, I beg you, George." She clambered into the back with my drowsing sister and leaned against the door, then stretched her legs out on the seat. "Look, I'm so comfy," she said.

George obeyed.

I didn't intend to nap. Besides, my mother hadn't left me much room. I wanted to make sure that the dusty roads and goats were as boring on the way home as they'd been on the way there, and I wanted to feel disconnected and misunderstood. At least, I hoped I was misunderstood. I needed to figure out how to thwart my mother's trick of knowing what I was thinking. I had to learn to think things she couldn't detect. I could practice while she napped.

"George," my mother said.

"Yes?" He turned halfway back.

"You hadn't really 'forgotten' about Byron's signature, had you?"

"I wanted it to be a surprise," he said.

"It was," said my father.

I scrunched up against my window and pretended to sleep. We'd left the headland and begun to ride along the scrubby plain that lay below Sounion when my mother poked her foot into my leg and said, "You think this is just a waste of time and it doesn't interest you and why are we dragging you all over the place, don't you?"

I could have killed her.

"I don't think that," I said. My voice was squeaky and artificial.

"I know what you're thinking," she said.

The summer went on and on that way. To Epidaurus, to sit in the top tier of the raked stone banks and hear a pebble ping on the stage hundreds of feet below. To Delphi, to drink the sacred mountain water in the marble basin from a wooden cup that had hung there on a chain for millennia. "They must have to get a new cup every twenty years or so," my father observed.

"Maybe it's a magic cup," said my mother. "Maybe it's a four-thousand-year-old cup." My father didn't think so. "Annette," he said, "don't be ridiculous." To Eleusis, to walk the Sacred Way and get hotter than I'd ever been anywhere, including the Acropolis at noon, and to go into a low, wide, rubbly cave that was the entrance to the underworld. "That's why it's so hot here," my mother told me. She was in a good mood, and so was my father. The trip to Sounion had done something to remove her resistance to traveling: thus, our constant goings-around.

Was there really an underworld? Had that crisscrossed stub of stone in the Delphi Museum called the Omphalos really marked the navel of the universe? In Cambridge it would have been easy to answer these questions. The answer would be, No, but that's what the Greeks thought. In Greece, at the entrance to the underworld, the answer wasn't so clear.

The air around these spots was zingy, like a pre-thunderstorm, crackly atmosphere. Things felt thick and thin at the same time. I could understand the thick part: thousands of people walking here and looking at these things and thinking they were important for thousands of years would make a place feel heavy and full. The thin was what worried me. It frightened me. In these places the veil or screen—whatever kept us in the everyday, regular world—had shredded or fallen away so that I could see through to another place, almost. I could know that there *was* another place. I could feel the underworld in the rubbly cave. It was a dank, vibrating something that was there in the back, implacable and big. You could pretend it wasn't there but it was there anyhow. It reminded me of first seeing the Parthenon, except the opposite. At the Parthenon, the world had unfolded enough for me to see a balance and quiet that was inside everything. At the entrance to the underworld, I got a whiff of a huge, shapeless violence, like an ocean, that lay beneath the surface of the day-to-day.

The worst part was that neither the balance nor the violence had anything to do with me. I was a speck. All these things I felt, I didn't really feel them in myself. I was only passing through them. They were a kind of weather. They were the essential weather of the world. If I got close to them then I got wet or hot or frightened or whatever they had to offer.

Greece was a long lesson in my insignificance.

The dolphins with their taut shiny grins followed us as we sailed down to Crete, hotter and hotter. The deck was white with quick-dried salt, and the brass tarnished overnight. My mother wore her shrug in the evenings, though it wasn't chilly. Islands left and right, then a day of open water. At the museum at Heraklion, my mother said, "It's Egypt."

"It's a kind of confluence point," my father said.

I could see what she meant about Egypt. To begin with, amazingly hot, even inside the dark museum. Then, everyone in the paintings was sideways, like Egyptians. And the feeling that there was no depth to things was also Egyptian. The paintings were basically bas-reliefs, and I didn't like that. Bas-relief had a strange attitude toward people, as if people weren't quite real. In Crete, it occurred to me that it might be an incapacity, not an attitude. Those Cretans couldn't see things any other way. The *kouros* in the Acropolis Museum who'd stepped out of his stone—in order to kick me in the ear—was beyond them. The Cretans were still stuck in the stone. Like the Egyptians, they were living in a two-dimensional, symbolic sort of universe.

It was a colorful universe, though. The women wore red and

yellow clothes and terrific, messy updos that reminded me of some of Frederika's hair experiments from long ago. Their eyes were lined with black makeup that swirled out at the corners. The only bad thing was the shape of their dresses. Their dresses were cut down below the chest so that their breasts stuck out. In fact, their dresses were a kind of reverse bra. They made the breasts push out and forward, but they exposed them, rather than covering them. I couldn't bear seeing the things on my own chest that I was still hoping wouldn't turn out to be breasts, so the idea that anyone else could see them, and that a person would want to stick them out like that, was a nightmare. Just being in the same room with pictures of these dresses embarrassed me.

Then a hot bus came along to take us to Knossos.

The palace—which wasn't anything like what I thought of as a palace—was enormous: a vast, weedy expanse with traces of things. It was more of a floor plan than a structure. Fallen-down walls and bits of doorways made the outlines of what had once been rooms. One long-ago room was filled with vases taller than I was. "They're for storing oil," my father said. Some parts, though, looked as good as new. There was a porch with thick red-and-black columns, and there were intact walls covered with bright paintings of fish jumping around in the ocean and curly-haired Cretan women with their breasts pointing out.

No Labyrinth. No Minotaur. I stood at the periphery of the wrecked buildings and looked out over the cliffs where Icarus had tried to fly. Everything was quiet and still.

"Those are reconstructions," my father told me when we were in the bus going back to Heraklion. "That porch, and the throne room. Who knows if it really looked like that."

"It looked convincing to me," my mother said.

"Cement," my father muttered.

On to Rhodes, on to Patmos, on to Naxos and Mykonos. The air was hot and the sea was dark. Every evening at dusk, when the ship sailed on to the next island, we were escorted for the first mile or so by the local fishing fleet with their lanterns lit in the prows of their wooden boats. In every village the glaring whitewashed box-shaped houses crowded the hills like a raggedy staircase. The church was always at the top, its stucco dome the only curve in a maze of right angles. We went into one of these churches: nothing inside except a blunt stucco altar above which was painted a big, heavy-lidded eye.

"The Eye of God," my father said.

The last stop was Delos. Not everyone got off the boat. But we did.

Delos seemed empty except for a bunch of stone lions in a row. They were crouched above a beach, leaning toward the sea with their mouths open in a stony roar. Because they were so old, they'd been weathered to a nice, nearly soft finish that was smooth and inviting. I climbed up on one and sat on its back. It was peaceful there and breezy, a cool, fresh breeze very different from the hot winds that had pursued us through the Cyclades all the way from Crete.

A green lizard walked onto my lion's foot. As it was zipping off the stone platform where my lion squatted, it turned yellow.

My parents suddenly popped up.

"You're here!" my mother said. "We were looking for you up at the temple."

"Oh," I said. "I didn't know there was anything else here."

"This is Apollo's birthplace," my mother said. "There's tons of stuff here. Well, never mind—it's time to go back to the boat."

"You shouldn't be sitting on that sculpture," my father said.

I scooted down off the lion.

"We were getting worried about you," my mother said.

"I was just here," I said. "I like it here. I think I saw a chameleon. It was green, then it went all yellow."

"You're a chameleon," my mother said.

My sister was the only one of us who could speak any Greek, the kitchen chatter she'd learned from Kula. Because she was a four-year-old, she spoke at a basic level. The rest of us couldn't manage even that. My mother's classical bits didn't go very far, I was too shy and self-conscious to risk more than Hello, Thank you, and Good-bye, and my father didn't bother. He believed that loud, slow, Greek-accented English would do the job. It did, but only with people who spoke English, and they thought he was making fun of them with his supposedly helpful Greek intonations.

Every morning Kula walked my sister to the Montessori kindergarten two blocks from our apartment and I got on a bus to the American school near the army base half an hour outside of town. I was in sixth grade now, and my parents said that school was too important for me to waste a year or even part of a year trying to learn Greek. So my first encounter with real Americans took place nearly four thousand miles from home. I'd never met people like this before. Cambridge might have had them, but I didn't go to school with them.

They chewed gum—totally taboo in our house. They ate sandwiches on soft white bread, another household no-no: whole wheat, please, or rye. The boys were tall and many were chunky. Most of the girls had breasts, and if they didn't, they were pretending to by wearing bras they didn't need. They had jingly charm bracelets with poodles and Eiffel Towers dangling off. Everyone wore bright-white sneakers, which they kept clean by painting them with white shoe polish during Friday recess. I missed my red Keds, but they would have been out of place.

Red Keds, however, would have been better than what I was wearing.

With her infallible style sense, my mother had sniffed out a dressmaker who had a weaver at her disposal. You could invent a fabric—I'd like a fine gray wool with a red pinstripe—and two weeks later the weaver had woven it and the dressmaker had run up a skirt, tailor-made to your design. I had a blue dress of heavy cotton with a Peter Pan collar and a white embroidered frieze around the hemline. I had a skirt of the gray wool with the red pinstripe. I had another skirt, multicolored stripes like Jacob's coat, that fell in big box pleats, and I had my leftover-from-the-summer sundresses from Filene's Basement warmed up by a green cardigan. The dressmaker had also created four white middy blouses, one with a collar embroidered in red for special occasions, to go with the skirts. To complete my outfit I had sandals from the outdoor market in the Plaka, where they sold scary brassieres shaped like torpedoes that made me worry about the eventual size of the breasts I was still pretending I didn't have. These sandals, though not as good as the gladiator ones from Florence, were of the same genre and, like them, had soles made of old tires. I didn't fit in, and my clothes were the badge of how different I was from my classmates.

They weren't afraid of school. They thought school was a kind of joke or a kind of game. They didn't listen when the teacher talked, they didn't sit still when she said to sit still, they didn't care if they couldn't follow the lesson because they weren't trying to follow the lesson. They passed notes and doodled and looked out the window and interrupted. Mrs. Mezitis, I need to go to the bathroom, Mrs. Mezitis, I broke my pencil, I want another,

Mrs. Mezitis, my tummy hurts, I have to go to the nurse. I'd done plenty of doodling and looking out the window at school in Cambridge, but I'd been furtive about it. I knew how important it was to pay attention. Nobody had ever told my classmates in Greece to pay attention. For them, going to school was a sport like dodgeball: The point was to avoid learning anything.

And to see what they could get away with. A boy named Craig sat behind me and kicked my chair all day. Sometimes he kicked so hard that I turned around, which was what he wanted. Then he'd stick his tongue out or jam his finger up his nose and wiggle it or make a mean scrunchy face. I tried not to react. Then after a few days, he did something so disgusting that I yelped. He turned his eyelids inside out, so his eyes were rimmed with ridges of wet, red, inside-the-eyelid skin. It made my own eyes hurt just to look at them.

"Mrs. Mezitis," I said, the first words I addressed to her, "Craig has done something horrible to his eyeballs."

But of course his eyeballs were back to normal and I was a snitch.

"I don't see what you're complaining about," she said.

Mrs. Mezitis was pale and dry. She had wrinkly hair that she tried to tame into a pageboy, but it frizzed in resistance. She was an American married to a Greek and she was a patriot. The one moment of the day she displayed anything like enthusiasm was reciting the Pledge of Allegiance in the mornings. With her bony hand clutched to her chest, she stood erect, facing the flag that drooped from the pole beside the blackboard.

I didn't know the Pledge of Allegiance. It wasn't part of the Cambridge catechism. But it was short, and I learned it in a day or two. Mrs. Mezitis always emphasized the words *under God*.

At dinnertime my parents demanded tidbits about school. It was the rule: Everyone had to tell about his or her day. The army school didn't offer me much. Craig stuck his finger up his nose wasn't a good tidbit. But at Wednesday dinner the first week, I could recite the Pledge of Allegiance.

"Reactionaries," my mother said. She snorted. "That *under God* thing is a McCarthyite addition. Typical. You don't have to say that."

"Everybody says it," I said. I didn't want yet another thing to make me stick out.

"I mean the God stuff," my mother said.

"I'm not supposed to say that?"

"You do what you want," my father put in. He gave my mother a look—one of those looks I didn't understand.

God wasn't a member of our household. I'd met him in the cafeteria in first grade, at my school with the cement playground across the street from home in Cambridge, when everyone folded hands and said, Thank you, God, for our food, before we ate lunch.

When I got home, I'd asked my mother, "Who's God?"

She was stumped, for once.

"Well," she said. "Well, some people believe in God."

"But who is it?" I asked.

She didn't answer.

"Do we believe in God?" I asked.

She shook her head.

"Can I believe in God?" A daring bid for independence.

"If that's what you want," she said.

I got the feeling it wouldn't be a good idea. God embarrassed my mother, and if I believed in him, that would be embarrassing too.

Five years later, God had popped up again. And just like last time, he provoked an unusual diffidence in my parents. You do what you want was not their general position on my behavior.

You do what we say was more like it. I was puzzled and I was suspicious: Maybe the question of whether to believe in God was a test of my character. I didn't want to fail it.

The next morning when we stood to recite the Pledge of Allegiance, I omitted the words *under God,* though I did move my lips as if I were saying something. Not saying the pledge would be asking for trouble, but saying the God thing would be betraying my parents in a way that I hadn't figured out.

At home in Cambridge, we had a teacher for English and a teacher for history and a teacher for science and so forth. The history teacher thought history was the greatest. The math teacher couldn't wait to explain algebra. Mrs. Mezitis was responsible for teaching all of our subjects, and she was equally uninspiring about every one of them.

The exchange about Craig's eyeballs was a preview of how Mrs. Mezitis and I were not going to get along.

Science class: "Matter comes in three forms," she told us. "Solid, liquid, and gas. Can anyone name three substances with these three different forms?"

Nobody did.

"Anyone?"

"Turds are solid," Craig offered. "Sometimes."

Mrs. Mezitis ignored him. She picked up her coffee cup and banged it—a little harder than necessary—on her desk. "A desk," she said. "A desk is solid."

"Water is a liquid, right?" said a girl named Lindsey, who had lived in Japan for four years.

"Right," said Mrs. Mezitis. "And how about a gas?"

"Gas," said Craig.

"Give someone else a chance, Craig," said Mrs. Mezitis. "Anyhow, gasoline is a liquid."

Craig kicked my chair. "I didn't mean gasoline," he said.

Nobody could think of a gas.

"Air," she said. "Air is a gas. Okay. The desk is a solid, water is a liquid, and air is a gas. Do you understand?"

I raised my hand. "What about mayonnaise? What's that?" I asked.

Mrs. Mezitis stiffened. "Don't ask foolish questions that waste our time."

"Or Silly Putty?" I went on. "What about that?"

"That will be enough out of you," she said.

At dinner I reported the mayonnaise interchange.

"That is not a foolish question," my father said. "That is a good question. And the answer is, it's a colloidal suspension. The solid molecules are suspended in liquid in such a way that it forms something between solid and liquid."

"Why didn't she say that?" I asked him.

"Maybe she didn't know it," he said. "That's my bet. Shocking, really."

This made me very happy. She was a dope, Mrs. Mezitis. I'd thought she might be, and now I knew it. My father had as much as said so.

"What about Silly Putty?" I asked my father.

"I don't really understand Silly Putty," he said. "It must be some kind of suspension, but it's a different kind from mayonnaise. Mayonnaise tends toward the liquid and Silly Putty tends toward the solid end of the spectrum. George might know. He had some training as an engineer."

"It drips," I said. "Like if you leave it on the edge of a table, it drips down to the floor."

"Yes, but it doesn't come apart," said my father. "It oozes in one mass. It's very strange."

"You can make copies with it," I said.

My father cocked his head. "Copies?"

"If you press it on a newspaper, it makes a copy."

"Oh." He waved his hand. "That's not interesting."

There was always a point at which what I thought was interesting or important bored the person I was talking to. With my father, that point was farther away than it was with Mrs. Mezitis, but I had now arrived at it. I decided to think about my father's dismissal of Mrs. Mezitis rather than his dismissal of me. If he thought she didn't know what she was talking about (and that seemed to be what he thought) then I could be like the other kids and not pay attention to her without worrying.

As usual, my parents were having a lot more fun than I was. They had a knack for it. They loved to meet new people and try unfamiliar foods and dash from place to place seeing sights. They were avid for life; they wanted to eat experience. I wanted to stay home and read, and if I had to go out, I wanted to do something I'd already done, something predictable. It was as if they were the children, excited by all the new things, and I was the adult, anxious and stuck in my ways.

In the afternoons when I returned from school, my mother was often taking a nap. She needed one because many nights a week she and my father were out until two or three in the morning at tavernas where dinner was served at eleven. Then there was a floor show, with a band and a singer. "The songs are all about misery," she said. "Their favorite is 'Cloudy Sunday.'"

"Can you sing it?"

My mother could play the piano but she wasn't much of a singer. She gave it a whirl, though. *"Sinefiasmeni Kiriaki,"* she sang. "You make my life black," was the next line.

"It's so yowly and wailing," I said.

"It's a lament," said my mother. "I thought it was a love song the first time I heard it, but it's about the Sunday the Nazis invaded Greece."

After singing, there was dancing. "But only for the men," she told me. "First they drink ouzo, then they throw the glasses on the floor, then they dance. Two guys hold on to one handkerchief, I guess so they can pretend that they aren't exactly holding hands." She laughed. "And they aren't, exactly."

"I want to come," I said. It was odd, but I did want to go. It seemed to be something I could watch rather than something I would have to do.

"You could never stay up that late," my mother said. "I can barely stay up that late."

"On a weekend?"

"Maybe." She yawned. "Oh, why not," she said. "You can come with us this Friday."

I hadn't expected her to say yes. Sometimes I felt her standards were slipping when it came to my behavior.

"Can we go to the one with the dancing?" I asked.

"They're all like that," my mother said. "Anyhow, we go where Andy takes us."

My father and Andy had been assistant professors together at Harvard after the war, back when Andy was an American. Now he was Greek again. He was part of a revered left-wing family. "Andy will be premier of Greece someday," my father had said at dinner one night. "First the old man, then Andy." As always, he was right. He didn't foresee that they were both going to be political prisoners as well, but nobody knows everything.

Andy had a huge, friendly face and a nice American wife named Maggie. "You look so sophisticated," she said to me when they arrived on Friday. "I can't believe you're only ten."

"I'm almost eleven," I said.

My mother had dressed me up: my gray skirt with a white

blouse and a red wool shawl she'd loaned me for the evening. She'd also let me wear her Victorian bracelet, the one that snapped open and had a chain as fine as a thread so that even when you undid it, it wouldn't fall off. It was a gold oval enameled black on the outer face, with five pearls embedded in it and a gold filigree incised in the enamel. My father's father, the communist diamond dealer, had received it in payment for a debt during the Depression. There wasn't much he could do with it—it wasn't a diamond—so he gave it to my mother when my parents got married. It was a bit tight on her. I was hoping this loan would become permanent.

Andy and Maggie and my parents sat around on the sofas drinking Scotch and eating fish roe on crackers until it was late enough to go to the taverna. My mother insisted that I have cucumber soup and cold potatoes in the kitchen with Kula and my sister. "Otherwise, you'll fall asleep because you're hungry," she said.

"But I want to eat with you, there," I said.

"You can do both," she said.

Finally, around ten, it was time to go.

Everybody got into Andy's little French car that hissed when you sat down. My father was in the front with Andy, and I was in the back between my mother and Maggie and their competing perfumes.

My mother smelled the way she always did: dry, sandalwood-y, tobacco-y, as if her cigarettes had been sweetened and bottled. Maggie smelled of lily of the valley. Her perfume made me feel sad. It was delicious, but at the precise moment I got a full taste of it, it would vanish. That was why it was sad. It was like an essence of nostalgia. Part of the smell was its quality of slipping away just when you thought you'd got hold of it.

"Diorissimo?" my mother asked.

Maggie nodded.

"You can only wear that if you don't smoke," my mother said.

My mother and her assertions. I'd often hated her for them. They seemed arbitrary or maybe designed to thwart whatever I wanted to do. Now I just wondered how she knew these things. What made her so sure that the shawl I had wanted to borrow, the red-and-green-striped silk, was "too grownup" for me? Where did she get the information that charm bracelets were vulgar—which she couldn't wait to tell me when I described my classmates. Why did she know who could wear a perfume she never used? My mother knew these things the way my father knew the succession of the kings of England. The difference was, if I wanted to check on my father, I could look up the succession of the kings of England in an encyclopedia. If I wanted to check on my mother, there wasn't any book to consult. She was the encyclopedia. I didn't think this was fair. That night, though, as we prowled the dark backstreets of Athens, with Andy leaning out the window to look for a lively dinner spot, I didn't care about the unfairness. My mother had a body of knowledge, and I wanted to find out where she'd got it and maybe get some too.

"Does it say on the bottle that you can't use Maggie's perfume if you smoke?" I asked my mother.

"I doubt it," she said.

"So how come you know that?" I asked.

"It says so on my nose," my mother answered.

That didn't help.

"Eureka!" said Andy. He turned backward toward me. "That means, I have found it. And I have."

I knew that *eureka* meant I have found it. Did Andy think I didn't know anything?

Andy drove the car up onto the sidewalk at an angle, and we all got out.

"Is it okay to leave the car like that?" I asked.

"You're such a worrywart," my mother said. "Relax."

I couldn't see why Andy thought this was a good place to have dinner. To begin with, it was closed. But that was just the outer part, a café with the chairs turned upside down on their tables. Inside there was a bar with a row of empty stools and a long, shiny shelf of bottles. The bar was also closed. At the back of the room was a doorway hung with a plastic-bead curtain of a sort favored by Athenian restaurants. They came in many garish color combinations, purple and yellow, red and green like a Christmas ornament. They always gave a touch of mystery to what lay beyond, and they chinked and muttered when you passed through them. This was an elegant one, blue and white, like the Greek flag. We passed through it, and the curtain whispered in my ear.

"Time to grow up," it said.

By twelve-thirty I was so tired that the skin of my face hurt. I'd eaten shish kebab (Ask for souvlaki, my mother told me, because shish kebab is Turkish and they don't like that) and baklava, and for a while that had kept me awake. The singer had wailed her songs; a lot of people sang along. Now the waiters were delivering short, smoky glasses of ouzo, and the singer was moving from table to table with her assistant the cameraman. She draped her arm around my father's neck and put her cheek against his head. I was horrified. How could she do that? He would get mad. But he looked quite happy. A blast of light from the flashbulb, and then she moved on to Andy and kissed his cheek. I looked at my mother and Maggie to see what they thought. They were laughing.

"One more! One more with Andreas!" said the singer, leaning in closer.

The cameraman backed up so he could fit the entire table in the frame.

The empty bottle of retsina, the napkins in little heaps, the overflowing ashtray, the tablecloth limp and littered with broken bread. My mother in a low-cut silk blouse. Maggie in profile, smiling above her pearls. The singer holding Andy's chin in her outstretched palm, his head on display like a trophy. My father with drooping, tipsy eyes and his bow tie askew. My shoulder, hunched and exhausted, wrapped in the borrowed red shawl. The name and address of the restaurant or of the photographer are stamped on the back of the photograph in purple ink now so faded it's almost illegible. One of the words seems to be *Endymion.* And we're all preserved there, like him, in our beautiful youth.

After that the dancing started and I fell asleep in my chair.

My November birthday was behind me by the time my mother decided we should go to Mycenae. The white summer light had subsided, and though the edges of things were still dazzly, the world was less tiring to look at. Now and then there were days of rain when our marble apartment became as cold and dank as the coffin-house in London.

This rain had caused a family of cockroaches to germinate in the depths of my toilet. They usually scampered around near the outlet at the bottom, but they sometimes walked up to the rim below the seat, where they lurked, waving their black antennae and, as in London, making me completely constipated. I could pee, because I could arch my back and shoot my pee into the bowl. Sitting was the problem. If I sat, I felt their crackly many legs skittering about on my behind. I felt that even though it wasn't happening and had never happened. It might happen, and the idea of it was ghastly.

We were planning a real, four-day trip. I was going to miss Thursday and Friday at school. George was coming with us; he and my father were taking two days off from their so-called work. We had two nights reserved at La Belle Hélène, the archaeologists' hotel in Mycenae. Then we were going on to Nauplion to see the remnants of Venetian rule. I couldn't wait. I was finally going to meet my second family, the House of Atreus.

"I don't think it will be too cold," George said at dinner the Tuesday before we left.

Kula had made one of her trademark terrible dinners. She had three or four of them. This was the tough lamb stewed with tomatoes and accompanied by a bowl of boiled potatoes, which she dotted with limp parsley, drowned in second-rate olive oil ("Why? Why?" my mother said. "In the land where olive oil was born!"), and placed with averted eyes before my father: an offering to the godhead. Kula was in awe of my father. When he got home in the afternoons from doing nothing at Doxiadis, she scuttled up behind him as he sat on the sofa, bringing a dish of glistening black olives or three peeled figs on a plate. Every morning the lotus-orange awaited him at the breakfast table, some days adorned with a jasmine blossom. "She's in love with you," my mother said. "No, no," said my father. "To her, I am Zeus." "That's just what I mean," my mother said. "It's not the same," said my father. "Anyhow, I enjoy being Zeus." "Who wouldn't?" said my mother.

"At least during the day," George went on. "The nights could be quite chilly. And it might be cold in the day if it's windy. And since it's high up, it might be—"

"In short," my mother cut in, "prepare for everything."

"That would be wise," said George. "It's often very windy, even in the summer. Have you got scarves, for instance?"

"I have a lot of scarves," my mother said, "and I will bring them all."

My father shook his head. He didn't like scarves. He didn't like hats or gloves either. He liked to stride out the front door with his overcoat unbuttoned and flapping around him. In Cambridge this often was not possible. But we were here, in Greece, where he could do as he wanted.

"I'll bring that black one for you, just in case," my mother told him.

"I don't need it," he said.

"Do we have to Look Nice?" I asked. Looking Nice meant uncomfortable clothes for visiting people we didn't really know or going to fussy restaurants where there was nothing I wanted to eat.

"Maybe once, in Nauplion," my mother said. "Bring the new middy blouse with the red embroidery on the collar."

Kula was back with a plate of melon slices.

My mother put a hand on George's starched bright-white cuff. "George, can you explain to Kula that we want to use the good olive oil? I can't seem to get that across."

George lifted his head toward the ceiling and moved his chin in Kula's direction. She skated over to his side on her noiseless felt slippers and stood at attention. Sharp, curt instructions from George; whispery protests from Kula.

"She says it's very expensive," he told my mother.

"I am paying for it. And it's what I want." My mother lit a cigarette for emphasis.

George explained that. Kula bowed her head. As she scooted back to the kitchen, she glanced at my mother, the smoke-goddess of extravagance, and looked away quickly, before my mother saw.

My mother saw. It was impossible not to see how much Kula hated us. We didn't know how to have a servant. Kula knew how to be a servant and that was all she knew. But she couldn't do it alone, and none of us could play our parts.

My father came the closest. That was probably why she worshipped him. He was naturally imperious, so the expressions on his face and his way of flicking his hand at something he wanted or something he wanted taken away were familiar and correct in Kula's eyes. It didn't matter that he couldn't speak Greek. Maybe it was better: no words to dilute his desires. They had come to an arrangement. Kula deposited sculpted fruit in front of him, and he ignored her existence unless he wanted her to remove a dirty plate, and that suited them both.

My mother was the problem.

If she had George around to back her up, my mother could make an occasional show of command, over the olive oil, for instance. But she couldn't maintain any authority. Her usual methods were seduction and charm. She wooed people and made them eager to please her by giving them the feeling that she appreciated them. Maybe she even did appreciate them. (It was hard for me to tell.) None of this was any use with Kula. Kula was not going to be enfolded into the family à la Frederika, coddled into behaving in a helpful way. Kula's position was below, and she was sticking to it.

My mother's feints at camaraderie in botched Greek got Kula upset. She would hide in the back kitchen. This was her inviolate space, off-limits to us, where she slept on a camp bed beside the crusty two-burner stove. Once, my mother had tried to go in there. Kula darted up in an unusual display of personality and flapped her arms as if shooing out vermin: Forbidden, forbidden, she'd said.

Two kitchens and she can't make a decent dinner, was my mother's complaint. But her real complaint was, I don't understand her and therefore I can't get her to do what I want.

George, naturally, was the source of Kula, who was the niece or the sister or the cousin of a woman who worked for his mother on the island of Aegina. During our first months, my mother had many consultations with George about Kula and what to do with her.

My mother was horrified by the back kitchen. "There's no window, there's no shower, her bed is jammed next to the stove. It's terrible."

"That kitchen is as big as the main floor of her house on Aegina where she lived with two other people," George said. "This is the Grande Bretagne, for her. She can wash at the sink. She's here in Athens with a secure job. You do not need to worry about it."

"But she could have her own bedroom," my mother said. "We have several extra."

George shook his head. "You are being sentimental."

This caused a rift between them.

"He's a heartless bastard," my mother reported to my father. "Like all communists."

"You're generalizing," said my father.

"From experience," my mother said.

"Why are communists heartless?" I asked.

"They look at the big picture," my father told me.

"Their theories are more important than reality," my mother said.

She forgave George within the week, because she was fond of

him and because she needed him. We all did. Each time George showed up, with his thin black tie, his cuff links fashioned from antique drachmas shining in his perfectly ironed sleeves, and replete with his knowledge of where to find the most honey-saturated baklava, the darkest mavrodaphne, the least-bumpy road to Eleusis, the person to bribe in order to see the largest, loveliest Pantocrator mosaic in Athens (in a church under restoration that had been closed to the public for years), we all relaxed. George would help. George would explain it, or organize it, or get rid of it. My father, initially resistant, had turned into his biggest fan, even to the point of defending the communist outlook.

"You have to see it in context," my father said. He was talking to me, but my mother made a face. "Nazis or communists. That was his choice. You can't be surprised he picked the communists."

"That was *then,*" my mother said. "Anyhow, you—" she added. She didn't finish her sentence. It was a reference to the communist diamond-dealing grandfather, who'd sent my father to communist Hebrew after-school every day. My mother had been raised a socialist.

"I don't understand why George said you were sentimental," I said. In fact, I understood almost nothing about my mother's quarrel with George, or about the communist-versus-socialist arguments that now and then took place between my parents.

"Concern for the individual is a bourgeois value," my mother said. "One person's situation isn't important. *They* say."

"I thought communism was about equality, that everybody is as important as everybody else," I said.

"Right," said my mother.

"Are we bourgeois?" I asked.

My father looked around at the chandeliers and the gilded

mirrors and the matching beige silk sofas across the room from the dining table. "I'd say so," he said. "We're certainly doing a good imitation of it."

"The bourgeoisie should be so lucky," my mother said. "We're living like tsars." She put her head in her hands and pulled her hair. "Oh, god, this country. I really can't take it."

"Annette," said my father in the tone he used when I was being especially balky.

My mother hated it here too, I saw. This surprising realization cheered me up.

But that, as my mother would say, was then. Now, several months later, two days before our journey to Mycenae, my mother was cheerily asking George what to pack and doing a good imitation of looking forward to the trip.

No imitations for me. I was buzzing with anticipation. I was sure that, like the Parthenon, Mycenae would still be what it had been—not a bunch of broken pieces like Knossos or a map of something it once was, like the Sacred Way at Eleusis. Up there on the citadel where Clytemnestra had unfurled the crimson carpet and Cassandra had said farewell to the sun, I was going to feel the pulse of the old, cursed bloodline. I knew it. All that family murder: I wanted to see its locus.

Wednesday night I was packing the little green suitcase my mother had got me before we left Cambridge for Greece when I felt a ripping sort of belly pain. I was used to bad belly feelings from constipation, and I kept on packing. Then there was another rip, somewhat worse. Also, everything in the excretory area felt peculiar, full and soggy. I went to the bathroom and looked into the toilet to check on the cockroach population: none. I sat down.

When I relaxed my knees, my underpants stretched out between them, and there I saw a little heap of dirt. It was dark and fragmented, chips of what I hoped was not poop. When I touched it, it crackled liked dried mud. I peed; the toilet paper (useless, glazed Greek toilet paper) came away with a red glob of jelly on it. Blood.

I was going to die without seeing Cambridge again.

I went back to packing. But I couldn't resist going to sit on the toilet every few minutes to check for blood. First I had to check for cockroaches. Each time I checked, there were no roaches but there was blood. It wasn't like nice, regular blood from a cut. It came in nasty jiggling blobs, as if it were carrying my insides along with it. That explained why I felt I was ripping. I was. Whatever was causing the blood was ripping me apart.

I didn't want to sit on the bed in case I bled on the blanket. I didn't want to sit on the toilet because I felt I'd used up my cockroach-free minutes. For quite a while after I finished packing I stood at the window watching the tangled Athenian streets revving up for their nightly explosion of activity. As I stood there I felt the blood oozing out of me, adding to the mess in my underwear.

Eventually I went looking for my mother.

She was rummaging in her bedroom closet. The big khaki suitcase with the leather edging was open on the bed.

"What?" she said, with her head still in the closet.

"I have blood," I said. I'd come up with this phrase while standing at my window. I was pleased with it, because it was true, it wasn't hysterical, and it seemed to strike the right tone. As soon as I'd said it, though, I started wailing. "There's blood down there that just keeps coming and coming and it hurts."

My mother emerged from the closet and sat down next to the suitcase. She patted the empty part of the bed beside her. "Come here," she said. She patted again.

"But the blood!"

"Don't be afraid of the blood," she said. "The blood is fine."

"I'm going to bleed on the bed! I don't want to bleed on the bed!" I was getting wound up.

She reached into the suitcase and took out the black scarf my father wasn't going to wear and put it on the bed. "Sit on that, if you're so worried about it."

I sat down.

"This is a big day," my mother said. "This is your first period, and it's an important moment."

I stared at her. "It is?"

"Yes. Now you're a woman."

I kept staring at her. "What does that mean?"

"Let's see." My mother was gathering some sort of speech, I could tell. "It means that you have become physically mature. Physically, you're a grownup."

"I am not a grownup," I said.

"No," she said. "But now you can have a baby."

"I don't want to have a baby," I said.

"That's good," said my mother.

"So what's the point? I don't want all this blood."

"It's normal. It's completely normal and fine and it's not going to hurt you. It means you're healthy and you're growing the way you're supposed to. It's good."

"What's good about it," I said. It wasn't a question. "And it hurts."

"It can be a bit painful in the beginning," my mother said. "That doesn't last, usually. It gets better as your body gets used to it."

"You mean I'm just going to be having blood forever, just leaking out blood all the time! Why didn't you tell me about this?"

"I did," my mother said. "But you weren't listening."

"When?" I had no memory of her telling me anything.

"Back in Cambridge," she said. "When the—ah—chest development started."

"Oh." If she had told me, then she was right; I hadn't listened. "But—but now always blood? All the time?"

"No. Just once a month for a few days."

"Like two days?" I asked.

"A bit longer than that," she said. "Maybe five days."

"Five days!"

She nodded. "Could be six," she said.

Even my low-grade arithmetic was good enough to show me that this meant nearly a quarter of my life was going to be devoted to bleeding. I put my head into my hands. "Why?" I said. "Why?"

"Every month your uterus gets nice and soft so that if you were having a baby, it would have a good place to grow. But then if there's no baby, the uterus gets rid of all that and starts again the next month, making a fresh new spot in case of a baby. That's why."

That wasn't really what I wanted to know.

"But I don't want a baby," I said. "What's a uterus?"

"A place where the babies grow."

"Can't we tell it not to bother?" I asked.

"Nope," my mother said. She got up and opened the top drawer of her bureau. "Now let's get you fixed up," she said. "I'll give you a belt and some pads." She poked around in the drawer for a minute. "I can't find an extra belt, but here's a pad." She pulled a long, thick bandage-y thing out of the drawer and handed it to me. "Just put that in your underwear for the night. In the morning, before we go to Mycenae, we'll get everything you need."

"I don't like belts," I said. "Belts make me itchy."

"You need this belt," my mother said.

I held the pad away from me. "One pad a day?" I asked.

"No. You need several pads a day, at least three."

I bowed my head. Belts and pads and hot, sore insides and nothing I could do about it. Maybe she was wrong. Maybe it wouldn't come back. Maybe it was just this one time. And what about my father! What would he think of me?

"Don't tell Daddy," I said. "Please, please, don't tell him."

"Okay," said my mother.

But I knew she would tell him and they would talk about it and there wasn't anything I could do to stop them, just as I couldn't do anything to stop the blood.

George led the way in the rattly Fiat, down the coast to the Isthmus of Corinth and over onto the Peloponnese. The day was bright and still. Hawks were hanging above the fields. There was nothing anywhere: no towns, no ruins, no traffic except one dusty bus barreling toward us, going north.

"This is the plain of Argos," my father said. "Right?" he asked my mother. She had the guidebook.

"Mmm," she said.

"The Argives," he told me. "Those who went to Troy."

He was trying to be nice to me, probably because of what my mother had told him about my situation. I refused to answer.

"Are you awake?" he asked.

"Argus had a hundred eyes," I said.

"That was somebody else," my mother said.

"Are you sure?" my father asked. "Look in the guidebook."

"He was guarding Io after she got turned into a cow," I said. "Because he had a hundred eyes."

"I don't think that's right," my mother said.

"What does the guidebook say?" my father asked.

After a while, my mother said, "It's confusing. There seem to be two of them. There was Argos, who built the *Argo*. And there was Argus, with a *u,* who had a hundred eyes. The plain is named after the first guy, so I'm right. But she's right about the other guy and his hundred eyes."

I knew I was right. It should have been an even more satisfying rightness because my mother had said I was wrong, but I couldn't enjoy it. All I could think about was how uncomfortable I was. I was wedged onto a thick, damp pad with a scratchy elastic belt taut across my belly. Every time the car went over a bump, and it went over a lot of them, the clammy pad jammed up against me. My head hurt. My legs felt as if they were being poked by needles. I smelled funny too, like rusty metal. My entire body had become a foreign object that didn't feel like me anymore. Probably I'd remembered Argus and Io not because we were crossing the plain where she'd been transformed but because my long-ago nightmare of being turned into a cow had come true. Like Io, I was stuck in this condition, which wasn't my real self.

"Whoops," said my father, putting the brakes on hard. "I see we have arrived."

George had pulled off the road and parked the Fiat under an olive tree. We drove in beside him. It was the usual Greek arrangement: no sign, nothing to hint at a sight worth seeing nearby. Up ahead of us was a big hill, but there were big hills in every direction, and this one didn't look especially promising.

"We walk up?" my father asked George. He tilted his head toward the hill in a Greek gesture; he was learning.

"The archaeologists have a road, but it's very rocky and full of ruts—you call them *ruts*?"

"Yes," said my father.

"That road is okay for a truck. I think the cars will be too banged around by it. We can walk up on it, though. And there are also donkey paths, which are steep but quicker."

My mother was holding her big red-and-black Greek bag, which was filled with scarves and hats. "It's so warm," she said. "It's a really nice day. Let's walk on the road."

"Did you bring the wine?" my father asked her.

She lifted the bag at him.

My father and George put my sister between them and started walking. My mother shouldered the bag, lit a cigarette, and turned toward me.

"Coming?" she said.

She made me so mad that I wanted to eat a rock. I imagined crushing a rock with my furious teeth or, just as satisfying, having my teeth crushed by a rock and spitting them out at her. Of course I was coming. What could I do but tag around after them? Anyhow, Mycenae was the one thing I wanted to see in Greece. I didn't need a lecture from my father on its importance, and I didn't need to hear my mother recite poetry about it, and I didn't need to look in the guidebook. There was a Mycenae in my head already, full of people and stories. All I needed was the place itself.

I followed my mother up the twisty road, going slowly so as not to catch up with her, so as to fall, little by little, quite far behind her. Low, spicy plants—rosemary, thyme, myrtle—grew beside and sometimes on the road. If I stepped on them, puffs of fragrant oil came up to me. Despite George's warnings, it was windless. The pad shifted around between my legs as I walked. Now and then I felt a gush of blood, which came out hot and quickly cooled. It was hateful, almost like peeing in my pants, and it was worrisome because I didn't know how much blood the pad could absorb.

I trudged up through the switchbacks. As I got higher, the wind started. I could hear my parents and George talking, but I couldn't see them, and the wind tossed their voices around in a confusing way. One minute they seemed to be right above me, the next they seemed far off to one side or another. I was getting chilly. I'd worn only a sweater and hadn't, of course, taken one of the scarves or hats my mother had stuffed into her bag. I kept my head down to blunt the wind and to watch my step on the road. Also, to show, though nobody was looking, how bad I felt and how hard it was for me to walk with my blood and my pad and my wrenched-up insides. Windy, windy, then suddenly, the wind was gone. I'd entered a passageway between two huge stone walls. I looked up and saw the lions, on their gate.

The entrance beneath them was an almost square opening that seemed small at first, but, looking around, I decided it was small only in comparison to the size of the walls. I walked into it and stopped on the granite threshold, which was scored as if it had been raked—with a rake of the gods, a rake that could carve lines in granite. The opening was bigger than it looked. It was at least twice my height, and the slab that went across the top to hold the lions' stone triangle was so thick that I couldn't imagine how anybody had gotten it up the hill and put it there.

At the Parthenon I'd felt that something had been peeled back to let me see beneath. Things were different here. There was nothing to peel. I was looking at it straight on. I was standing on a hill fortified before the start of history, before there were flourishes like fluted columns or stone acanthus toppings to pretty up the situation. Everything was a big square declaration of power: We are strong, we built these enormous walls, we can crush you, go away.

I liked it. I went through the gate.

It was a brutal place, and it was unapologetic about that. It wasn't trying to beguile anyone with its perfection the way the temples did. It was a good spot to plan and carry out murders. The terrible wind was rushing across the hilltop, bending the grass that had infiltrated the ring of gravestones and the foundations of the palace buildings and some of the crevices in the tight stone courses of the walls.

My parents and George had got themselves nicely set, sitting on the ground against a broken wall, out of the wind. They were drinking their wine and eating bread and hunks of salami sawn off with my father's pocketknife. My sister was cozied up next to my mother reading her animal-alphabet book, her perpetual owl beside her.

I hated them for getting comfortable, which seemed a kind of desecration of this cursed place. I didn't want to eat salami and bread, so I was mad about that. But the really bad thing was that they looked complete without me.

I could see they'd be happy if I stayed by the Lion Gate, kicking at stones and bleeding, instead of coming over to be with them. They were enjoying their lunch and looking forward to their post-lunch pleasures. My father was going to drink another glass of wine while my mother blew her smoke at the mountains. George and my sister were going to take little naps. If I went over there, I would disrupt everything. I didn't fit into their schedule. I would complain about lunch. I would complain about sitting on the ground (because I didn't want to sit on my soggy horrid pad). Even if I resolved not to complain no matter what, not to say what I didn't want to eat or didn't want to do, my presence would be sulky in a way I couldn't control, and my mother would say, "You're in a mood." When she said, "You're in a mood," she meant, You're in a bad mood. She made me feel that having any sort of mood at all was forbidden. And though she hadn't said anything yet, she was right.

My bad mood was the sum of several contradictory moods. I was wistful and sorry for myself, because I wanted to sit with them and be comfy and warm, but they didn't want me. Why didn't they want me? They never did. I also felt the opposite. I couldn't believe I was related to them. I didn't even want to look at them. I wouldn't sit with them if they were the last people in the world or the only people up on the citadel of Mycenae—which they were. Also, how could they be so cavalier about being here, chewing their salami as if this were a normal spot for a picnic? Cannibalism, human sacrifice, matricide, murder: Just about every bad thing there was had happened up here, and they didn't care. What was the matter with them? They always had to look in the guidebook to know what was going on.

But I could smell it and taste it: blood everywhere. Buoyed by how perceptive I was, I headed over to them.

"Hah!" my mother said when she saw me. " 'These roofs. Look up!' "

There weren't any roofs. It was all in ruins.

"There." My mother pointed. " 'There is a dancing troupe that never leaves.' "

I looked up but they weren't there. It had been a long time since they'd been there.

George opened his eyes. "Don't provoke the Furies," he said, half asleep.

My mother laughed.

George sat upright. "I am serious," he said.

What if time didn't always move forward? What if there were places where time got stuck or became circular, where it was now but it was also all the times before now and everything was happening all at the same moment? That could explain why, though I didn't see the dancing troupe, I knew they were there on the roof that wasn't there now but had been there, once. George also seemed to think they were up on the roof. Maybe he was just being extremely careful in a George-like manner, covering all the bases. Or maybe he knew things we didn't know.

I knew something too, even if I wasn't sure what it was. The difference between this place and a regular place was like the difference between knowing the melody and then hearing it played by an orchestra. Everyday life was just one line of song that ran from yesterday through today and into tomorrow, going along a narrow path. And then—these crazy places in Greece! Suddenly, huge symphonic chords whose bottom notes boomed so far down there was no knowing where they came from. The noise of time was enormous, but the places themselves were quiet. Like the underworld—nothing there except the click of crickets. That made it easier to hear the thrum of the menacing, subterranean ocean. And here at Mycenae the only sound was the intermittent hiss of wind, a whispered accompaniment to the screeching on the roof, clanging metal wheels on granite thresholds, the thump as the ax meets bone.

Perhaps my mother was quoting Cassandra in the same way she'd quoted Byron at Sounion, as a citation of a line that applied to this spot. I hoped so. I hoped she couldn't actually see the Furies dancing.

I didn't want to think she could do that. I wanted to be the only one sensitive enough to feel all the horrors of Mycenae. It was okay if George felt them—he was a Greek. But if my mother felt that sort of thing, we would have too much in common. I didn't like that idea at all.

I'd always known I wouldn't be like her when I grew up, because we were totally different. Clothes: She loved them, I hated them. Furniture: I didn't care one whit about furniture or paint colors or how the living room was arranged, and she spent hours on that. The piano was her special thing, but I was no good at it and that was fine with me. All her twisty, twirly ways of getting people to do what she wanted: Those were nasty methods I was never going to use. I wasn't like her. I was like my father.

Except my father had to look in the guidebook. He had to look it up in the encyclopedia. He had to check on it in the dictionary or the concordance or the collected works of. Whereas my mother knew. She just knew.

They were packing up, brushing off crumbs and dust. My father jammed the cork back into the wine bottle. I wasn't going to get even a bite of the salami and bread I didn't want.

"You did not eat," George said.

He was the only one who cared about me.

"At the café beside La Belle Hélène they have very good sweets of the spoon," he told me. "I will get you a beautiful fig. It's the best one."

"Oh, she doesn't like them," my mother said.

I didn't like figs and I didn't like sweets of the spoon, which were candied fruits served dripping with honey, but I wanted one anyhow, because George was being nice.

"Apricot," he said. "Orange. Whatever you like."

"If you think the fig is the best one, then I would like to have that," I said.

My mother raised her eyebrows. My jab had hit. I was pleased.

And now it was time to go. She checked in the bag: sunglasses, wine bottle, scarves, owl, all set. We headed back toward the terrible gate.

I'd wanted to walk with George, but he'd teamed up with my father so they could discuss whether to go to Nemea or Tiryns the next day. George was for Nemea. "Tiryns is just a shadow of Mycenae," he said. "At Nemea is the nice piece of the temple for Zeus."

I was in my usual position behind everyone. "Any lions?" I called to them.

My father granted me an appreciative snort. "Were there ever any lions?" he asked George.

First I was happy that he thought my question worth repeating, then I was mad because he thought it hadn't really been asked until *he* had asked it.

"Jackals, probably," said George.

My insides were beginning to feel very bad. Something in there was opening and closing like a fist, squeezing out blood with each movement. My back hurt. The pad seemed to be used up. It was leaking at the sides, making tickly dribbles down my thighs that chafed my skin against my blue jeans. Soon, blood was going to reach my ankles and emerge into public. Then what?

I had to get another pad. I hustled up to my mother, who was close to the gate, holding my sister's hand.

"Do you have another pad thing in there?" I asked her.

"Oh," she said. It was down at the bottom. She lifted my sweater a little and popped the pad under it. "Go behind the wall over there," she told me. "I'll wait."

I wanted her to wait. I was surprised she'd offered to. "You don't have to wait," I said.

She didn't bother to respond. She waved her fingers at the wall and then at me. My father and George were approaching. She waved her fingers at them too.

"Go on," she said. "We'll be along soon."

My sister said, "I'm going with Daddy."

My mother handed her off to my father, and I trudged over to my wall and went behind it.

I pulled down my blue jeans and squatted. It was wonderful to feel the air on my dank bottom parts. When I got my pad unhooked from the little prongs of the belt, I had a good look at it. It was a combination of hard and gooey, black and stiff around the edges and bright with fresh pink blooms in the center. My upper legs were streaked with thin rivulets that itched. I decided to pee. I looked down to see if I had peed blood, but the earth was so parched that my pee had gone straight into it like a needle. I stayed squatting for a minute to let things dry out before strapping myself onto a new pad.

When I stood up I felt better. The clean pad was soft and nice. Peeing had helped too; my sensations were so mixed up I hadn't even known I needed to pee.

The old pad lay at my feet. It looked like a thick red worm. I poked it with my sneaker. All that blood had come from inside me: strange. Could I just leave it there? I decided I could. It was going to dry up and fall apart soon, probably, I hoped.

I liked leaving my blood on the ground. Mycenae was the right place for it.

Home

We were home, after many more things.

A white horse in a field in Thessaly on the day of the earthquake, when the ground rippled like water. The wicker baskets that hauled us to the top of Meteora to eat bread and feta with musty-smelling monks. The bees frantic in the bowl of honey at Sunday brunch in Kifissia with the professors from Tübingen who had first disapproved and then helped when I fainted on the Acropolis. They were a couple; I hadn't known that was possible. My parents went to Istanbul for ten days and Frederika came from Sweden to babysit once more. My mother thought Freddy and George? But he was too busy to come over that week, so they never met. Besides, Frederika had a nice Swedish boyfriend, Anders, who was a civil engineer. My mother said that wouldn't last. "You're too romantic to be married to an engineer," she told Frederika.

The years of wandering were over. We were home and we were staying home.

"Frederika will come back to live with us again, won't she?" I asked my mother.

"You're both so grown up now, we don't need her," my mother said. "But she's always welcome. She might. I don't think she's planning to, though."

I wanted her back so I could reconstruct life as it had been. It was just barely possible—I felt that. There was enough of the old me, the one who knew nothing about bleeding and eternity, to have one last round of childhood. If Frederika came back, we could try on makeup and laugh about how silly we looked. She could tell me what to do and I could not do it and she would love me anyhow, and the world would be safe for a little while longer.

But she wasn't coming back. She was going to stay in Sweden and marry Anders and have two daughters and then divorce him. My mother was always right.

We came home in August. After the dry glitter of Greece, Cambridge felt thicker and stickier than I remembered it. When I pressed my finger into the tar of our street, it left a hole. My attic bedroom smelled of heavy, unused air. The backyard was a tangle, the closets were stuffed with clothes that didn't fit us, the cupboards were full of boxes of spaghetti turning to dust and cans of tomato soup that my mother said looked "dubious." The inside of the unplugged refrigerator made me think of an empty swimming pool, sad without its contents and with a whiff of chlorine. It was a haunted house, and our old selves were the ghosts.

Pinch was another ghost. The Bigelows had taken her for the year, as they'd done when we went to England. But this time, she died. My mother didn't tell me until we were on the second leg of our journey home, the twelve-hour flight from Rome to Boston.

"She was an old cat," my mother said. "She was more than ten."

"When did she die?" I asked. I couldn't believe my mother hadn't told me. "Did she die last week or something?"

"Oh, no," said my mother. "Sometime in the spring, April, I think."

"Why didn't you tell me then?"

"I felt the news could wait," she said. "There wasn't any point in upsetting you."

"But all this time I thought she was alive. I thought when we got home, she'd be there."

"That's kind of nice, isn't it?" said my mother. "She lived another four months, for you."

• • •

I didn't know what to do with my days. I made bicycle pilgrimages to the important places: the candy store across the street from the Bigelows' (who were on the beach in Wellfleet with the other psychoanalysts), where Roger and I had bought bull's-eye caramels and Squirrel Nut bars with our pennies; the gloom of Gray Gardens East, where I'd enjoyed feeling sorry for myself; even the boggy riverside fields of my detestable school, where soon enough I'd be back in the classroom, bored to death. At each place I was surprised by how small, how faded, how insignificant it was.

I couldn't locate the problem—I couldn't tell if the problem was "real" or just something the matter with me. Maybe while I was away Cambridge had gotten worn out and dirty and unappealing. A worse thought was that it had always been like this, but I hadn't known it. Or maybe it was both. Maybe I'd changed and Cambridge had also changed.

In Harvard Square bits of scrap paper were scooting around the empty streets and everything was asleep, waiting for September. Veritas mugs and spiral notebooks lazed on the shelves of the Harvard Coop. The Out of Town News was deserted. There weren't any French graduate students looking for *Le Monde* or homesick midwestern kids buying the *Chicago Tribune,* just a few locals grabbing packs of Chesterfields and Lucky Strikes. I walked my bike into the Yard: nobody and nothing. The enormous colonial trees rustled their dusty hot leaves above me.

I stood beside my bicycle, looking at Memorial Church, where in the spring a platform would be built to hold the faculty and the Latin orator and the sheriff of Middlesex County and everyone else needed to enact commencement. My mother and I always sat in the audience and tried to find my father, in his black robe, among the rest of the professors in their black robes.

The choir sang a hymn, "Domine Salvum Fac," that made me shiver every year.

I wondered if I would shiver this coming spring. I didn't think so. What had thrilled me was the idea of how many years—hundreds!—this scene had taken place in this spot, and of how old the rituals and costumes were. I had felt that I was part of a big, old thing.

But I wasn't really part of it. And it wasn't very old. It was a nice ceremony on a pretty June morning in a small town in America, and I was a bystander.

If I shut my eyes I could see the dark, turbulent Aegean, sacred to Poseidon, thrashing at the headlands of Sounion. I could see the almost-smiling girls of the Acropolis. Those things were old. I wasn't part of them either.

I got back on my bike and went home. I was home now.

But it was no good pretending. I had become a stateless person.

My mother was purging the house. Everything chipped, broken, lidless, outgrown, or disliked had to go. Out, out, onto the curb for the trashmen.

"What about the Goodwill?" my father asked. "Someone could use this stuff."

"I haven't got time to go there," my mother said.

"I'll do it," said my father. "We'll do it." He turned to me and nodded my agreement for me.

I didn't care. I had nothing else to do. I felt chipped, lidless, and broken. Maybe I would go stand at the curb on Monday morning and wait for the maw of the garbage truck to eat me up.

Every afternoon for most of a week my father and I gathered the boxes and old shopping bags full of the detritus of the past and shoved them into the Chevrolet. Then we went all the way across town, past the building where Alexander Graham Bell had received the first telephone call, and the NECCO factory, breathing out clouds of sugar and chocolate, beyond the railroad tracks to the half-empty stretch between Central Square and MIT.

A few guys were always lounging against the Goodwill building, smoking, when we pulled up. They didn't look at us as we made our several trips from the car to the back of the store, where a squinty lady ruled over stacks of stuff. She pointed: "Kitchen left, clothes right," she said. She said that every day, refusing to remember us from the day before.

"Those people don't like us," I said on the way home.

"Why should they?" said my father. "The way they see it, we've got everything and they've got nothing, or not much."

"Is that true?" I asked him.

"It's not untrue," he said.

"But we're giving them our extra stuff, so they can have some things they need."

"Charity underscores disparity," said my father.

"You were the one who wanted to give them things," I objected. "Mummy wanted to throw it all out. If you don't believe in charity—"

"I didn't say I don't believe in it," my father interrupted. "I said it shows up the difference between the ones who have and the ones who don't have. That doesn't mean it isn't worth doing."

"And it doesn't matter if they don't like us?"

"You don't help people because you want them to like you," my father said. "You do it because they need help, and because you can help. They don't have to like you for it. In fact, they will probably dislike you. That isn't important."

"Daddy," I said. "Are you a communist?"

My father made an Ingrid-y noise, *pffff,* blowing air out in a rush. "Hardly," he said. "I wouldn't be on the economics faculty if I were. Though," he muttered, "there have been a few."

"What happened to them?" I asked.

"Gone. Purged." He waved his hand at the rearview mirror.

"Mummy says you're a communist."

"It's a family joke," he said.

One more thing I wasn't in on. "I don't get it," I said.

"It's not that funny," he said.

Labor Day weekend. The Bigelows were coming for dinner.

"I thought they were on the Cape," I said to my mother.

"They decided to leave early, so as not to get stuck in the Monday-night traffic. And to see us." She had a roast of beef in the oven and heaps of tomatoes and corn on the counter. The corn-water pot was boiling away. "Shuck these," she said, jerking her elbow at the corn.

I liked shucking corn, because it was a permitted mess. I sat on the floor and spread the business section of *The New York Times* in front of me. The silk felt wet, though it wasn't. Some ears peeled easily, and some I had to struggle with, but there was always one moment when the whole casing gave way and the bright, fresh kernels appeared, with their sweet vegetable smell. Something about corn was sad. Like the huge tomatoes, many so ripe they were splitting at the top, corn signaled the end of summer.

The doorbell rang before I'd finished shucking.

"Perfect timing," said my mother. "We don't want the corn to sit around and get old."

The Bigelows hadn't changed at all.

"How wonderful to see you again," said A.A. "The travelers return."

"We brought beach-plum jelly," Ingrid said, "because we wanted to bring oysters but we were afraid they would die in the car."

"Mama, you thought that. I told you just put them in a bucket of seawater," Roger said.

"I'm glad you didn't," my mother said. "We want to start right in with the corn, unless"—she looked worried—"you've had it up to here with corn."

"Never enough corn," said A.A.

"You grew up," Ingrid said to me. She scowled.

I could see that Roger wanted to hug me. He looked from side to side, he blinked, he looked at the floor. Then he walked over to me in a robotic shuffle and put his arms around me like pincers, his hands sticking straight out behind my back so as not to overdo the contact.

"Hi," he said.

"Hi," I said.

"Have we got time for Campari and soda?" my father asked my mother.

"Sure. Why not? Campari and corn." She slid the ears into the pot one by one. "How many minutes do you do?" she asked Ingrid.

"Two after the boil."

"We had roast corn on the beach," Roger said. "You roast it in the shell."

My father said, "It's called a husk."

"Hey!" said Roger. "I learned the longest word in the English language. Do you want to know what it is?"

I nodded. It was cozy to be with Roger again.

My father opened his mouth to say the word, and my mother poked him with her wooden spoon. "Wait," she whispered.

"Okay." Roger drew a breath. "Antidisestablishmentarianism."

"But do you know what it means?" my father asked him.

"Something about church?" Roger hunched his shoulders.

Before my father could correct and expand on that, my mother said, "You have to pick up the pot and drain it because I can't lift it."

It was time to eat. "Each person take one thing to the table," my mother said. She handed the heavy, steaming dish of corn to my father and picked up the roast, oozing on its wooden board. A.A. took the tomatoes in oil with red onions cut paper-thin. Ingrid took the bowl of horseradish mixed with sour cream to put on the slices of beef. I took the wicker basket of hot little rolls cut from a tube of dough that lived in the freezer ("pretty good for premade," according to my mother), and Roger took the virgin log of butter on the yellow plate from Italy. My father zipped back into the kitchen to put all the drinks on a tray and carry them in too.

"Now," said A.A., "tell us everything. I could see from your letters, Annette, that the luxurious life was a bit of a strain."

"I guess I'd rather make my own dinner," she said.

"Why not, if you can cook like this," said A.A.

My mother was pleased.

"The entire Doxiadis operation turned out to be a boondoggle," my father said. "Doxiadis has a theory he calls Ekistics. The science of human habitation." He fluttered his hand above his head. "It's all up in the clouds. As far as I could see, everyone there was his nephew or his cousin or his pal from the Resistance, and they spent a lot of time in cafés spinning out no-hope plans for cities they wanted to create on the southern coast of

Greece. Nobody in the government paid any attention to them. It was extremely frustrating."

"Must have been," A.A. murmured.

"They're in terrible shape," my father went on. "The economy is a shambles. Well, the whole place is a shambles. For instance, there isn't even one traffic light in Athens. They're heading for either a Communist takeover, which won't help, or a military coup, which will make things worse. The last thing on their minds is urban planning—which I can understand. They've got more important problems. Everybody's suspicious of everybody else, What did your uncle do during the war sort of thing, and they're all scraping along at a subsistence level."

"Or at a nonsubsistence level," my mother put in. "They're living on potatoes and nettles."

"We never ate any nettles," I said.

"We did," my mother said. "We ate them in a taverna on Crete."

"You know, we used to eat nettles in Sweden. They were a special spring treat," Ingrid said.

"Don't they sting?" I asked.

"Uncooked," said Ingrid. "Cooked, no."

"Nettles stinging your tongue," Roger said with an appreciative shudder.

"But they don't!" Ingrid said in her screechy, you-don't-know-what-you're-talking-about voice. "I explained!"

My father wanted to quash the nettle digression. "Where they'd be without the Marshall Plan is anybody's guess if this is where they are with it."

"So for you," A.A. said, "it must have been a disappointment. All the trouble of moving abroad and then not finding any way to help. Especially since they'd been so eager."

"Well, they were deluded," my father said. "Doxiadis had some fantasy that an economics professor from Harvard could solve everything."

"That *you* could," A.A. said.

My father said, "A professor from Podunk Technical College could have not helped them just as well as I did. Or didn't."

"But without the cachet," my mother said.

"Still," A.A. said. "To see Knossos, to see Delphi and Olympus . . . "

"We never got to Olympus," said my mother. "Anyhow, it's just a mountain."

"You really didn't like it there," said Ingrid.

"But it *is* fantastic," said my father. "It's—I can't describe it. To be sitting in the theater at Epidaurus, where Sophocles was first performed. Your head spins."

"Because it's too hot and there's nowhere to eat, so you're running low on potatoes," my mother said.

"Annette!" My father was shocked.

"Okay, I'm exaggerating," my mother admitted. "Delphi was particularly lovely. And you do have that strange sensation of the centuries rolling back."

I stared at her. She'd had that feeling too?

"Maybe next year, instead of Wellfleet, we'll go," A.A. said to Ingrid.

"Kind of expensive," said Ingrid.

"What do you think, Roger?" A.A. asked.

"You said we were going to Kitty Hawk, to see the airplane things," said Roger.

"You should have come to visit while we were there," my mother said. "We had two hundred extra bedrooms."

My father made a face. He didn't like my mother's overstatements.

"But what was the problem?" Ingrid asked my mother.

"I think it was living in Athens," she said. "It's a hideous city, dirty, sprawling, disorganized."

"Needs a dose of Ekistics, bad," said my father.

"It needs something, all right." My mother shook her head. "It might be the contrast, because the landscape of Attica is so beautiful. The sea and sky and the rocks are all unchanged, of course. Then in the middle of it, this *blot*. You keep pinching yourself, I'm in Athens! But to believe it, you have to be an epigrapher and an archaeologist and to know the plays and Thucydides and Pausanius, and if you aren't a good enough historian, which I'm not, you feel guilty all the time—you feel you're wasting an opportunity. And you are. Maybe my imagination wasn't up to it. I just couldn't see past the mess of the present."

"You had to do a kind of mental excavation every day to appreciate it—is that what you mean?" asked A.A.

My mother nodded. "Yes, otherwise you get stuck in the difficulties of daily life, and there are plenty of those. No food in the markets, repairmen are three days late, everybody lies all the time. About everything."

"Almost everything," my father said.

"Think of one instance when they didn't lie. You can't!"

"George didn't lie," my father said.

"He lied constantly!" My mother was getting mad. "It's a two-hour trip. No, it isn't—it's a four-hour trip. The boat will stop for two days in Crete. But it doesn't; it stays for half a day. The owner of this restaurant will give us a discount. But no, he won't, or he's not the owner anymore. It's reflexive, perpetual, needless lying."

"They want to please," my father said. "They tell you what you want to hear."

"I want to hear the truth," my mother said. She stood up. "Chocolate roll, anyone?"

"You made chocolate roll?" My father was surprised and delighted.

"Why not," my mother said. "It's a celebration to be home and to be eating with the Bigelows."

"We're glad you're back too," Ingrid said. "But not as glad as you are, I see."

Sometimes I couldn't understand what Ingrid meant. Wasn't she happy to see us? A.A. and Roger seemed really pleased. Maybe she didn't like us—me, in particular. Maybe she'd enjoyed having a year off from including me at dinner several times a week and contending with the messes Roger and I made together.

I looked over at Roger, who was sitting across from me. His head was still too big for the rest of him. I wondered if he was ever going to grow into it.

My mother pointed at the plates, and I got up to clear the table. A.A. got up too.

"No, no," my mother said. "She can do it."

For a moment, I missed Greece, where Kula had done all the chores I had to do at home. But I didn't want to be back there. I wanted to be in a place where I could be happy, and that wasn't Greece. It didn't seem to be Cambridge anymore either. Once, though, it had been. Hadn't it been?

I cleared the table. I tipped the corncobs into the trash. I stacked the dishes beside the sink the way my mother liked. When I went back to the table, Roger was talking about how great seventh grade was going to be. "It's the Civil War and all those battles."

I sat there eating chocolate roll while my father and A.A. discussed the chances of Senator Kennedy's becoming president. A.A. thought it was likely.

My father didn't. "Nixon's such a car salesman, he'll convince the whole country that if they don't elect him, the Soviets are going to drop a bomb on us. And everybody knows his name. Nobody knows a thing about Jack Kennedy."

"Everybody knows that Nixon is a snake," my mother said.

My father jerked his chin up in the Greek gesture of dismissal he'd adopted.

"We might be ready for a turn to the left," said A.A. "And he's so young and charming. That helps."

"At least he's got your vote," my father said.

"I wish I could vote for Norman Thomas the way I used to," said A.A. "Maybe I'll write him in."

My mother smiled. "My mother would have loved you," she said to A.A. "Did you know that she ran for mayor of Philadelphia on the Socialist ticket?"

"Really! How did she do?" A.A. asked.

"About as well as Norman Thomas," said my mother.

My mother loaded the dishwasher while my father wrapped the remains of the roast in aluminum foil and slid the tomatoes into a smaller bowl.

"Now I feel we're really home," said my mother. "Having a dinner like that."

"Yes," said my father. "I guess I'd better look in on the office on Monday."

"I wish you would cut the grass in back," said my mother. "Monday's a holiday."

"Even better. Nobody will bother me," my father said. "I'm sure there's a huge pile of mail."

"Inviting you to conferences that happened in February," my mother said. "You could cut it tomorrow."

"Can we get another cat?" I asked.

"Oh, god," said my father.

"What do you care?" my mother said to him. "It's not like it's a dog you have to walk."

"They're always underfoot," he said.

I opened the back door and went into the yard.

It was a sea of tall grass topped with tiny wheat ears of seed. Stars and mosquitoes and fireflies and fast-chirping crickets. The night was very dark and warm and big.

I stood knee-deep in the dewy stalks and I felt as big as the night. I had a booming, echoing feeling in my chest, a throbby sort of feeling, as if I had lost something wonderful. My childhood—it was gone!

But it hadn't been wonderful.

This was what was wonderful, standing alone in the big, soft night rewriting the past to make myself miss what had never been. Now that it was over, I could turn the past into anything I wanted. I could revise the empty space inside me so that it had a better shape: the outline of a happy childhood.

A NOTE ABOUT THE AUTHOR

Susanna Kaysen has written the novels *Asa, As I Knew Him* and *Far Afield* and the memoirs *Girl, Interrupted* and *The Camera My Mother Gave Me*. She lives in Cambridge, Massachusetts.

A NOTE ON THE TYPE

This book was set in Adobe Garamond. Designed for the Adobe Corporation by Robert Slimbach, the fonts are based on types first cut by Claude Garamond (c. 1480–1561). He gave to his letters a certain elegance and feeling of movement that won their creator an immediate reputation.

COMPOSED BY North Market Street Graphics, Lancaster, Pennsylvania

PRINTED AND BOUND BY Berryville Graphics, Berryville, Virginia

DESIGNED BY Iris Weinstein